MISSING

The sensible thing to do was to shove the awkward corpse of Anita Chesney into Pending, as unsolvable.

Mendoza stood beside the Ferrari, the heat reflected starkly from the pavement—always ten degrees hotter in the valley. The boys in his office joked about his crystal ball, but perhaps the main reason why Luis Rodolfo Vincente Mendoza had a reputation as a detective was his passion for tidiness. The loose ends, the unfinished patterns, annoyed him.

He would really like to know what happened to Anita Chesney, that rainy March day fifty-one months ago.

———————— ★ ————————

SHANNON
DELL

Cold Trail

WORLDWIDE.®

TORONTO • NEW YORK • LONDON • PARIS
AMSTERDAM • STOCKHOLM • HAMBURG
ATHENS • MILAN • TOKYO • SYDNEY

For
Carroll and Evelyn Buck
Tried and True Friends

COLD TRAIL

A Worldwide Mystery/July 1989

First published by William Morrow & Company, Inc.

ISBN 0-373-26027-X

The end crowns all,
And that old common arbitrator, Time,
Will one day end it.
—SHAKESPEARE, *Troilus and Cressida*

ONE

"THAT," said Alison, coming back to the kitchen from the telephone in the hall, "was the fence man. It's going to cost ten thousand dollars."

Mendoza set his coffee cup down rather sharply. *"¡Socorro!"*

"Well, after all it's nearly four and a half acres," said Alison. "And we might as well do everything right to start with. While money's still worth anything."

"They do say," observed Máiri MacTaggart, straightening from loading the dishwasher, "that it's more costly to rebuild an old house than build a new one."

"But look what we'll have," said Alison. "Nobody builds houses like that these days."

Mendoza got up and yanked down his cuffs. "I'll just remind you, *cara*, that it isn't necessary to do everything at once. You shouldn't be running around in this heat."

"Oh, I'm fine. I suppose the air conditioning will be the last thing in. Anyway, if I get any bigger I won't be able to get behind the steering wheel, to go running around. Thank heaven there's only two months to go." The new baby, either James or Luisa, was due at the end of July.

Mendoza picked up his hat. "Well, I'm off. Just don't try to do too much at once, *amada*."

"No, no," said Alison. Mrs. MacTaggart pushed levers and started the dishwasher. The twins, of course, had departed on the bus for their private nursery school half an hour ago. The cats were all out, and Cedric, the Old English sheepdog. The Ferrari slid past the window down the drive, and Alison and Máiri looked at each other.

"It's an awful lot of money, that is." Máiri shook her tight silver curls.

"I know—but it's going to be a house," said Alison. "It's just, there's so much to be done." Ever since she'd discovered her hundred-year-old *estancia*, the old winery in the hills above Burbank, she'd been finding out just how much it was going to cost to remodel and modernize it: it was one thing after another. The escrow had closed out a month ago, and after consulting the construction company, plumbers, electricians, and now the fence man, Alison was rather appalled at what she'd got into; but it was indeed going to be a *house*—a separate suite for Máiri, a playroom for the children, a studio to encourage her to paint again—and there was also the old winery building, tentatively scheduled to become a stable for two ponies.

"Och, well," said Máiri, "at least you're making work for a crew of men. I wonder if any you've been talking to could fix yon swing."

"Oh, I expect any handyman can do that." The double swing in the backyard had withstood a year of vigorous use by the twins, and yesterday two of its iron hooks had parted from the frame. Mendoza was far from being a handyman. "There's bound to be one in the classified ads," said Alison, still thinking about the fence. "And I've got to see that plumber at nine-thirty, I'd better get dressed."

"Just as the man says, all this gadding about. Time and enough after the bairn's here."

"But I want to get things started. It's going to take ages anyway," said Alison, untying her robe.

MENDOZA WASN'T THINKING about Alison's *estancia* as he drove downtown; he could count on Máiri to keep her from running around too fast, or so he hoped. There wasn't much on hand of real interest at the office, the usual never-ending greed and mayhem; his chief concern at the moment was that rapist-killer. They knew who he was and there was an

A.P.B. out; Mendoza wondered if it had turned him up overnight.

It hadn't. When he came into the office Sergeant Lake told him that and added that the night watch had left them a new heist job.

"Surprise, surprise," said Mendoza. It was Monday, so John Palliser was off. In the detective office, Hackett and Henry Glasser were talking desultorily, nobody else there.

"Morning, Luis," said Hackett. His bulk was slouched in his desk chair. "I suppose Jimmy told you about the heist. Tom and Jase are out on that, and George just went to look at a new body. Nick's down in R. and I. with that pharmacist looking at mug-shots." The pharmacist had got robbed on Saturday night, knocked around a little when he put up a fight.

"No bets he'll pick one." Mendoza went on into his office and sat down at the desk, picked up the report centered on the blotter. It was an autopsy report on a Jane Doe, found last Thursday afternoon in Pershing Square, D.O.A. He glanced at it, grunted and passed it to Hackett. "As expected, an O.D. These damn fool kids. She looked about seventeen." She wasn't on any missing list; her prints had been sent to the FBI and NCIC, but it was a long chance she'd ever been printed.

Hackett squinted at the report, held it farther away and finally at arm's length; Mendoza watched him sardonically and said, "When are you going to give in, Arturo?"

"Damn it, I suppose you're right, but it came on so sudden—there's never been anything wrong with my eyes—" For the last six weeks Hackett had been squinting at reports, holding them at various distances and complaining about smudged typing and illegible writing.

"The years of paperwork catching up to you," said Mendoza. "Admit it, and go see an eye doctor."

"I suppose I'll have to, damn it. Damn it," said Hackett, "I'm due in court this morning—the Holt arraignment—and I don't like it, Luis. Something about it smells a little, but I can't put my finger on it.''

"The evidence looked straight enough.''

"Such as it was,'' said Hackett. "But I don't like it. And where in hell did that .32 casing come from? Fulger was shot with a .22.''

"That is a little funny, but seven witnesses pointed out Holt—''

"And I still don't like it,'' said Hackett. "Not that there's much I can do about it.''

The phone on the desk buzzed, Lake putting through a call; Mendoza shoved the right button. "Robbery-Homicide, Mendoza.''

"This is Patrolman Montez, sir. We just got a call down here on Sixty-second Place, and it's a body.''

"What's the address?'' Mendoza took it down. "Have you called an ambulance? What's it look like?''

"Oh, we won't need an ambulance,'' said Montez, sounding rather grimly amused. "It looks like it's been a body a long, long time, Lieutenant, and I'd say you'll be lucky to find out who it was.''

"You don't say. Well, somebody'll be coming—just preserve the scene. Something new,'' said Mendoza, putting down the phone. "You'll be heading for court—'' He went out to get Glasser, and found the communal office empty. Lake said the pharmacist had picked a mug-shot in five minutes and Galeano had taken Glasser off hunting. "Well, once in a while we do get a fluke. Call the lab and tell somebody to meet me at this address. Talk about women's work.'' Mendoza went out to the elevators, down to the parking lot, and headed the Ferrari up Temple to hit Broadway.

A good way down Broadway, to Sixty-second Street, he turned to find the little cul-de-sac labeled Sixty-second Place. The black and white was parked near the end of the short street, and next to it loomed a big truck; four men in

tan jump suits were talking to the two uniformed patrolmen. Mendoza slid the Ferrari into a red-painted zone behind the truck and got out.

This was all, now, a black area, most of it old and run-
down. Los Angeles was a city in flux these days; the real inner city, the oldest part of it, once the shabbiest of all, had
been face-lifted with glittering new civic buildings, and
where some of the oldest drab department stores had been,
new underground malls had been constructed to attract back
the suburban shoppers. But fanning out from the inner city
were still hundreds of drab old streets, dirty and tired and
lined with ancient buildings, business or residential; here
and there a new apartment had appeared, but for the most
part these streets hadn't changed much since Mendoza was
first riding a squad car twenty-five years ago.

Pocketing his keys, he went up to the little group of men.
"Where's the body?"

"Gah!" said the biggest civilian, and made a face. He was
a bulldog-faced middle-aged man, looking tough, but he
shuddered. "I don't never want to see a thing like that again.
Oh, Jesus. Go out on an ordinary job, nice summer day, and
right away run into a thing like that! You boys can have it!"

"It's under the house," said Montez with a jerk of his
thumb. "The place has been condemned, and when Mr.
Simpson here turned up with his crew to knock it down, they
came across the body."

"Never had such a shock in my life," said one of the crew
plaintively. "You have to see what shape a building's in,
foundations and so on, see how to take it down. Not but
what this place looks like I could knock it down with a
hammer, but I went in under the porch there to have a look,
and first off I thought it was a drunk crawled in there and
then when I got my flashlight on it—my God. Just like Bill
says, thing like that shakes you. A corpse yet."

Mendoza regarded the house somewhat balefully; he had
on a new suit. The little street had three ramshackle apart-

ment houses on one side, two four-family places on the
other, and in between, three single houses. All the buildings were ancient, neglected, but the small single house
standing alone at the dead end, facing the street, was obviously the oldest: a small frame house hardly larger than a
garage, long unpainted, all of its visible windows broken, a
derelict of a house sitting on a niggardly lot about thirty feet
wide.

Montez offered Mendoza his flashlight. "It's only about
six feet in from the porch."

"Thank you so much," said Mendoza, handing him his
hat, and went up the raggedly broken cement walk to the
house. There was a tiny square porch, a gaping hole under
two sides of it where boards had been torn out. He had to
lie flat to crawl in; the house was raised barely three feet off
the ground. It wasn't as dark as he'd expected, but he
switched on the flash. The place had been built on the
sketchiest foundation, and there was only bare earth here.
Somewhere above, the floor was broken, letting in light. He
circled the flashlight, found what he was looking for, and
held the beam steady, conscious of the faint, pervasive odor
of dry rot and dusty earth. The first of the summer heat had
arrived early, and it was very hot and close in that little
space. Dim light from the broken flooring above slanted
down to help the flashlight.

It looked at first glance quite like a drunk sleeping it off.
A huddled dark figure, head lolling to one shoulder. But the
beam of light was merciless on what showed of the face: a
brittle-looking, grinning, shrunken mummified face. It was
difficult to tell much about the clothes: what looked like a
dark coat, something colored under it. The flash moved:
thin legs with tatters of cloth or flesh: one high-heeled shoe.
The corpse had been female.

He crawled out backwards, stood up and began brushing
himself down. The lab truck was just pulling up to the curb.
"You can see what I mean," said Montez.

"In all my years on this force," said Mendoza, handing him back the flashlight, "I can only remember one other corpse under a house. I found that one myself, and as I recall it gave us the hell of a lot of trouble. Besides getting Art Hackett involved in matrimony. But that one was a lot fresher than this."

Marx and Horder came up and after a look demanded what in hell he expected them to do with that. "Just look for anything," said Mendoza. "You're the trained lab men." He watched them crawl back into the hole with camera and strobe lights and lab-bag, and turned to Simpson. "I suppose you know who owns the house?"

"The city, I guess," said Simpson. "I do wrecking work for the city and county mostly. It was the city gave us this job—Planning Commission office. That's all I know. Except by the look of the signs on the place, it's been condemned a hell of a long time. I've known places to stand for years before the city gets round to having 'em down."

Which was helpful; but there'd be records somewhere. If that turned out to be relevant. Mendoza lit a cigarette, staring absently at the hole under the porch. "And so what now?" asked Simpson. "I don't guess you guys'll want us to go ahead and knock it down? I better call the city and tell them."

Mendoza didn't say that he doubted there'd be any useful clues to the corpse lying around that house. You never knew. As he finished the cigarette, Horder came slithering out of the hole and stood up. He had a plastic evidence bag in one hand. "There's no use poking around there much, Lieutenant. We'll get some photos and that's about all. But we might have a break right off." He held up the bag. "About all you can tell, it was a woman—and there was a handbag right beside her. What's left of one."

"*Así*, just fancy that. Think you can get anything from it?"

Horder shrugged. "Have a try. I'd have a rough guess that body's years old, and it and the handbag didn't have much protection in there from rain or heat either—that whole space'd be flooded in a heavy rain, and like an oven in summer. God knows what might be left in the bag. I'll say right off, forget about getting any prints, probably. I'll call the morgue-wagon, they might as well come get it."

Mendoza looked around the dirty, narrow little street. Many of the residents here would be at work, but he could see a dozen or so dark faces at windows in those apartments. Probably a good many of the people here weren't too fond of cops. He could see this corpse getting shoved into Pending right away; but they had to go through the motions. He left Marx and Horder to deal with the body, told Simpson the Planning Commission would let him know about the job, and drove back to Parker Center.

Hackett had left for central court; Grace and Landers had brought in a suspect on one of the heist jobs and were questioning him. Mendoza told Lake to get him the Planning Commission, and anticipating a session with bureaucracy sat back and swiveled around in his desk chair to view the clear outline of the Hollywood hills. As he pulled the trigger of the pearl-handled revolver that was his latest desk lighter, the phone buzzed at him. "I've got somebody in the Planning office," said Lake, "but they don't seem too sure which department you ought to talk to."

Inevitably, Mendoza took it from there, and got passed around, explaining patiently, until he got a Ronald Lightfoot who apparently knew what he was doing and had access to some pertinent information. He left Mendoza hanging on while he went to consult maps, again to look up dates, and finally advised him to contact the County Tax Collector's Office for more facts.

By twelve o'clock, when Hackett came back, Mendoza had a little sheaf of notes and was contemplating them meditatively. "Well, short and sweet," said Hackett. "Arraigned for Murder Two. And I don't like it."

"There's nothing you can do about it now," said Mendoza inattentively. "We've got enough continuing cases to work. And this new one—or rather an old one—what we can do about that I don't know either. Probably not much. Let's go have lunch and I'll tell you about it."

In the outer office they picked up Grace and Landers, who had just let the suspect go. "Up in the air," said Grace, brushing his mustache in a habitual gesture. "He might be, he mightn't be. Nothing to say. He's got the right pedigree for it—"

"And how many other punks have too," said Landers. As they went out to the corridor they met Galeano and Glasser just coming in.

"Wasted morning?" asked Mendoza, eyeing them. "I thought that pharmacist was a little quick on the draw."

"Oh, so did I," said Nick Galeano, "but we have to go by the book. He could have been right. That's him, he says after about three minutes of looking, so we had to check it out. One Salvatore Rodino, and he's got a pedigree of armed robbery, and with the pharmacist so positive we might have nailed him for the job. Only he's got an alibi. He was in the middle of his whole family, about thirty-five people, celebrating his grandparents' golden anniversary."

"It's a frustrating job," said Mendoza. "Come and have lunch and hear about the new one. Come to think, Art, you said there was another new body—George not back yet?"

"Apparently not. I don't know what, Jimmy just said a body."

Settled at one of the big tables at Federico's on North Broadway, they heard about the lady under the house. "Talk about a cold trail," said Mendoza, bringing out his sheaf of notes. "I wouldn't even guess how long it's been there—let Bainbridge try to pin it down. I've got this and that on the house, but what legwork that might give us—I

asked for information going back nine or ten years, to give
it leeway. At that time the house was owned by Robert
James Leigh, that is he had a loan on it with a local savings-and-loan and was making payments. Sporadically. The
following year he defaulted on the payments, and finally the
savings-and-loan company repossessed the property. Then
it was sold, on another loan, to a Manfred Willing. He made
four payments and then stopped. Of course they sent him
the polite reminders, only he didn't answer his mail, and finally somebody went to see him and found a family named
Jones living there, who said they paid rent to a Mr. Willis. I
got this off the record, by the way, this Lightfoot in the
Planning Commission office knows somebody at the savings-and-loan firm. They finally discovered Willing in jail—
as Willis—for burglary. Not long after that the house was
transferred into his wife's name, and she kept up the payments for about six months and then stopped. Let's see, that
was about five and a half years ago. About then, when they
were looking for her, somebody called in a complaint to the
Board of Health and an inspector came out, and after the
usual rigmarole the place was condemned. That house and
the two apartments on either side are still owned by the savings-and-loan company, and they've delayed doing anything about the house because they're getting some Federal
money—read, yours and mine—for a big new housing pro-
ject there. Now the loan's come through, and that whole
block is due to come down. When the place got condemned, the people living there said they'd been paying rent
to Mrs. Willis but she hadn't been around lately, and in fact
neither the savings-and-loan company, the Board of Health
or the Planning Commission ever turned her up. They had
an address for her, on Seventieth, but she wasn't there.''

"Aha," said Hackett. "So maybe she ended up under her
own house."

"I don't think it's so simple." Mendoza drank black coffee and lit a new cigarette. "I rather think that corpse was a

white woman. At any rate, they had a lot of trouble getting the tenants out. A Mr. and Mrs. Rex Jones, and a Buford Talmadge, and Wilma Smith—you guess, relatives or just friends. The house has been standing empty and condemned for four years and eight months.''

''And just now they get round to taking it down,'' said Grace. ''On account of the Federal money. I suppose in the meantime it's been a hideout for the neighborhood kids, or a nice quiet place for the local lovers. Or has it?''

Mendoza shook his head. ''No information. But that's another thing. Given that area, that particular backwater, and that kind of people, do you think we'd get much information asking around?''

''About a million to one,'' said Landers. His perennially youthful face wore a shrewd look. ''Floating population, and those tenants—probably on welfare-floating off God knows where. And even if we found them—''

''Oh, yes, indeedy,'' said Jason Grace. He passed a hand over his brown face, rubbed the mustache back and forth. ''Any of you ever read Irvin S. Cobb?''

''Why?'' asked Hackett. ''Some, I think, years ago.''

''Well, Mr. Cobb says somewhere that colored folk are about the most secretive race there is. If you can generalize about any group of people—which you can't, but there are some general trends, you might say—he may have a little something there. And anyway, that kind of people—they wouldn't be all eager and anxious to help us out.''

The waiter brought their plates and Hackett eyed his steak glumly. ''It'll go in Pending, even if we get some identification. And I still don't like the Holt thing.''

Galeano sampled his sandwich and said tersely, ''That .32 casing. It's funny, I'll grant you, Art. But in a place like that, and what we heard from Piggott and Schenke about that crowd, all the confusion and noise and milling around, somebody else could have had a gun. What we do know,

that .32 slug, wherever it is, didn't have one damned thing
to do with Fulger getting shot. It was a .22 killed him.''

"Yes, and we never found it," said Hackett morosely. He
was fiddling with the menu, testing his eyes by moving it
back and forth. "Damn it, I didn't think eye trouble could
come on so sudden— And I know there were seven witnesses said they saw Holt with a gun, saw him fire it—but
I'd feel better about it if we'd found the gun.''

"Considering the general atmosphere, so would I," admitted Galeano.

The night watch had gone out first on that one, last
month, and by Piggott's report it had been a wild scene. A
Negro bar and dance hall down on Vernon, about a hundred
customers there as well as two barkeeps and a five-piece
combo. Fracases of this or that sort not uncommon at such
a place, but it had a good reputation; it wasn't a dive. About
nine o'clock that night the nearest squad car had been
chased out there on a 415 call. By the time the patrolmen got
there, there was a dead man in the street outside and an excited, yelling crowd all around. It took a while to sort out
those with any relevant information. What Piggott and
Schenke had got, finally, was a typical little sordid tale.

Jody Holt, twenty-four, unemployed, had been sitting at
a table with his sisters, Gloria Holt, twenty-two, and Be-
atrice Linker, twenty-seven, and her husband George,
twenty-eight, a waiter working at a restaurant up in Hollywood. About half an hour before the disturbance, Kathy
Fulger, twenty-four, a clerk at a drugstore in the area, came
up to sit with them. She was an old friend of the Holt family, had lived next door to them since they were all children
together. They were, everybody said, just having some
drinks and talking, nobody high, when Kathy's husband
Lester showed up. He was, everybody said, a mean son of a
bitch even when he was sober, and twice as mean drunk; he
started to slap her around, accused her of two-timing him,
and dragged her out the door. She was crying and scream-

ing, the Holt girls yelling at him to leave Kathy alone, and George Linker tried to pull him away from the girl and got knocked down and out. In the street outside, Fulger went on beating his wife, and a crowd surged around them for several minutes before a single shot was fired and Fulger fell dead. Subsequently, out of the crowd of witnesses seven people swore that they'd seen Jody Holt waving a gun around, seen him fire it. Holt denied he'd had a gun; his sisters and brother-in-law denied it. But he had a pedigree, one count of armed robbery as a juvenile, one count of burglary.

The evidence was there, and not bad evidence; just a little slim. The collected reports and statements went into the D.A.'s office, and the warrant came through for Holt's arrest. It wasn't a big thing, just a violent family squabble ending in a man's death, the kind of thing that happened rather monotonously in any big city. None of the people involved were interesting or important. Fulger had been a mean bully nobody would miss; Holt was just a little punk who, if he wasn't in jail on this charge, probably would have been presently on another.

But that night, in looking the place over to make an initial report, Piggott and Schenke had picked up that .32 casing, the ejected shell case from an automatic pistol. It had been on the floor twelve feet from the table where Holt was sitting, toward the door to the street. The slug that killed Fulger had still been in his skull, and Ballistics had pinned it down as a .22 Colt revolver.

It was a very extraneous thing, that .32 shell casing. The bartenders—one of whom was the owner of the place, Randolph Kellerman—couldn't say where it had come from. The place was swept out every day, and it hadn't been there that morning.

Nearly a week had elapsed between the shooting and Holt's arrest; he had had ample time to get rid of the .22.

"Those witnesses," said Grace now in his soft voice. "I wasn't on it—pretty credible witnesses?"

"That was what tipped the scale," said Hackett. "All decent types, most of 'em excited, but absolutely sure. All of them have clean records, all but one in regular jobs, and that one's in construction, just laid off temporarily. Four men and three women. It's not a cheap gin mill, that place, more a family hangout where people go for a little fun without spending much money."

"It's out of our hands now anyway," said Galeano. He finished his second cup of coffee. "And I suppose we'd better get back to work."

Higgins came up behind him and pulled up a chair from the next table. "The rest of you can. I'd better brief the boss on the latest body." As usual he looked a little rumpled and untidy, his craggy face as much a badge of his job as the one in his breast pocket. "You'll be hearing about it, not that I think it'll make much work for us. It's a cold trail but kind of a simple one."

"So I might as well hear about it too." Hackett yawned and sat back. Higgins told the waiter to bring him the steak sandwich, and lit a cigarette over coffee.

"Another cold trail," said Mendoza meditatively. "Yes?"

"People," said Higgins. "Doing what comes naturally. It was a Mrs. Hilda Lewis called in. She manages this old apartment over on Fresno in Boyle Heights. Not particular about tenants as long as they pay the rent and don't bother anybody. The place is owned by a savings-and-loan company. She tells me this apartment's been vacant about ten days, two weeks—one of the tenants, a Leroy Riggs, just told her they were moving, and they went. She hadn't got round to cleaning the place yet because the rent was paid to the first. Then yesterday some of the other tenants on the third floor complained about a terrible smell, and she thought maybe Riggs had left out some food— So after she looked, and called cops, and I got there, she says it's Sylvia, well, Sylvia Swain she called herself, well, she lived there with Riggs—''

"So we go look for Leroy," said Hackett.

"They're both in Records. Sylvia had a pedigree for soliciting back to age nineteen—she just turned forty. He's only twenty-seven, pedigree of possession, B. and E., one count of burglary, one count of pimping. Mrs. Lewis says they'd been living there for five years—that was after I'd seen the records and went back to ask her some more—and, well, she knew Sylvia was a pro but live and let live and they were quiet tenants. I haven't checked, but I could guess that quite a few of the female tenants there might be in the same line of work."

"People," said Hackett through a yawn. "He strangle her or what?"

"Couldn't say—wait for the autopsy report. It looked more as if she'd been beaten up, but she's been dead ten days at least, that could be just cyanosis. Anyway, Leroy doesn't seem to be a very bright boy. I just put out an A.P.B. on him."

"*Bueno,*" said Mendoza. "Now you'd better hear what you missed," and he told him about the body under the condemned house.

Higgins said uninterestedly, "We'll never get anywhere on one like that. Probably never get it identified." Hackett was moving the menu back and forth again. "If you'd stop dragging your heels and admit you need glasses, Art—there's nothing queer about it, after all you're no youngster—"

"I'm only a year older than you. Damn it, it came on so sudden—"

AT THREE-THIRTY that afternoon a sheriff's deputy spotted the rapist-killer's car out in the valley, and him in it, and picked him up. Mendoza and Higgins had handled that case, a very nasty one with one three-year-old dead and another still in the hospital, so they forgot about Leroy temporarily to talk to the rapist. His name was Jack Thatcher, and he had quite a record, they'd found when they finally identified him—pedigrees of child rape and molestation in five states. Only once had he been locked up in jail, for ninety days; the other judges had handed him probation with mandatory psychiatric treatment.

Neither Mendoza nor Higgins thought much of psychiatric treatment, or of the ones like Thatcher. They had some good evidence on him but it would be nice to get a confession as well. They talked to him for an hour and didn't get one, so they took him down to the jail and booked him in. The warrant had been issued on Saturday.

At five-thirty Mendoza called the lab. "Don't tell me it's too early to ask," he told Horder. "You should be able to guess whether you'll get anything, at least. That handbag."

"Oh, yes," said Horder. "The detective novels all the time have the scientific lab men pulling off marvels of intricate detection. Just occasionally we do, and it's usually pretty simple lab work. In this case, an infrared camera and an enlarger."

"Elucidate," said Mendoza.

"Well, you can have the handbag tomorrow. For whatever use it may be—I don't think much. And what was in it, which wasn't much. Handkerchief, cosmetics, cigarettes, lighter. Everything's rotted away, you can just barely see what they were. But some are worse than the rest. There was a billfold. What was in it was just slightly better protected than the clothes or the handbag itself. No, for God's sake, you can't make out anything even under a microscope. We used tweezers to separate the little plastic slots, and we think there are—or were—a couple of credit cards, and what could be a driver's license."

"*¡Parece mentira!* You think you can raise something?"

"Have a try anyway. We'll probably know one way or the other sometime tomorrow."

After debating with himself, Mendoza called Bainbridge's office and asked if he'd had time to look at that corpse. He talked to Bainbridge himself, who said as it happened he'd been at loose ends when it came in, and he had. Casually. "You won't expect an autopsy report on that one tomorrow, I hope. If you ever get the body identified, it'll be through dental records. Good God, Luis, of course I haven't the slightest idea what killed the woman."

"Or how long ago?"

Bainbridge snorted. "No way to pin that down. Depending on where it was, extremes of temperature and so on, anywhere between six months and five years. You'll get a report sometime."

At least they had Thatcher. Something accomplished; now if another soft-headed judge didn't hand him over to the headshrinkers again— And as usual the other new ones coming along, two heist jobs now: Leroy: Jane Doe was still unidentified, and no autopsy report yet on what looked like a suicide last Friday afternoon. Doubtless more new ones to come.

Mendoza got his hat and started out, and found their policewoman, Wanda Larsen, arguing with Henry Glasser in the anteroom. "I'm just as much qualified to question suspects as you are, Henry! Now you've all finally condescended to letting me get some street experience— And I shot a better score than you last month!"

There was a sullen-eyed blond lout waiting on the bench opposite Sergeant Lake.

"We seldom shoot suspects under questioning," said Glasser, poker-faced. "I'm just prejudiced lady—I somehow don't feel that a willowy blonde would get very far trying to scare a tough punk like this one. I'd rather team up with Higgins."

Mendoza regarded them benevolently and left them still arguing.

He drove home to Rayo Grande Avenue—with all the remodelling and plumbing and electricity to go into the hundred-year-old *estancia*, not to mention the ten-thousand-dollar fence and the stable for the ponies, it might be Christmas or next spring before they actually moved—and was pounced on by both the twins and Alison.

"Daddy, come look at my picture, Miss Turtle let me bring it home because I got a gold star for it—" Terry, impetuous and more feminine every day.

"Miss Thirkell, Terry," said Alison. "Luis, this swing—"

"Mama says we can't swing no more, Daddy, you get a new one—" Johnny shouting to drown out Terry.

"Luis—"

"One at a time, *por favor*. I'll see the picture in a minute, *niña*." They got the twins quieted down after a while, Mendoza inspected the picture and promised to read to them before bed. Máiri shepherded them off for baths, and Alison said everything was in the oven, if he wanted a drink before dinner. Cedric was sprawled on the sectional sound asleep, and cats were distributed about in various favorite places—El Señor on the credenza, Bast and Sheba coiled together in Alison's armchair, Nefertite in Mendoza's.

He was, inevitably, pursued to the kitchen by El Señor, and poured him half an ounce of rye in a saucer. Coming back with his own rye and Alison's sherry, he asked, "What about the swing?"

"It's the most frustrating thing. A perfectly simple little job—for anyone who knows how to do it, and I must say it's also frustrating that you can't drive a nail straight—we've called four numbers from the classified ads, repairs, handymen, and nobody will come! One man said he only does small appliances, but the other three said they couldn't be bothered with such a small job. It's just a matter of screwing those brackets in, I should think." Alison, who, like most redhaired people, had a temper, looked belligerent. "I think I could do it myself if I knew just how to go at it. But honestly—"

"There must be some handyman willing to do it. Just keep trying, *cara*."

"A lot of help you are. And you know, it's belatedly dawned on me that we're going to need more help for that big a house—this one is quite enough for Máiri and me now we've lost Bertha." Their longtime household domestic, Bertha, had suffered a broken hip last month and was permanently retired. "And of course I was a fool to mention ponies—the twins can't wait, and I don't know the first thing about ponies and neither do you, and how we could shop intelligently—and we'll have to find somebody to look after them—and the yard, not that I want much formal landscaping, but there'll be some lawn, and pruning shrubs and so on—"

"Now don't dither, my love," said Mendoza. "Take one thing at a time, and it'll all work out. It seems to me the first order of business should be producing this new offspring. After that, you can get on to conferring with the plumber—"

"Oh, I've done that," said Alison. "They've only drawn up one set of remodeling plans or I could show you. Four and a half bathrooms. And the electrician—about eighty outlets, and a microwave oven because we both think it'd be interesting—I found out today the air conditioning'll be the first thing in, on account of ducts in all the ceilings. And the tile people are coming next week to start repairing all the floors—I'm just going to have area rugs, a real Spanish feeling—"

"Just don't try to do too much."

"But what to do about the swing—it's maddening."

"I expect some solution will present itself," said Mendoza vaguely. He was thinking about the lady under the condemned house.

AT ELEVEN O'CLOCK on Tuesday morning he and John Palliser had just finished an abortive interrogation of a possible suspect on one of the heist jobs, and let him go for want of any conclusive evidence, when Marx and Horder came up from S.I.D.

"We'd like some appreciation for this job, Lieutenant," said Marx. "Personally I thought it was wasted effort, but Bill wanted to try."

"You've got something?"

Horder was holding a big manila envelope. "I didn't hope we'd get this much." But before he opened it, he laid the handbag on Mendoza's desk—half rotted away, an odor of desiccation clinging to it. "There were three—well, things— that could have been credit cards. Felt as if they'd been that stiff and thick. I thought if we got anything, it'd be from one of those, trying with infrared. I was wrong. They were too far gone. But the driver's license was in the first slot, further protected by the flap of the billfold, and it hadn't got stuck to the next plastic slot like the credit cards. But I'm damned surprised at how much we raised." He opened the envelope and slid a still-damp glossy 8 by 10 print before Mendoza.

There wasn't much detail, and it needed a magnifying glass to make it out. But it was probably enough. At the top of the print big blurred letters showed: *CA I OR A DR S LIC E*. Just below to the left, quite clearly legible, the legend *Expires on birthday 1974*. The license number was just a blur, but directly under it—"*Maravilloso*" said Mendoza. "You've got all the appreciation you can deal with, boys." Just under that blur were more legible letters, visible under the glass. *Anita An Ch n y*—no number, but below that, *Cum land R Gl d le, CA*.

"That's a beautiful job, and thanks so much," said Mendoza. "Sometimes you earn your keep."

Horder looked at the print thoughtfully. "And while technically speaking we're not detectives," he said, "we do some thinking too. If that turns out to be a positive I.D., will you tell me just how in hell a dame from Glendale—respectable, conservative, upper-middle-class Glendale—got stashed dead under a ramshackle house in the middle of the inner city?"

"I wish I knew," said Mendoza.

TWO

EVERYBODY BUT HACKETT was out, hunting the possible suspects in the heists, men listed in Records with the likely pedigrees: all too often an exercise in futility, but the kind of thing they got paid to do. And they were shorthanded, with Rich Conway unexpectedly laid low with an emergency appendectomy last week.

Hackett looked at the print respectfully and said, "Now that'd be one big fat miracle, if you've got that corpse identified so soon."

"Mmh, yes, there is that," said Mendoza. "The marvels of science, but there's no guarantee that the handbag belonged to the corpse. But by all probabilities—and I think we bypass our own Missing Persons. If she was reported missing anywhere in the country, the record would get sent to us eventually, but—mmh, yes, *Expires in 1974*—the stack of back records on microfilm—"

"And there's at least part of an address here."

"Shortcut," said Mendoza. "If she's in Glendale's records, there wouldn't be so many to paw through. So come on, let's go and ask." He flipped a hand at the lab men. "And thanks very much for the nice work."

He swung the Ferrari into the parking lot of the Glendale Police building at a quarter to twelve. This force was about a tenth the size of the LAPD, but it had a reputation as a good one. The headquarters building was new and handsome, light and dark gray cement slab, with wide steps in front. Hackett showed the badge to the desk sergeant and they climbed shallow stairs to the detective office on the second floor. Only one man was in, a Detective Dahlman, who listened to Mendoza's story, looked at the print, and shook his head.

"Doesn't ring a bell with me, but we can have a look in Records. CHE what, A, B, C, D, could be almost any vowel—but with part of an address showing—that's got to be Cumberland Road, classy section of town. Let's see if it's in Records." He took them downstairs to their little R. and I. office and showed the print to a rather plain blonde girl, who looked interested. "How far back should we try?"

"Expires in 1974," said Mendoza. "And that house has been empty four years and eight months. Suppose we start with 1973." The blonde, having copied down the legible lettering from the print, vanished into a rear office, and Dahlman excused himself.

"We're always shorthanded, and this damned heat wave—half a dozen new things turning up just the last couple of days. If there's anything here, Betty'll get it for you."

Hackett's stomach was rumbling twenty minutes later when Betty came back with a page of Xeroxed typing. "This is the only file it can be, sir. It was March 1974, missing person report, and I expect Sergeant Costello could fill you in on details, he handled the case."

Hackett looked over Mendoza's shoulder to scan the terse lines: she'd copied only the initial missing report, filed by John Bryan Chesney, an address on Cumberland Road, Glendale. Anita Ann Chesney, white Caucasian female, aged forty, five-two, a hundred and five pounds, hair light brown frosted, eyes blue. Her car also missing, a two-door three-year-old Dodge, white, plate number such and such.

"There are some follow-up reports if you'd like to see them, sir."

"I think we'll try Sergeant Costello first," said Mendoza. They went back upstairs; a couple of other men had come in now, and Dahlman introduced them to Costello, a blue-chinned tough who stared at the print, at the Xeroxed page, and passed a massive hand over his jaw.

"I'll be damned," he said. "That one. You think you've found this woman? Down on your beat? I will be good and Goddamned."

"Do you remember anything about it?" asked Mendoza.

"That I do. Look, I was just about to go out to lunch," said Costello abruptly. "Might as well kill two birds with one stone, hah?" He led them ten blocks to a small, bright, clean place on a busy corner, where a pert waitress exchanged chaff with him, whisked away with their orders and back with a full pot of coffee. "So," said Costello, facing them across the little table in the booth. "I expect you want anything I remember. Which is chiefly the husband. John Chesney."

"What about him?" Hackett bent to Mendoza's lighter.

"Well—" Costello looked uncomfortable "—I was sorry for the man. He was wild, that is he was cooperative at first, willing to answer any questions—you could sympathize with him, if it happened like he said. According to him, his wife must have been kidnapped, murdered—they were all gay and happy, no arguments, no trouble, happy family, no reason for her to walk out, he was struck all of a heap. He leaves for work that morning, everything just as usual, when he gets home she's gone, the kids say she was gone when they got home from school. So far as he knew she'd just been going out to lunch with a girl friend in Pasadena, should have been home by three-thirty or four."

"And you didn't buy it?" asked Mendoza. "What's the background for the Chesneys?"

"Well, I couldn't buy it, after I looked around," said Costello, stirring sugar into his coffee, "because I've got some common sense and I've been a cop awhile. She was a grown woman, and it was broad daylight. Oh, we looked— we did the legwork on it. The neighbors saw her drive off about eleven-fifteen that morning, looking perfectly normal—she waved at them. They couldn't say whether she had any luggage in the car. Husband says none missing. The woman she was meeting for lunch expected her to show up at about twelve-thirty, claims she never saw her. Well, they were old friends, so she could have been covering up. I still don't know whether she was. But it wasn't as if Mrs. Chesney would've been passing through any rough areas—''

"Very respectable section of town," agreed Mendoza lazily.

"Sure. We looked around, what else? The husband couldn't say how much money she might have had, cash that is, but she had her checkbook." Costello was silent and then said, "Damn it, I got annoyed at him later on, I got the feeling he had to be covering up something—the way he kept telling it over and over, it was all sweetness and light, they'd never had an argument since their wedding day, no reason for her to walk out without warning—''

"And you think she did?" asked Hackett.

"Damn it, I don't know," said Costello. "I did once. You asked about backgrounds. Well, Chesney was doing all right, his own realty business, but he wasn't a millionaire. Nobody kidnapped the woman. She drove off free as a bird, just never turned up at the girl friend's—if that woman wasn't lying—never came home, and she wasn't mixed up in any accident, taken to any hospital or jail. She was in the middle of the city, crowds all around, and like you say a respectable area. She couldn't have been held up or abducted. And when her car turned up—''

"Oh, it did? Where?" The waitress came back with their orders and Costello attacked his sandwich hungrily.

"It was either two or three days later, we could look it up. It was parked in the public lot at the Union Station—we had an A.P.B. out on it, naturally, and one of your boys spotted it. We towed it in and looked at it, and there was nothing. But nothing." Costello spread his hands eloquently. "She'd never been printed, so we couldn't check that, but there were a couple of unknown latents on the dash, probably hers—a woman's anyway. The car was absolutely clean, no blood, no dirt, no mess—nothing to say she hadn't just parked it and walked away."

"Which you think she did." Mendoza poured more coffee.

"Damn it, I did. We poked around the station. I found a ticket agent who said a woman kind of like that description had bought a ticket to Chicago from him, paid for it in cash, that day. He was vague about the time, but it was a coach fare on a train leaving about four that afternoon. I had a theory by then," said Costello with a short laugh. "I thought it made sense. I thought Chesney had been covering up a row, maybe on account of the kids, and she'd just walked off to scare him a little."

"It might look like that," said Hackett. "The kids?"

"Teenagers—boy and girl. Nice kids. Nice people," said Costello. "Upper-class people. You know? Not the kind of married couple who can have a big fight, yelling and hitting, and make up an hour later. Never argue in front of the kids, everything battened down, all smooth on the surface. It just looked to me as if there could have been a row, the kids not knowing—oh, I asked 'em, and they said Mom and Dad never had arguments, officer—about money, or another woman, or whatever, and she got in a huff and took off. Probably, I thought, she'd turn up in a week or two, all over her mad. Only she didn't." Costello lit a cigarette and blew smoke in twin flares from his nostrils. "And I changed my mind."

"Why?" asked Mendoza.

"Time," said Costello tersely. He refilled his coffee cup. "Chesney kept pestering us for nearly a year, believe it or not. I never knew when he was going to show up, hadn't we found out anything, what were we doing about it, did we know any more. And offering wild suggestions. She'd been knocked on the head for her diamond ring, the girl friend was hiding her for some reason—" Costello shrugged. "I ask you. She did have a couple of good pieces of jewelry on, by the way, and we put the description out on the pawnbrokers' hot list, but none of it ever showed. Nothing says the girl friend was anything but completely honest—another nice woman, grass widow with plenty of money. So then the way I read it, it was funny Mrs. Chesney didn't turn up of her own accord, the way it looked she'd gone. And the more I thought about it, I thought—up to the time you walked in just now—she must have had a brainstorm. It didn't seem likely, it doesn't happen often, but people do."

"Sudden attack of amnesia?" said Hackett.

"It does happen. For one thing, there were no checks written on her account after that day. Chesney didn't think she'd have had over fifty or sixty bucks on her, but he wasn't sure, he didn't know just what she had in her checking account—"

"Separate one?"

"Yeah, she had some money of her own, four-five thousand a year, from her parents. That was another thing, they hadn't any relatives at all—both only children, their parents dead, no cousins or aunts or uncles. Nobody for her to run to. She could have had a brainstorm of some kind, and for no reason or any reason gone downtown, got on that train to Chicago, and vanished into the blue."

"But they usually turn up," said Hackett. "You followed that idea up?"

"Call me thorough. After about two months, when that's what it looked like to me, I did. Asked the Chicago boys if a woman of her description had showed anywhere, amnesia victim, psycho case, incompetent, in jail or a hospital. And nobody had. So then I thought—sometimes you grasp at straws—maybe she'd just stepped into another personality—like that stage play—forgot who she was, and was maybe quietly waiting on table in the Loop somewhere as Sally Smith—"

"In any case," said Mendoza, "it never crossed your mind that Chesney had anything to do with her vanishing away?"

Costello gave him a cynical glance. "I said I'd been a cop awhile. That was one of the first things I checked out—not that there was any remote idea in my head that she was dead, no evidence of that at all. She was alive and well when she left the house at eleven-fifteen that morning. He'd left for the office at seven-forty—the kids saw him go. And between eleven-fifteen and the time he got home at six-thirty Chesney was in somebody's company every minute, except for the odd five minutes in the lavatory—his partner, secretaries, clients."

"*De veras.*" Mendoza finished his coffee. "Well, we'll have to look him up, get her dentist's name, see if we can get the corpse definitely identified. It looks as if it's got to be her, but just how in hell she could have ended up down there— Has Chesney been pestering you lately?"

"No. It was about a year later he quit coming around to ask why we weren't still looking for her. We ran it into the ground, Mendoza. There was nowhere else to look, ask questions. And everything that showed on it—or didn't show—led us to the conclusion that she'd gone voluntarily. I don't know if he finally realized that, accepted it, or not. I was just grateful he got out of our hair."

"Understandable. What's the realty firm?"

"Chesney and Willard, out on Glenoaks. This is the damnedest—well, after all the legwork I did on it," said Costello, "I'll be interested in what you turn up. If it is her. And if it is, all I can say is it must have been magic. Abracadabra. Little green men from Mars snatching up her and the Dodge off the Pasadena freeway—" He shook his head. "It's more likely she just dropped the handbag, in the middle of an amnesia attack, and your corpse picked it up. Or is it? I couldn't say."

"Well, we'll hope to find out," said Mendoza. "Thanks very much—we'll be in touch."

In the Ferrari, instead of turning out of the lot onto Glenoaks Boulevard, he went straight up Brand, looking for Cumberland Road. "But amnesia victims," said Hackett, "practically always turn up somewhere."

"On the rare occasion they don't." Mendoza was peering at street signs. He had to follow several side streets, avoiding dead ends, to get as far north as Cumberland. He drove slowly along it looking at house numbers; it was a broad, quiet street with very well-bred-looking houses behind immaculately groomed yards. The Chesney house was a gray French-Normandy stucco on a corner. "Very nice," said Mendoza. "But I suppose there won't be anybody at home now." However, he parked and they went up to push the doorbell.

After a moment the door was opened by a nice-looking dark-haired woman. She stared at Mendoza's question. "Chesney? I'm afraid— Oh, that was the name of the people we bought the house from. I'm afraid I don't know where they moved. It was two and a half years ago, I don't know if the post office— It was through a realtor, Mr. Willard over on Glenoaks, he might know."

"So," said Mendoza, switching on the ignition, "does the plot thicken? Chesney, after protesting too much, also vanishing away?"

"Your torturous mind," said Hackett. "Obviously, they didn't need that big a house any more—or he couldn't afford the taxes any more, way they've been going up."

"Es posible," admitted Mendoza. But five minutes later as he pulled the Ferrari to the curb he added, "Or is it?" The realty office was housed in a smart new brick and stucco building, looking prosperous; and the sign on the window read *Willard and Pollock.*

Inside, the atmosphere was stark modern. There were doors to two private offices, seven or eight desks scattered

about, but nobody visible but a redheaded secretary indus-
triously typing at an L-shaped desk near the door. She
looked up brightly. "Can I help you?"

"We're looking for Mr. Chesney," said Mendoza.

The smile faltered. "I'm sorry, I never heard of a Mr.
Chesney. None of our salespeople—"

"Mr. Willard, then."

"Mr. Willard's out, but he said he'd be back by five. If
you'd like to leave your name—"

Mendoza gave her a card. "Would you ask him to call me
if he gets back before six, please. It's rather urgent."

"Yes, sir, certainly." Her mouth dropped open and stayed
that way as she glanced at the card. She stared after them as
they went out; she looked excited.

CHASING DOWN the heist suspects was rather like making
bricks without straw, and about as rewarding. Lacking any
positive identification, you hunted up men with appropri-
ate pedigrees out of Records, and fetched them in to lean on
them—if you found them—in the usually vain hope that one
of them would say, "Oh, yeah, I done that job, how'd you
know?" On occasion it did happen, so it had to be tried.

Nick Galeano was tired of talking to the stupid pros, and
just as glad to get out of more of it when a new call came in
just as he got back from lunch. Higgins was talking to a
shrewish-looking woman at his desk, Glasser was talking to
Wanda Larsen at his, and nobody else was in. The squad-car
man had said, homicide. Galeano said amiably, "Either of
you like to go out on a new corpse with me?"

"Certainly," said Wanda, getting up instantly. She was
hot for street experience; give her a few years, thought Galeano, and she wouldn't find the job so exciting. Unless, of
course, she got married and quit. There was a little speculation on the grapevine about Wanda and Glasser, but nobody knew anything for sure.

It was Adams Boulevard; they took Galeano's car. He didn't offer any conversation on the way; he was ruminating about Marta Fleming. And a little about himself. He surprised himself a bit, settled bachelor suddenly thinking about getting married. Suddenly falling for that prickly German girl. But a good girl; he hadn't got her to come and meet his mother yet, but he would. Marta had some definite old-fashioned ideas about how widows should behave, but damn it, the man had been dead nearly five months. Marta hadn't had much out of life the last few years; he'd like to try to make life some better for her. And now he knew just how to make her laugh.

It was her day off from the restaurant where she worked, and she hadn't a night class at the high school where she was taking stenography and typing. She'd agreed to go to dinner with him; he hoped he could get off a little early. He was going to take her to that place in Burbank everybody raved over; he'd never been there himself.

When they spotted the address on Adams, another squad car had joined the first and a noisy crowd, all black, was being held at bay by the uniformed men. It wasn't a belligerent crowd, but anxious and excited. As Galeano and Wanda got out of the car, they caught snatches of comment— "Somebody said Mr. Hanley took sick—" "Don't hear no ambulance comin'—" "Lord God, sure hope nothin' serious—" "They more cops? Can't be the doctor, he got no bag—" "I was in there just a while ago, he's O.K. then—"

"What've we got?" asked Galeano of the first patrolman. They were holding the crowd at the curb with some difficulty, the other two guarding the door of the little corner store. A faded legend on the awning said *Groceries Wine Beer Tobacco*.

"The proprietor, looks like," said one of the uniformed men. "This lady here's the one called in." He and his partner had her between the crowd and the door, waiting agitatedly; she was a thin, very black woman in her thirties, wearing a blindingly bright pink housedress. She had one arm around a thin black youngster in jeans. "Mrs. Hooper."

"O.K.," said Galeano. He went over there, Wanda following him, and showed the badge to the woman. He didn't have to ask questions; she started to talk rapidly, compulsively.

"I knew there hadda be something wrong, just like I told these officers, see, I'd sent Tommy here to get a six-pack of beer, gettin' so hot in our place, and he come back and said Mr. Hanley wasn't there, he hadda go to the drugstore up the street and the man kind of argued about sellin' it to him, I mean Mr. Hanley knows ever'body along here and knows Tommy'd just be buyin' it for me or Dave, that's my husband, but I knew there hadda be somethin' wrong, Mr. Hanley's always there, open seven to six, eats his lunch right in the back room, but Tommy said he called his name real loud and he wasn't there—so I come to look, and Lordy, Lord, that poor old man—nice old man, he was awful good about givin' credit to folk down on their luck, he carried us a whole month time Dave lost his job—"

Galeano left her gabbling at Wanda, telling it all over again, and went past the second team of patrolmen into the store. It was a little, old-fashioned place, very stuffy and hot. There was a double freezer case, only a couple of unshaded bulbs for light at the rear, narrow shelves crammed neatly with the usual cartons, all the staples. There was a scarred old wooden counter at one side, with an old-fashioned cash register at one end. Galeano went around the counter and looked.

Mr. Hanley looked curiously dignified in death, a portly old black man with gray kinky hair. His gold metal glasses were smashed on the floor beside him, blood had soaked the gray hair and flowed down his neck and chest; on his other side, as if dropped in haste once used, was a short thick chunk of two-by-four, with blood on one end. The drawer of the cash register was open, and there wasn't any paper money in it, only coins.

Galeano bent and felt the man's hand. It was quite warm, warm as life. A hot day, and no air conditioning in here, but he didn't think Hanley was long dead. Less than an hour, maybe. And this busy street, people and businesses all around— This would make some legwork.

He went out to the nearest squad car and called up a mobile lab truck. It didn't look like anything complicated; there might be prints all over that register, even the two-by-four; the lab could lift prints from almost anything these days.

While he was at it, he called the office and asked for some help. They'd have to ask questions at every place around here. Sergeant Lake said Landers was just in, he and Glasser would be down.

LANDERS HAD JUST come back after another session with the pharmacist, Kenneth Lowe, and the only nice thing about it was that from where he sat opposite a stack of mugshot books, he could see his wife at her desk out there in the ante-room of Records and Information—slim, flaxen-haired Phil, neat in her navy uniform.

The pharmacist wasn't nearly so good to look at. He was very much on the defensive, and surly. "Well, it sure looked like the one held me up—I thought it was. It's you says he wasn't the one—"

"He wasn't. We'd just like you to look some more, Mr. Lowe, and take your time—look carefully and don't jump to conclusions. I know it's confusing to look at so many different faces, but if you'd just—"

Nothing conclusive had come of it, of course. Lowe, once bitten, was reluctant to commit himself and the most he would do was point out one shot and say it might be him, or somebody who looked like him.

Landers noted the name and thanked him. "The citizenry," he grumbled to Phil as Lowe went out. "Well, let's have a look at the pedigree and see if it fits." Phil looked it up for him and it did: Jerome Becker, two counts of armed robbery. Unfortunately he was still in Folsom doing time.

"You can't win 'em all," said Landers. "Unless I get tied up on something, I'll take you out to dinner."

"We can't afford it," said Phil. "The timer just turned the roast on three minutes ago, and we're having spinach salad and new potatoes with parsley."

"Oh, well," said Landers, "I ought to go see Rich in the hospital tonight, anyway."

He didn't suppose they'd ever drop on Lowe's heist man. He didn't much care one way or the other. When Lake chased him and Glasser down to Adams Boulevard and they heard about Mr. Hanley, he groaned and said to Galeano, "Why do these things always happen in a heat wave? We'll have to talk to a hundred people here, and probably nobody can tell us anything. Who notices a customer going into a grocery store?"

"Somebody might have, if he came out with blood on him," said Galeano.

It was Jason Grace's day off. He got up a little later than usual, and before it got too hot went out and mowed the lawn, back and front, of the colonial-style house in View Park. Virginia came out after a while and put the baby on a blanket under the apple tree, and drove off to the market.

Grace watched plump brown Celia Ann with amusement as she tottered here and there, still unsteady on her legs. When Virginia got back and had put the groceries away, she came out to the backyard and said, "I've turned the air conditioning on—you'd both better come in out of the sun." She watched Celia staggering after a butterfly, and laughed, and then said, "You know, Jase, it doesn't seem to be going to happen, does it? One of our own."

"Doesn't seem to, Ginny."

"And she's nearly fifteen months old. If we're going to look for another, we'd better start."

"I guess we had," said Grace gently.

HACKETT HAD JUST EMERGED from an interrogation room, helping Palliser to question one of the heist suspects, and glancing at his watch noted absently that it was only an hour to end of shift, when Lake buzzed him.

"I've got Gloria Holt and her mother here," he said expressionlessly, "asking for you."

"Oh, hell," said Hackett unhappily. "All right." He didn't know why he should waste time on them. It was over and done.

They came in drearily and sat down beside his desk, looking at him in silence. Gloria was a good-looking girl, smartly dressed; her mother had the same neat regular features and pale brown skin.

"I—we just wanted to ask you," Gloria began, "if—if there isn't something more to do. For Jody. You've been nice, Mr. Hackett—Jody said all of you were nice to him, even when you think he did it. But he never did, Mr. Hackett, he never killed Les Fulger. I tried to explain before—sure, he knew Kathy but she was never his girl, just a friend, he wouldn't go killing over her—"

"Well, you see," said Hackett, "seven witnesses—"

"I never thought I'd be saying, thank God Daddy's dead. It just about killed him when Jody got in that trouble as a kid—we've always been honest, respectable people and— It just isn't right!" Gloria uttered an involuntary sob.

Hackett was aware of that. They weren't riffraff, but solid citizens. Jody was the only one of the family who'd ever been in police trouble. "You see, Miss Holt, it's out of our hands now. He's been arraigned and he'll have to stand trial."

"But those people, they're all wrong—he never had a gun—Bea said we were fools to come see you, what should you care, but you were polite to us yesterday in court and I thought—"

"We don't want to waste your time, Mr. Hackett," said Mrs. Holt quietly. "I can see there's nothing much you can do now. But you being a policeman, you'll know something about courts and lawyers and so on—like Gloria says, we never had any call to—" and her smile was bitter. "What I want to ask you, about that lawyer the judge appointed for Jody—is there some way we could get a different one?"

"Why?" asked Hackett. "Who is he?" That detail had come in writing from the court clerk; he hadn't seen it. Most cops had a nodding familiarity with the Public Defender's office.

"His name's Morrison. He doesn't *care*—he thinks Jody's guilty, he told him it'd be a waste of time to say he's not, try to fight. He said just plead guilty and it'd probably only be a three-to-five-year sentence. *Only!* said Gloria.

"I don't like the man," said her mother. "Even aside from that. Mr. Hackett, I tried to bring all my children up right as good Christians. Jody got into that trouble that time, got in with some bad boys in high school, and he was punished for it. That's all past, he goes to church regular like the rest of us, he's had a pretty steady job driving a truck for this moving company, till they went out of business. He's straightened up, he's a good boy. He never did what you say. But one thing I do know, as a Christian, Mr. Hackett—it's just as sinful to tell a lie and say you're guilty of something when you're not, as the other way round."

"I see," said Hackett meaninglessly. He placed Morrison after thought: a dapper, cynical-eyed young Negro. "Jody can petition the court for another attorney, but I don't know that it'd do much good. There's always a back-log of cases, all the attorneys tied up for months—" He hesitated, and then said, "Look, maybe it would help if I talked to Jody —and Morrison."

"Would you, please—explain that Jody's got to say he isn't guilty, because he *isn't*—"

"We'd surely be grateful for anything you could do, Mr. Hackett."

"I'll see what I can do," said Hackett. And of course there wasn't anything, but as he'd told Luis, he didn't feel easy about Jody Holt. Seven witnesses—but after this many years as a cop, you got the gut feelings.

When they'd gone he went across the hall to tell Luis about it; but he was on the phone, talking absorbedly, swiveled around to face the window. It was six o'clock. Hackett got his hat and went out.

He took longer than usual to get home, because he was driving more cautiously these days; he could see traffic lights all right, but not pedestrians, or boys on bicycles, until he was on top of them. He was feeling more indignant than surprised: such infirmities happened to other people. He might have to fight a continual battle to keep pounds off, but so did other men: failing eyesight was something else again, obscurely alarming.

He came in the back door and found Angel standing over the stove. "You're late, darling. Dinner in ten minutes." Five-year-old Mark came at a run to greet Daddy, Sheila after him on shorter three-year-old legs. Hackett took a step toward them, Angel said, "Look—" and the big gray Persian got between his legs and sent him sprawling flat. The floor shook, and his family immediately erupted in gales of mirth.

"Daddy fell down! You look funny, Daddy!"

"Funny!" echoed Sheila, giggling.

"For heaven's sake, Art, Boy was right in front of you!"

"That's right," said Hackett, getting up stiffly, "laugh at your elders. Ow. This is getting serious, damn it—I never saw hide nor hair of him—damn it, I think I've torn my shirt—''

"Well, never mind," said Angel briskly. "You've got an appointment on Thursday morning with a Dr. Rumbold. He's an ophthalmologist—I thought we'd better be sure it's just middle-aged farsightedness—''

"What the hell do you mean, middle-aged?"

Angel cocked her brown head at him. "I wonder how you'll look in glasses."

HIGGINS TOOK OFF a little early, feeling tired. He didn't much like Mrs. Lewis, and suspected she knew more about what went on in that apartment building than she was letting on. Not that it mattered much. The A.P.B. would turn up Leroy Riggs sometime, and eventually an autopsy report would tell them how Sylvia Swain had died.

He felt better when he got home, to Mary and the kids: Steve and Laura, Bert Dwyer's good kids, and their own Margaret Emily, surer on her fat legs every day. Steve, looking more like Bert all the time, had some new snapshots to show him, and Laura of course was at the piano.

"Tough day, George?" asked Mary. "You've got time for a drink before dinner."

"I'll take you up on that," said Higgins gratefully.

THE NIGHT WATCH came on, Piggott and Schenke first, Shogart a little later. Schenke had taken to crossword puzzles lately; he was a patient man and a tolerant one, but when Shogart switched on the beat-calls on his transistor radio, Schenke's mouth drew tighter and tighter. Finally he put the puzzle away and went down the hall for coffee. Piggott wandered after him.

"I swear to God, Matt, I'm going to ask for a transfer back to day watch. That fat slob—''

"Now, Bob," said Piggott. "He's never got used to the change, you know." Shogart was a holdover from the old

Robbery office, merged with Homicide a couple of years ago. He only had a year to go to retirement. He'd vaguely resented the younger men coming in, the new superior officers. "He's just marking time."

"I know that," said Schenke, "but it's damned annoying. Why he has to have that damned radio on—"

It was a welcome break, five minutes later, when they got a call: a heist at an all-night market on Third. They both went out on it, leaving Shogart dozing lightly and the radio blaring about a 415 on Wilshire.

"How are the tropical fish?" asked Schenke on the way.

"Oh, fine. I'd kind of like to try breeding some again, but Prudence says over her dead body."

ALISON STILL HADN'T found a handyman to fix the swing. She now had acquired an unmanageably large remodeling plan on construction paper, which she had spread out on the living-room floor after dinner, and only nodded vaguely at Mendoza's announcement that he was going out again.

"So, go. Maybe by the time you get back I'll have this figured out so I can explain it to you. I don't understand all these builders' symbols, if that's what they are—" She was sprawled out on the floor, red hair tousled. "And it's no help that James-or-Luisa keeps getting in the way." The cats, fascinated by a new game, came to investigate. Mendoza left them at it and went out into a gratefully cool night; the hot nights would come later, with the city baked through.

On the phone at ten minutes of six, Willard had sounded incredulous to the point of incoherence. "I don't think—on the phone—really, I can hardly believe—I'm sorry, did you say Lieutenant, I'm not making much sense, but if you could possibly—either my office or home, I must hear about this at once—of course you don't know what a personal shock—" The appointment made, he had rung off instantly. He hadn't mentioned Chesney's name, given Mendoza a chance to ask.

Somewhat intrigued, Mendoza cruised up Glenoaks Boulevard in Burbank looking for Frederic Street. This wasn't too far from the four and a half acres, the estancia and old winery that were to be Alison's *La Casa del Gente Feliz*, the house of happy people. When he found it, Frederic Street was not very long, with newish, small houses and well-kept yards. At the Willards' there was a very bright porch light, and the door was opened five seconds after he pressed the bell.

"I apologize for dithering at you on the phone, Lieutenant. But this is so incredible—you caught me a hell of a way off base, shall we say. Sit down. My wife."

Willard was a short plump, bald man with steady dark eyes. His wife looked a good deal younger, a trim blonde with a friendly smile. "Can we offer you coffee, Lieutenant?"

"Thanks very much."

She went to get it, and Willard sat down suddenly on the couch opposite the chair Mendoza had taken. This small living room was pleasant, neat, rather nondescript. "You said—you've found Anita. After all these years. Incredible's the wrong word. My God, what this will do to Ann and Bryan—" He brought out a handkerchief to polish his bald skull.

"We don't know yet, Mr. Willard. We want to talk to Mr. Chesney. Very probably dental records will be the only definite way to identify the body. Could you tell me—"

Willard stared at him. "You don't know," he said. His wife came back with a tray, set it on the coffee table. "Ruth, they don't know about John. I thought—"

"Then we'd better tell them, hadn't we?" she said calmly. "It's queer how things work out, Alan, but now we know Nita's dead—well, we knew she must be—it's all right, you know. They'll be together, and all right. Cream or sugar, Lieutenant?''

"Neither. Chesney's dead?" asked Mendoza.

Willard uttered a long sigh and sank back on the couch. "Yes. You see, this hits me—hits us—pretty personally. John and I weren't just business partners, but lifelong friends—we were in school together. I was his best man—he was mine. Our kids grew up together—our two boys—Ann and Bryan. I don't know if I can explain it—or whether I have to—what a—a fundamental shock that was to him. Nita—it isn't a thing that happens, somebody just disappearing. Ordinary people—an ordinary family—doing ordinary things. You know? Bryan and our Bob both fifteen, mixed up in Scouting—Ann was in high school—I remember we'd just made that deal for the new shopping center in Thousand Oaks, a nice profit—" He stopped. "Look. Look. What John said to me, the police asking questions about another man, whether she drank, gambled, quarrels between them—a lot of crap! Excuse me, but it was. They were an ordinary quiet couple, John and Nita—didn't run around to nightclubs, didn't drink, oh, one before dinner—it was a lot of garbage! Nita was a homebody. Just that day, she was going out to lunch with an old friend, Felicia Russell—only she just never came home. And the police asking all the questions—but they never found out anything. You don't know what it did to John. If you're married, a happy marriage, just try to imagine—"

"I expect he can," said Mrs. Willard, looking at Mendoza thoughtfully. "Nita had just ordered some new drapes, for one thing. And she was having a dinner party for six couples the week after she—went."

"I see," said Mendoza. "You saw each other fairly frequently? You'd have known if there was any friction between them?"

"Friction!" said Willard. "They were both quiet, easygoing people. I tried to tell the police—they asked me questions too, but I don't suppose that sergeant—he looked like a gangster—ever meets respectable ordinary people! And finally they just stopped looking, decided she'd left him after a fight—which is just silly. What it was like for him— He used to drive over the way she'd have been going, that day, asking questions, did you see, did you notice— And he was very bitter about the police. He couldn't seem to make them understand— At the last, he planned it all out, you know. He was always a smart businessman,'' said Willard simply. "The house was nearly paid off. He took some of the profit from that Thousand Oaks deal, and got it clear. That was three years ago this month. God!'' said Willard. "If I'd suspected—but he was keeping up the front, I thought he seemed a bit better, more himself, that last month. It was a Friday—I'd just closed a deal on an acre in Glenoaks Canyon—'' Willard shut his eyes. "He said, 'So long, Al, see you in the morning,' and off he went. And that night after the kids were in bed he went out to the garage and started the car with the doors shut— He left me a letter. And one for the kids. He felt they were pretty well grown, could get along without him, then—Ann was nineteen, Bryan nearly seventeen. He knew we'd do our best for the kids.''

"You wanted to know about the dentist,'' said his wife gently. "They went to Dr. Streicher on Central in Glendale.''

"But—finding her now—you didn't say where or how— what in God's name happened?''

"I haven't the slightest idea yet,'' said Mendoza. "I'll want the Chesneys' address, and this Russell woman.'' They nodded at him dumbly.

THREE

On Wednesday morning Mendoza came in a little late, and collected everybody there in his office—Hackett, Palliser, Grace. "God knows what ramifications might turn up to work on this one, you'd all better have the background." As usual, he was dapper and elegant in silver gray Italian silk, snowy shirt, discreet dark tie. He lounged at the desk, over coffee from the machine down the hall, and gave them a succinct account of the Chesney thing; Hackett, who had heard most of it, listened patiently.

"I wonder why Costello didn't know he was dead. At any rate, he knew what he was doing—if a suicide ever does. He got all his affairs in order, changed his will in favor of the children, paid off the house clear, and took himself off. The girl was nineteen, the boy seventeen. Willard saw them through it, sold the house, and so on. There was enough capital to give them a modest income. Mrs. Chesney had left what she had to the children outright, but of course that's in limbo, she couldn't be presumed legally dead for another three years from now. At the moment, the son and daughter are living together in Glendale, Ann Chesney working as a steno somewhere, Bryan attending Glendale College."

"You're presuming the corpse is Anita Chesney," said Hackett.

"We'll know soon enough." Mendoza grinned. "According to the yellow pages, Dr. Streicher's office is closed on Wednesdays, so I got hold of him at home last night after I saw the Willards. I don't think he'd ever talked to a police officer before, he was as thrilled as a ten-year-old. Asked to help the police—one of his patients maybe murdered! He'd have fetched his records and rushed right down then—I convinced him our surgeon would appreciate him more this morning. I'd take a bet he's at the morgue now routing out Bainbridge."

"I suppose it's got to be her," said Palliser, smoothing the line of his admirably straight nose absently. "But what a funny thing. No handle. How in hell could she have landed down there?"

"You could," said Grace, "build all sorts of stories, but maybe we'd better wait for some facts—whether it is her, how she died and when. Speculation isn't our job."

"Tell the man," said Hackett. "You know him, Jase."

"Maybe speculate is all we can do here." Mendoza sat back and blew smoke at the ceiling. "I don't know that we'd get much from an autopsy. That house—oh, yes, that condemned house—and dates. If we speculate that she did land there, somehow, the day she disappeared, or even within a few days, that was early March four years ago. Four years and three months ago. Just a while, five months or so, since the house had been condemned and the tenants evicted. But that doesn't rule out the erstwhile tenants, who knew the house was empty—"

"Four of them," said Hackett. "I don't remember who they were except for Buford Talmadge, which is a hell-elegant name for a villain. But they were linked to the house most recently. They couldn't know she wouldn't be found right away. But, Luis, how would a crew like that have been in contact with Anita Chesney?"

"De veras," said Mendoza. "It's up in the air. A very pretty tangle. How the hell did she end up down there, boys? Costello says she'd have been driving through a very respectable area of town—true—Glendale, Eagle Rock, Pasadena—if she'd been accosted by anybody, ran into any trouble, there were helpful honest people all around."

Palliser said, "That's true enough, in town. But wouldn't she have been on the freeway? That one wouldn't be packed in the middle of the day."

"Oh, come on," said Grace. "He's playing games, John. The next thing he'll say, how do we know she was heading for Pasadena? Because everybody said so. I suppose we've all got some imagination. So she was being blackmailed by a former lover and had a date to pay him off? Down on Sixty-second? The date with the girlfriend was a blind and she was really off to meet a gigolo?"

"I haven't the slightest idea," said Mendoza. "But at the time everybody who knew her complained about the police having nasty minds. She doesn't really seem to have been that kind of woman, Jase."

"Let's wait for some facts," said Grace.

"We've got a few already." Mendoza reached to the side of his desk and drew the handbag towards him, where Horder had left it resting on a half-sheet of newspaper. It was desiccated and half rotted, but it was possible to see what it had been. A March day when Anita Chesney left home; whatever she had worn, she had carried a dark handbag, probably worn dark accessories, shoes, gloves. The bag had been black patent leather, a generous-sized envelope bag with double plastic handles. Mendoza picked it up by the bottom edges and suspended it over the sheet of newspaper, and a few objects slid out. "The lab's still got the billfold. There wasn't any money in it at all, or the remnants of any. Chesney said she'd have had a little wad of cash."

"But he also said he wasn't sure how much," said Hackett. "We don't know."

"Conforme." Mendoza's long fingers hovered over the objects on the paper. A faint smell of decay arose from that. A once-gold-finished compact, much corroded, probably a good one originally but mass-produced. There were a few grains of fingerprint-powder clinging to it. A wadded-up

mess of scarlet paper—probably there wouldn't have been anything left of it if it hadn't been in the handbag—which had been a nearly full pack of Pall Mall cigarettes. A folded handkerchief, stained with mold and mildew as was the handbag. A book of matches. A rusted butane lighter. And that was all.

"I thought she was supposed to have a checkbook," said Hackett. "Costello said—"

"But she didn't sign any checks after that day," Mendoza reminded him. "At least—mmh—no checks on her account, genuine or not, were presented. Costello wouldn't have missed that. Maybe she didn't have it with her."

"But the inference is, she was robbed. You really haven't got many solid facts," said Grace.

Mendoza's hand paused over the bag. "Oh, yes," he said. "'She fell among thieves.' Well, we know a couple of things. She didn't carry a cigarette case—just cigarettes, loose. Rather odd for a woman. There could have been both cash and the checkbook, and the thieves smart enough not to try forgery. But just how the hell—that ramshackle place in the middle of the inner city—"

"You're supposed to be the one with the crystal ball," said Hackett. "Meanwhile, until we know it was her, there are more definite things to work. Did anybody tell you about the new heist?"

They left him there brooding over the handbag, cigarette in the corner of his mouth.

"That's the kind of thing," said Grace with a smile, "he gets a lot of mileage out of. No handle all right—even if she's definitely identified, there's not a solitary lead pointing anywhere. It's damn tedious hunting the heist men, but at least you know where you are, more or less. I suppose somebody'd better go get a statement from the latest victim."

Mendoza had shoved the handbag to one side and had the deck of cards out, practicing the crooked poker deals, when

Dr. Bainbridge bustled into his office at ten-thirty. The doctor was balder and tubbier than ever, with the inevitable black cigar in one hand.

"You do come across the damnedest things, Luis," he said interestedly. "I had this eager beaver dentist descend on me just as I got to my office and found your note about that corpse. He was game, I will say. Not used to corpses, especially one in that state, and at one point I thought he was going to pass out on me, but he pulled himself together and we checked through the whole list. Fillings, bridge, caps and so on. Which all showed up to match his records. I was surprised—never thought you'd get an I.D. for that one."

"So it was Anita Chesney."

"By all the dental charts. What led you to the dentist?"

Mendoza told him absently. "Well, it had to be her. But beyond that—one great void. No handle you can say. *¡Vaya por Dios!* Cumberland Road—that house—and Sixty-second Place—'¿Qué sé yo?—* Listen, Bainbridge, I'd like a full autopsy report as soon as you can get to it."

"I doubt if it'll give you much," said Bainbridge comfortably. "One thing I can tell you right off the bat—she wasn't shot, or knocked on the head—there's no skull damage at all. If she was shot elsewhere, unless the slug's in her or nicked a bone, there probably won't be anything to show. If she was strangled, or knifed, ditto. The corpse is partly mummified, partly skeletal. It's just luck she had some distinctive dental work—if she'd had a set of perfect teeth, the driver's license would just have given you a presumed I.D. I'll have a look and send you a report, but I have a suspicion the identification's all you'll get from the body." He ambled out.

"*¡Porvida!*" said Mendoza, annoyed; and then he laughed. The identification was the hell of a lot more than he had expected. He picked up the phone and dialed Willard's office, found him in, and passed on the news.

"Well," said Willard. "I don't know what to say. It just seems—impossible."

"I'd like to see the Chesneys. I suppose Miss Chesney will be at work—do you know the firm?"

"I—Lieutenant, would you let me call and tell them? This isn't going to be easy for them. I can set up a meeting—say at their apartment? That might be easier—any time you say."

"Quite all right. One o'clock? You'll let me know, then." Mendoza put down the phone and his eyes strayed to the handbag again; he brushed his mustache back and forth. She fell among thieves, he thought. But how, and when, and where? That quiet classy street in humdrum respectable Glendale, and Sixty-second Place—

YESTERDAY AFTERNOON they had wandered around down here, while the lab team was busy with Mr. Hanley and his little store, asking questions. Galeano hadn't expected much and they hadn't got much; you might think the more people there were around, the greater chance that somebody had noticed something, but it didn't always work out that way. There were a few places they hadn't covered before the end of shift. Galeano, Wanda and Landers headed down there this morning again.

"We'll have to get a statement from the Hooper woman anyway," said Galeano.

"And we didn't talk to the boy," Wanda reminded him. "Not that I suppose he noticed anything, but for the record—" They were in Galeano's car; Landers had taken off separately.

"Sure. You ever been to that Castaway restaurant in Burbank?"

"Mmh-hmm. Lovely," said Wanda. "Like the play. On a clear night you can see forever."

"Really something," agreed Galeano. Marta had loved it; she couldn't take her eyes off the spectacular view and he'd teased her that she didn't know what she was eating, not even looking at it. That was quite a place. "Art was telling me the other day—you know the Lieutenant and his wife have just bought a new place they're doing all over? Old place, a real estate. Art says it's not far from the Castaway place, they'll have about the same view, right down to the ocean."

"Fabulous," said Wanda. "Nice to be rich, Nick. Is it big enough for horses, I wonder?"

"I guess so, if they want some." He remembered Glasser saying something about Wanda being nuts on horses. Funny for a policewoman.

The Hoopers lived in an apartment, one of a row over a block of stores along Adams. When they found the right door and knocked, it was opened to a small bedlam. What looked like fifty little kids chasing around resolved to only five. Mrs. Hooper, again in the pink dress, smacked bottoms and bawled orders and reduced the noise to bearable level. "Excuse me, they're a handful—only two of 'em mine, I mind Mis' Ketch's an' Mis' Edgewood's while they're workin'. My other three are in school."

Wanda explained about the statement, which flurried her. "I don't write too good a hand, miss, I don't know—"

"Nothing like that, I'll just type out what you told us yesterday and you sign it after being sure it's right."

"Oh, I see. I guess I can do that."

"And we'd like to talk to Tommy. To see if he noticed anything in the store. I suppose he's in school."

"No, miss, he wasn't feelin' too good an' I kep' him home. He had the stomach cramps all night and a fever, kind of. I got him in bed."

"Well, suppose I just go over what you told us while Mr. Galeano talks to him." Wanda got out her notebook.

"I guess that chair's clean enough, miss—" She was looking doubtful, little nervous glances between them. Galeano went down the hall: the only way to go, as the kitchen opened out of the living room, a minute table and six chairs crowded at one end. The rooms were all small: off one side of the hall were three bedrooms and a tiny bath. Five kids, he thought. Seemingly decent citizens; the place was a little untidy, reasonably clean.

Tommy was lying on one of three cots in the back bedroom. He sat up when Galeano came in and said, "What you want?"

"Just a couple of answers, Tommy. When you went into Mr. Hanley's store yesterday, did you happen to notice anybody right outside, or just coming out?"

Tommy shook his head. "I didn't see anything. I just thought he wasn't there. And Ma had to get in such a fuss, and go look."

The man might not have been ten minutes dead then. The blood was still wet twenty minutes or so later, when they got there. "There were people on the street, though. Anybody you knew?"

Tommy squeezed his eyes shut, evidently thinking. "They was a bunch of big boys, a little ways down the block. Chip Bishop and Henry Wheelock and a couple I don't know their names. Mis' Day with her baby, she lives down the hall from us, she was just walkin' along. Some other people I didn't know."

That seemed to be all. Galeano thanked him gravely and went back to the living room, said, "Meet you back at the car," to Wanda, and went down to the street. Down the block Landers' long slim figure was leaning on the fender of Galeano's car; he beckoned.

"What's up?"

"Well," said Landers, "we might have a smell of a lead, Nick. I started out where we left off yesterday, the apartments over that building opposite Hanley's store." They'd talked to all the business people on the ground floor first. "This old fellow, Amos Gibson, says he was there all day yesterday—mostly is, he's pretty lame and doesn't get out much. Lives with his daughter and her husband, they both work. He saw all the excitement yesterday, and he says just a while before the squad cars came, maybe half an hour, he saw a young fellow go into Hanley's store. He knew him— a Chip Bishop, and a young hellion, he said, been in cop trouble.''

"You don't say," said Galeano. "Tommy noticed him on the street. Did Gibson see him come out?''

"Nope. He was looking at a magazine, just glanced up now and then, but he's sure it wasn't any longer than that before the squad cars came up."

"I think we'll take a look at Chip," said Galeano.

That was easier said than done. Several of the shopkeepers on that block knew him, but nobody knew where he lived. They got a description, collected Wanda, went back to the office and left her typing the statement while they asked Phil about Chip down in R. and I. She brought them his file in five minutes.

"There you are," said Landers. "Twenty now, six-one, a hundred and ninety. Assault, assault with intent, robbery from the person, attempted rape—what the hell's he doing walking around loose?—you needn't answer that— Just the type to knock over a poor old grocer for the few bucks in the register. The address is Thirty-seventh, but that was last year."

"Well, a place to start," said Galeano.

"I DON'T KNOW what else I can say to you, Jody," said Hackett. "If you want another lawyer you'll have to tell Mr. Morrison."

"Kind of polite, tell him I don't want him for my lawyer." Jody Holt didn't smile at the little sarcasm. He sat head down across from Hackett in the little interrogation room at the central jail, bare except for the wooden table and chairs. He wasn't a bad-looking young fellow, with the same thin sharp features as his mother, his skin darker. He had straight black hair cut surprisingly short; he was clean-shaven. The stubby hand that held Hackett's cigarette shook a little. "I—I—never thought it'd come to—me getting arrested. For that. It all happened so sudden."

"How do you mean? That night when Fulger—"

"No, sir, getting arrested. I—that thing happened, and it was terrible, man getting killed that way even if it was Les Fulger, he was a mean one. But I—well, I just told what I knew, the officers askin', an'—I thought—that was it. You an' the other officer, you come an' asked questions again, an' next thing—next thing you arrest me, say you think I did it—I never in the world expected—it isn't fair."

"You know all those witnesses say you had a gun, they saw you fire it."

Jody didn't look at him. "It's a lie," he said in a low voice. "I never."

"Well, you'll have to go in front of the judge now, Jody. If you want another lawyer, you tell Mr. Morrison. Maybe he'll be just as glad to get rid of you."

Jody didn't smile. "Say, plead guilty, get a three-to-five. For doin' nothin'."

"You want to claim you're not guilty, take a chance with a jury?" Naturally the busy, smart young public defender wouldn't want to get tied up in a long-drawn-out trial like that, the police evidence, those seven witnesses against Jody, the other witnesses. A guilty plea, sentence handed down, the matter closed.

"That's what Ma says to do. I guess it is. Not much chance, but maybe a better one, see." Jody glanced once at him, and down again.

Hackett got up. "You tell Morrison. He's supposed to be representing you, and if he's not doing it the way you want you're entitled to ask for another lawyer."

"He—kind of makes me nervous. Way he knows it all, way he—fancy clothes and all."

"Don't let that worry you, Jody. He's just got the gift of gab."

As Hackett turned to summon the warder, Jody said earnestly to his back, "I never killed that man. Ain't nobody goin' to make me say I did, Mr. Hackett."

Hackett looked after him as the warder led him down the hall. Damn it, he thought, against those seven solid witnesses, that sounded solid too. And Jody, slower-minded than his mother and sisters, didn't have the gift of gab.

Damn it, thought Hackett, wasting time. He drove up to the Hall of Justice and rode up to the floor where the Public Defender's office was. It was a place where a lot of ambitious young lawyers with no money for expensive offices could get a start. Some of them would learn a lot by the experience, go on to private practice creditably; some would be out for the fast buck, use the experience to develop into shysters.

Reg Morrison was in, working on a brief at a neat desk in the common office. He looked up as Hackett loomed over him, his eyes narrowed and he said, "What's biting you, Sergeant?" Even with his jacket off, tie loose, he had the same gift as Mendoza for exuding the utter fastidious neatness. He had a clever, narrow dark face, a faintly insolent expression.

"Jody Holt," said Hackett. "He wants a chance to plead not guilty, and you don't want to waste time on a trial. Give the poor devil a break, can't you?"

Morrison's white teeth flashed in a cynical grin. "Why the hell should I do that, Sergeant? Waste a lot of time on that little punk? What's the point? He did it, everybody knows that. He's got a pedigree behind him, this won't be the last time he's up in front of a judge. I've got a couple of suits coming up that'll be worth some publicity to me. And if you think I'm a cynic, sure I am, but I tell you no lie I gave that punk my best advice. With the evidence against him, his only chance is to cop a plea and hope for a short term."

Hackett hadn't any answer to that; there was too much truth in it. He shrugged and turned away. "Don't tell me, Sergeant," the mocking voice followed him, "you really think that punk's telling the truth, he says, I never done it?"

AT TWELVE-THIRTY a squad car in Hollywood called in to say that Leroy Riggs' car had been spotted turning into a lot on Sunset, and he'd been picked up. Grace and Palliser had been just about to go out to lunch. "Damnation," said Palliser, "George was on that—what was it, oh, that dead hooker in Boyle Heights. I don't know any of the details. You'd better call George, Jimmy. He'll cuss, but it can't be helped."

Higgins cussed; there were things to do on his day off, and he wasn't especially curious about how Sylvia Swain had got herself dead. But he'd have to come in to talk to Riggs; there wasn't anything to hold him on, they hadn't had an autopsy report or anything from the lab.

By the time he got to the office Hollywood had brought Riggs in, and a messenger had brought in a manila envelope from the lab, addressed to Higgins. Grace and Palliser were back then too, and Higgins filled them in on Swain rapidly. The envelope contained all the photos the lab men had taken at the scene. Higgins passed them around, grimacing a little at the reminders of that stinking corpse.

"It doesn't look as if there'd been a fight," said Palliser.

"No, I remember thinking it was all a lot neater and cleaner than you'd expect," said Higgins. "Except for the corpse, of course. Old place, and there was dust—the apartment had been shut up for a couple of weeks—but she seems to have been a reasonably good housekeeper."

"What killed her?"

"I don't know, no autopsy report yet." The corpse had been lying tidily on the bed, which was made; she'd been fully dressed in a white pantsuit, shoes and stockings. "Well, let's see what Riggs has to say."

What Riggs had to say was not much. He faced the two big men—Grace had a report to finish—in the interrogation room with anxious eyes and scared defiance. He was a weedy young fellow looking even younger than his twenty-seven years, superficially good-looking in an adolescent way, with wavy blond hair and pale blue eyes. He was very nattily dressed in sports clothes.

When they started to question him about Sylvia, he said in a thin yelp, "Sylvia's dead? What do you mean, she's dead? She was all right when I left—"

"And when was that?"

"Uh—I don't remember the exact day—"

"Mrs. Lewis says it was the fifteenth of last month. That's two weeks and a day. She tells us you told her you were both moving out."

Riggs shook his head. "The old bitch got it wrong, is all. I said I was moving."

"You'd lived with Miss Swain there for about five years, is that right? Had you had a quarrel with her?" It might have looked like a funny setup to anybody but experienced cops, the young Riggs and forty-year-old Sylvia, but they'd all come across combinations as funny before. You never knew what people would do.

"Yeah," he said after a minute, "that's it. A quarrel. She told me to get out. So I did. And she was all right—just fine. That was the last time I saw her."

And they would never prove any different. With the time elapsed before the body was found, the autopsy surgeon couldn't pin down the time to within twenty-four hours. They didn't even know that she'd been murdered.

"Listen," he said, "this is an awful shock. I didn't know— Listen, I thought a lot of Sylvia. And she didn't have any relations, any family, to pay for a funeral. I'd kind of like to do that, give her a nice funeral. Could I?"

Higgins and Palliser looked at each other. "If you've got the money, no reason you can't," said Higgins. "You can claim the body as soon as there's been an autopsy. But we'd like to have your present address."

"Oh," he said. He licked his lips nervously. "Yeah. Sure."

"Are you working anywhere?"

"I'm sort of looking around. I think I got a job lined up. Listen, this is a shock, honest—she was O.K. when I left, I don't know a thing about it."

"If you'd just leave your address with the sergeant on the way out," said Higgins, after a few more rounds of that. And as Riggs started out, "I don't know why I bothered to come in. Another one all up in the air."

"Like the boss's latest corpse," said Palliser. "That is a wild one. Jimmy was telling me it got identified, which is surprising enough. We don't often have mysteries thrown at us, and if you ask me, even his crystal ball couldn't fathom this one."

"Now that my afternoon's ruined, I may as well hear about it," said Higgins.

MENDOZA SAT FACING Anita Chesney's son and daughter in the neatly nondescript living room of an apartment which would be a far cry from the house on Cumberland Road. This was middle-class Glendale, respectable, nothing elegant. Chesney had managed to liquidate enough to leave them a modest income, augmented now by what Ann Chesney was earning, steno at a local brokerage.

They were both good-looking young people, and very evidently bright young people: the girl with short dark hair, rather a poker face, brilliant hazel eyes; her brother a six-footer with sandy hair and a good jaw.

There hadn't been any exclamations, how awful, how could it have happened, how was she found, where. All that they'd have said to Willard when he broke the news. And they weren't very fond of police.

The girl had just said to him, in a cool voice, "Uncle Alan told us you sounded reasonably intelligent and understanding, Lieutenant."

"I hope so," said Mendoza. There was an ashtray on the table beside him; he lit a cigarette.

"I don't know whether it's better or worse—knowing. And having it all again. I suppose you are—investigating. Going to ask all the questions over again."

"Annie," said Bryan. "They're just doing their job. They've got to."

She had been sitting on the arm of a big chair opposite Mendoza; she got up and sat down in it properly, stiffly upright. "Are you?" she asked. "Going to ask us all over again how much Mother and Dad quarreled, about what, or if she had a boyfriend or got drunk?"

"Occupational hazards, Miss Chesney," said Mendoza in his deep voice, only faintly sardonic. "Police meet a lot of people like that. They were questions that had to be asked, at the time. But you and Mr. Willard make the point—ordinary decent people."

"I'm sorry," she said. "I can see that—now. But to have it all over—it was bad enough then, it was just a nightmare, and then Dad—like that—but we'd just about got over everything. Picked up the pieces, started out new. And then this."

"I can appreciate that." He was giving them time.

"Do you know—how she died?" asked Bryan.

"We haven't had an autopsy report yet. They may not be able to find out."

"But then we'll never know anything more," said Ann. "You don't know, nobody who hasn't lived through it can possibly imagine what it was like— Wondering, trying to imagine what could have happened—and no way of finding out. Just a big blank. And that sergeant asking about—we'll never know now."

"We don't know until we look. Miss Chesney, I've got just a few questions for you. At that time, did your mother have any sort of household help?"

She looked surprised. "What's that got to— Well, yes, we did. A woman came once a week to do the heavy cleaning—wax floors, wash windows, things like that. Mother'd had her for years—five, anyway, I think. Nellie—Nellie—" She looked at her brother, who shook his head. "Nellie Truax," said Ann suddenly. "I don't know where she lived—I don't think I'd recognize the woman, I was usually at school when she came."

"White woman, Negro?"

"Oh, she was colored—the little I ever saw of her, she seemed a nice woman—middle-aged, I suppose."

"Mmh. The Glendale police told us that your father offered a number of theories at the time. Did he, or you, ever settle on any idea that seemed most plausible to you?"

It was Bryan who answered, roughly. "How could we? There wasn't any plausible idea, that'd hold water. She was only driving over to Pasadena to see Mrs. Russell. She did that a couple of times a month. She'd usually be home when Annie and I got in from school. Oh, we thought of a lot of things," he said wearily. "Her jewelry. She had quite a lot— Dad liked to give her things."

"Her diamond ring was the most valuable piece she had," said Ann. "We know that because she had it valued for the insurance company. She always wore it, it was—part of her. That was the reason Dad gave up thinking she'd been attacked in some way—you know, mugged. Because it never showed up. He said mostly the muggers, the kind of thieves who, oh, force their way into a car, like that, aren't professional robbers and don't know a fence, if that's the right word. They just pawn things. Her ring didn't turn up at any pawnshop, the police said, and I suppose they could find out that much."

"Besides, it couldn't have happened like that," said Bryan. "She wouldn't have been out of the car, just going to Pasadena, and nobody would try to force their way into a car in broad daylight in the middle of town. And naturally she'd never have picked up a hitchhiker."

There hadn't been any jewelry on the corpse. *She fell among thieves,* ran the refrain in Mendoza's mind. "Could you describe the ring?"

"There was an official description on the insurance policy," said Ann. "Yes, you see, she had it made. A jeweler here in town made it for her—Mr. Messing, he used to have the jewelry counter at Webbs' but now he's got his own store in the Galleria. The diamonds were my grandmother's. It's—it was—quite a large ring, a center diamond and two others either side. The center one was two and a half carats and the others one carat each. There were little emeralds all round the shank of the ring and around the diamonds. It was yellow gold."

Mendoza calculated rapidly. Worth quite a bit, that fancy piece would be, call it ten thousand on today's market—more. A third of that from a fence, a twentieth from a pawnbroker.

The girl leaned forward suddenly. "Have we got it across to you?" she asked intently. "That we were an ordinary happy family? Living ordinary happy lives? Dad going off to work every day, regular hours. Mother always there? Dinner at six-thirty, and she and I doing the dishes together. School homework. Mother and Dad talking or reading. Once in a while people in to dinner—Uncle Alan and Aunt Ruth—other ordinary people they knew. The alarm at six-thirty, and have a good day, darlings, and home in the afternoon. They were strict about my dating, and that was fine with me. A real square family, Lieutenant." She took a pack of cigarettes from the coffee table, lit one with a shaking hand. "You know, that was such an ordinary day, but I can remember every single second of it. I mean it started out an ordinary day. I had on a new dress, and Dad said it made me look too old, not his little girl any more. I was embarrassed. He left for work just before Bryan and I started to school, he kissed Mother at the door and she said, 'Have a good day, darling,' and he was just turning out of the drive when Bryan and I left. There was an English exam, I was a little worried about it. We had a lot of rain that year, and it started to rain in English class, about ten-thirty, I remember how it drummed on the windows—''

Bryan had got up and was standing with his back to them, looking out this window to the street below. "It was rather fun walking home in the rain—it'd started again by then— and I thought Mother'd be home, she'd been to lunch with Mrs. Russell but she'd be home then and maybe we'd start a fire in the fireplace. Bryan was late, he had a boxing class in the gym. And when I got home the doors were locked, Mother wasn't there. I thought she'd just got talking with Mrs. Russell, and I knew where we kept the spare key hidden in the garage. And when I went in the phone was ringing, and it was Mrs. Russell, and she said, 'Ann, I'm worried to death—where's Nita? She never got here, and I've been calling since one o'clock.' And she said I'd better call Dad, and I did.''

"All right," said Bryan stolidly, turning. "That's enough of an orgy, Ann. You don't need to go on, how we sat and worried, and Dad called everybody we know asking if they'd seen her, and nobody was hungry but we made hamburgers, and then about eight o'clock Dad called the police. I know this has brought it all up again for both of us, but we got over it once, and nothing's changed, is it? We always knew Mother must be dead, or she'd have come home.''

"I'm sorry," she said. "I'm sorry. I know.''

"Miss Chesney," asked Mendoza, "have you a picture of your mother?''

She looked up, faintly surprised. "Yes—'' She went out of the room, came back with a glossy photograph in a leatherette frame. "This was taken on her birthday the year before."

An echo of Bainbridge's voice—*partly mummified, partly skeletal*—and he thought with a little wry smile, what we all come to. He looked at the photograph with interest. Anita Chesney had been a pretty woman, more femininely pretty than her daughter: her hair rather loose around her round face—"light brown frosted," he remembered—little laugh wrinkles about large eyes, a pert straight nose, good teeth behind a wide smiling mouth.

She fell among thieves. It came to him, intriguingly, that even when they got handed the mysteries—as occasionally they did—they were tracking down villains: in this case, they would be trying to follow the trail of the victim. If there was any trail to pick up at all. A cold, cold trail, fifty-one months old.

"What do we do about a funeral?" asked Bryan abruptly.

Mendoza told him about claiming the body. "It isn't Mother," said Ann. "Tidy it away decently. I'm sorry I was rude, Lieutenant."

"If you are—investigating," said Bryan, "only I don't suppose it'd be possible to find out anything, this long after—well, I think—"

"Oh, what does it matter?" she said savagely. "As far as I'm concerned, let it go—it's over and done with." She went into the bedroom and shut the door.

"I guess that's right," said Bryan miserably. "If you ever do find out anything—" He left it there.

Mendoza disliked loose ends. Being here, he drove up to Glendale Police Headquarters and found Costello, rumpled and untidy, struggling with a typewriter over a 510 report. "Why didn't you know that Chesney's dead?" he asked him.

"What?" Costello stared up at him. "He is? When?"

"Three years ago this month. Suicide, and a plainclothes man would have been out on it—there'd have been an inquest."

"I will be damned," said Costello slowly. "Suicide. The poor bastard. Three years—I was in the hospital most of that month, I got shot up by a sniper on the freeway. But it's funny nobody mentioned—I'll bet you Ordway was on it. It wouldn't have been a big thing, I gather—straight suicide? Yes, well, there'd be one report, the inquest, and that's that. And before I got out of the hospital a drunk broadsided Ordway on his way home—he was D.O.A. Probably that's why I never heard about it. We're usually busy—the other guys might never have heard about it."

"I just wondered," said Mendoza. "Thanks for clearing that up."

"That corpse—" It was a question.

"Oh, it was Anita. Dental records."

"I will be Goddamned. Now how in the name of all that's holy did she get down on your beat?"

"*¿Quién sabe? ¡Sabe Dios!*" said Mendoza. He was wondering if it would be any use to talk to Felicia Russell, and deciding that to be thorough he ought to, sometime. The cleaning woman, Nellie Truax—they could have a look, most likely a vain one.

Bainbridge might come up with something at the autopsy.

They could have a stab at looking for those tenants from the house on Sixty-second Place. But they'd been five months evicted when Anita vanished away.

Of course, there was nothing to say she had died the same day she vanished. That was just assumption, perhaps logical, perhaps not.

The sensible thing to do here was to shove the awkward corpse of Anita Chesney into Pending, as unsolvable. Whatever had happened to her four years and three months ago, there was no remote lead to follow up now.

Mendoza stood beside the Ferrari, the heat reflected starkly from the pavement—always ten degrees hotter in the valley—and stared absently at the tropical greenery around the front of the headquarters building.

The boys in his own office joked about his crystal ball, but perhaps the main reason why Luis Rodolfo Vicente Mendoza had a reputation as a detective was his passion for tidiness. The loose ends, the unfinished patterns, annoyed him.

He would really like to know what had happened to Anita Chesney, that rainy March day fifty-one months ago.

AT ABOUT THE SAME TIME Lake was saying to Landers, "Did we ever know it to fail? Get a heat wave started, the bodies begin to pile up."

"Don't tell me." It was three-thirty. Landers and Grace had just finished talking to a suspect and let him go; Galeano and Glasser were shut up in an interrogation room with another. "What and where?"

"Little unusual—a Mr. Meriwether, and he bypassed the squad car, called in direct. It's Virgil Avenue," and Lake passed on the address.

"O.K., we're on it. Where," asked Landers, "is Art, by the way? I haven't laid eyes on him all day, and he hasn't been working the heists."

"I've got no idea. He's been acting absentminded lately—worried about his eyes maybe," said Lake.

FOUR

THE ADDRESS WAS close in on Virgil; a couple of blocks up and this, whatever it was, would have belonged to Hollywood division. When Landers and Grace got there, in Grace's little blue Elva, there weren't any signs of excitement outside. It was an old, solidly built middle-class apartment house, dull red brick, about thirty units on three floors, with garage spaces to each side and behind it.

In the square lobby, with the row of mailboxes on one wall, a burly-shouldered man eyed them and said, "You the cops? Yeah—" looking at Landers' proffered badge "—you sure don't look old enough to be a plainclothes cop, mister." Landers had got so used to hearing that, it didn't bother him so much these days. "Name of Kowalsky—I'm the manager here. I knew you wouldn't want anybody pawing around, I told them to keep out, once we saw she was dead. It's up on the top floor."

They followed him up narrow carpeted stairs to the third floor. Halfway down the hall on the right-hand side two more people were waiting, a man and a woman: the man middle-aged, paunchy, formally dressed in a dark suit and white shirt, the woman a plain sandy-haired female in her thirties, dowdy in a beige dress and flat heels. They looked excited and upset; they eyed Landers and Grace without speaking. "I guess you want to see it first," said Kowalsky. "Then we tell you what we know."

The apartment door was half open. Inside, a chain-lock dangled from the slot, broken. These old apartments had more generous-sized rooms, were more solidly built than newer ones; the living room was a good size, with a big window facing on a small balcony. It was nicely furnished; there were a number of well-tended house plants around, everything looked orderly except for the body on the floor and the coffee table pushed out of place.

The body was lying face up, legs twisted to one side. It was the body of a woman, a plain, rather pug-faced woman with reddish blonde hair, a thin body, wearing a blue cotton dress, white sandals over bare feet. A pair of shell-rimmed glasses was on the beige carpet two feet away, unbroken.

"She's been dead awhile," said Grace, looking closer. Where the bare arms were flung out, cyanotic marks were visible on the underparts.

They went back to the hall. "Her name's Susan Horgan," said Kowalsky. "She'd lived here for eight years. My God, she must've had a fit or something, all I can think. I hadn't seen her since Sunday."

"I'm Meriwether," said the other man fussily. "This is Miss Olson. I must explain—"

"Just a minute, sir," said Landers. "We'll have to get the lab up here. Is there a phone we can use?"

"My apartment, sure." Kowalsky was businesslike; Grace went away with him.

"We expected her back Monday," said Miss Olson agitatedly. "She'd been off with a summer cold. She called in to say she'd be back Monday, that was on Friday, but she wasn't. The office couldn't get an answer, and when she didn't come in today, and the registrar said there wasn't any answer to her phone, I thought—I went to Mr. Meriwether—"

"Hold it," said Landers. "The office where? You worked with her?"

"She was a teacher at San Marino Elementary School. I am the principal," said Meriwether. "Miss Olson is also a teacher. When she consulted me, I thought we had better investigate. As soon as classes were over, we came—it is only a few blocks. Mr. Kowalsky had a key—we got no answer to the bell, of course—but the chain was up. However, we could see Miss Horgan lying there, and of course she might have been alive—and he got a hacksaw to cut the chain. But—''

''It must have been a stroke,'' said Miss Olson breathlessly. ''She was only thirty-seven, poor thing, but with the chain up—she always kept the chains up, she was very conscious of the terrible crime rate, she told me as soon as she got inside she hooked the chain—''

''Yes?'' said Landers. He pushed the door open farther and went back in. He could see where the chain, a stout solid one, had been recently sawed in two: flecks of metal on the carpet underneath. There was a big brown sack standing on the little table just inside the door, and its contents had leaked a dark soggy stain and mess on the table, dropping to the carpet. Gingerly he peered into the sack. Packages of frozen vegetables, a couple of TV dinners, frozen orange juice concentrate. He looked at the body again. She was lying just in front of a long coffee table before the couch, the table was shoved crooked, and there was a visible dark bruise on her left temple. He felt of that gently, and it gave softly under his fingers.

''Depressed skull fracture,'' said Landers to himself. He straightened and looked into the open door at the right. A neat bedroom, nothing looked out of place—twin beds, a chiffonier. The other way, a door led into the kitchen and dinette area, a table and four chairs at the dinette end by a window. There was an outside door leading from the end of the kitchen; it would give on the same hall as the front door. When these places were built, more stringent fire regulations were in effect. That door was locked, and there was another solid chain firm in its slot.

Grace came in to join him. ''The lab's on the way. What's it look like?''

"I'll tell you, Jase," said Landers, "it looks like something out of a detective story. A locked room. Kowalsky had to use a hacksaw on that chain on the front door. And I don't think she had a stroke."

"Locked rooms don't happen in real life," said Grace. "You mean, à la John Dickson Carr? I don't believe it."

They looked, waiting for the lab men. The windows were all locked. There was an extra lock on the sliding glass door to the balcony, an arm that folded down across. On the bedroom window, where a fire escape came within five feet of the ledge there was another extra lock. Just in front of the little table inside the door was Susan Horgan's handbag, a sensible beige leather tote; it was on its side, a few contents spilled out: lipstick, compact, comb, Kleenex—and a big old-fashioned double coin purse, spilling coins but no paper money.

Grace looked at the body and said, "This is impossible, Tom."

"Locked room, like I said. It looks as if she'd just got home, put down the groceries, fastened the chain, and—"

"And," said Grace. "No telling how long she's been dead. The air conditioning's on. That mark on her temple could be just cyanosis."

"Feel it," said Landers. "Educated guess, she got knocked down against the coffee table. Only how did X get out?"

"Oh, don't be ridiculous," said Grace. "She fell down and hit the table after she'd put the chain up, only way it could have happened."

Scarne and Duke arrived with the lab equipment, and they left them to take photos and start dusting for prints. Duke said the morgue wagon would be coming. Landers talked to Kowalsky and Grace to Meriwether and Miss Olson, who had unexpectedly burst into floods of tears.

"Not that I really kn-knew her so well," she hiccuped, "but the poor thing! The poor thing! She'd been at San

Marino nearly ten years, but the last couple of years she just
hated it, living in the city—the awful crime rate—she was
scared to death, living alone. She came from Maricopa, she
got the job here because she had a married sister in Van
Nuys, but lately she just hated it, she had an application in
to the Maricopa school board—''

Meriwether couldn't add any information; Landers told
them they might want to talk to them again, other teachers
at the school. He got the married sister's name after Miss
Olson had cudgeled her memory. Scarne and Duke had finished taking photographs, and the wagon came for the body.
It was getting on for six o'clock then, and other tenants were
coming in, alarmed and astonished to find police on the
premises. They talked to a Cyrus Plenish who lived down
the hall, hadn't known Susan Horgan. ''Most of the people
here have regular jobs, they don't fraternize much—you
know, good morning if you pass in the hall.'' They talked to
a young and pretty Mrs. Eaton who lived on the left side of
the Horgan apartment, hadn't known her either except to
speak to. ''Except Mr. Kowalsky said how particular she was
about locking up. We've only lived here six months—she
didn't seem very friendly, always in a kind of hurry when-
ever you saw her.''

They talked to a young man who came plodding up the
stairs just as they were leaving at six-thirty. He said his name
was Sidney Putnam, and he lived in the apartment just to
the right of Susan Horgan's. He hadn't known her either,
and like Mrs. Eaton he hadn't heard a sound from that
apartment any time he was home. ''I didn't know her at
all,'' he said. ''I've only lived here a couple of months, just
came down here from Seattle.''

They left the lab men still poking around. The initial report could wait until morning. ''I'll be interested to hear,''
said Landers, ''what the boss says about this one. Locked
rooms yet.''

GALEANO AND GLASSER, hunting for Chip Bishop, didn't find him till four o'clock, at a pool hall said to be one of his haunts, on Jefferson Boulevard. They brought him in for questioning. He was a typical street lout, the kind they saw a lot of, and he was smart enough, experienced enough with cops, to know they hadn't a thing on him.

"So I was somewhere around when some dude knocked Hanley out," he said, lounging in the straight chair with an invisible swagger. "So what? I don't know nothin' about it. I dint even hear about it till next day, I guess I went off someplace before the fuzz showed." He was a little too fat, very black, with a big Afro and dirty, scruffy clothes that smelled of stale sweat.

"You have a job, Chip? What are you doing for money these days?" asked Glasser.

He leered at them. "What's with the bread? No sweat, fuzz. Ma gets another brat every year, all the more from the welfare—we do all right. I don't have to rob nobody."

They leaned on him without result. He was on probation, and they could probably get a search warrant without any difficulty, but it wasn't worth the asking. So far as they knew the only loot taken was anonymous cash, unidentifiable. Old Mr. Hanley had been a widower without any family; except for the neighborhood customers who had appreciated his credit, there wasn't anybody to mourn him.

"I was just hangin' around with some pals," said Chip. "They could tell you I dint do nothin'. Henry Wheelock 'n' Flake Henning, a couple others."

The pals were undoubtedly carbon copies of Chip, and their backup worthless. "That was a waste of time," said Glasser when they let him go.

Galeano shrugged. "Maybe. Wait for the lab report, Henry. Maybe they picked up some latents from the register. It wasn't a very brainy job, possibly spur of the moment." If they ever got anybody for it at all, it would be through such carelessly left prints, but it was a long chance.

You couldn't make bricks without straw. And it was end of shift.

Galeano was hungry, but instead of shoving a TV dinner in the oven, at his bachelor apartment, he showered and put on a clean shirt and went out of his way to the restaurant on Wilshire where Marta Fleming worked. She was on duty by then. She came up smiling to take his order, and he looked at her with concealed fondness. She was looking better these days, more cheerful, not so wary of life; maybe he'd begun to show her life wasn't so bad after all.

"The roast beef is very good tonight," she told him seriously, but there was a little smile in her dark eyes.

"Good," said Galeano comfortably. "You better bring me that. Not quite so fancy as last night. That's a nice place, isn't it?"

"Very beautiful, all the lights, the view. I have been writing my mother all about it today."

"We'll try it again." He watched her threading her way between the tables, her good rounded figure, her tawny blonde hair pinned up severely on the job. He wondered what she wrote about him, to her mother and sister in Germany. A nice stodgy policeman, not handsome or romantic but safe. Something like that. Settled-bachelor Galeano, stocky and dark, never very good-looking, and ten years older—he sighed at his coffee. Marta could probably do better for herself.

PIGGOTT AND SCHENKE came on night watch a little early, as usual. In the middle of the week things were usually a bit slower, even on this beat. They exchanged some desultory talk, and Schenke got out his latest crossword. Half an hour later they were still alone, and Schenke said, "E. M. goofing off? Isn't like him. Whatever else about him, he's conscientious."

"Maybe he called in sick." For want of anything else to do Piggott consulted the desk downstairs, but the desk sergeant didn't know anything. "Funny," said Piggott, picking up his paperback again. "He's usually right on the dot."

"Him and his transistor radio," grunted Schenke. Neither of them was missing Shogart.

Five minutes later the desk relayed a call up and Piggott took it. "Robbery-Homicide, Detective Piggott."

"This is Sergeant Connolly, Hollywood. You've got an E. M. Shogart on your squad—he just got shot up, up here. On a heist."

"What?" said Piggott.

"You'll know who to notify. We've got the witnesses here now, and Shogart's in Hollywood Receiving. He's pretty bad, Piggott. He walked in on the heist and tried to take the guy. You'd better get hold of his wife or whoever."

"Well, I'll be—" Piggott, that good fundamentalist Christian, wasn't a swearing man. "We'll be on it, thanks."

Schenke looked up the number and called Shogart's wife; there wasn't any way to break a thing like that gently, but she didn't go to pieces; she'd been a cop's wife a long time. Then they shot up to the Hollywood precinct in time to listen to the witnesses making statements.

"I didn't know he was a cop." The market manager, Frank Philips, was still excited, but in control: a flabby big man. "I knew him, he came in for cigarettes, candy, a lot of nights just before closing, but I never knew he was a cop. I might have known tonight, way he reacted—my God, I'd no more have tried to jump a guy with a gun, but he went right for him—this guy'd just come in, there was only one customer left, I was about to close up—and he pulls that gun—"

The customer was a Mrs. Hicks, young and rather pretty, still scared. "I just froze, I saw that gun—and then the other man, the one got shot, he was getting a carton of cigarettes in the next aisle, he yelled Drop it or something, and he had a gun too—"

"I might have known he was a cop!" said Philips. "It took the hell of a lot of guts to try to take that guy—looked like a cannon he had, and I guess they both fired at the same time, it sounded like Judgment Day—"

Connolly had a private word with them. "It's our baby, but you know we'll have a damned good try at getting him. That's a good man, Shogart. I rode in with him in the ambulance, he gave me a little before he passed out. The guy was young, big, black, plaid pants. Not much, but—" He stopped and then said awkwardly, "I saw he was wearing a scapular, I asked the hospital to get a priest, I guess he had the last rites. Just in case."

On the street outside, Schenke said, "Poor old E. M. Well, give the devil his due, Matt, he's a good cop. I hope to God he makes it."

"We'd better call the Lieutenant," said Piggott. "We'll put up a few prayers he makes it, Bob."

"*¡CÓMO!*" said Mendoza to the phone. He was standing shirtless in the hall, in the middle of undressing. "Well, our grouchy old E. M.—a cop to the last. Yes, let's hope it won't come to that. What about the heister?"

"Philips thought he might have winged him."

"*Así.* Where are you now?"

"The hospital. His wife's here. They aren't saying one way or the other—he's on the critical list, he took a slug in the chest and another in the stomach. God, I hope he'll pull through," said Schenke.

"Amen," said Mendoza seriously. He put the phone down and went back to the bedroom. Alison was sitting up in bed polishing her nails. "You'd hear about it anyway," said Mendoza, and told her about Shogart. Her mouth tightened a little; cops' wives never enjoy hearing about cops getting shot, but it really didn't happen all that frequently.

"I hope he'll be all right, Luis. I know he never—got close with the rest of you, but—"

"I'm betting on E. M. He's a tough one, *amada*. He'll pull through, and take retirement early—go out in a blaze of glory. More power to him."

After a little silence Alison said, "You were telling me about this—thing. The Chesney woman. What a thing. I don't see how you could ever find out anything."

"Eso es duro de pelar," said Mendoza rather vaguely. "A tough one."

She watched him buttoning his pajamas, keeping her mind off Detective Shogart with an effort. "Luis—just where in the name of goodness could you even start to investigate a thing like that?"

Mendoza finished winding his watch and stood gazing at it thoughtfully. "Now that, *mi vida*, is a very good question. A very good question indeed." He reached for the lamp switch. "Go to sleep and don't fuss about Shogart, *cara*. All good cops go to heaven, but I'm betting he'll make it."

"I know it doesn't happen often," said Alison into the dark.

"No. Don't worry—it's bad for James-or-Luisa."

ON THURSDAY MORNING, however, Mendoza didn't seem inclined to leave at the usual time. He called the office to ask about Shogart—"No change—he's still on the critical list"—and poured himself a third cup of coffee.

The twins, full of breakfast, tidy and clean all ready for nursery school, unaccountably vanished ten minutes before the bus was due, and Máiri MacTaggart was quartering the backyard, calling when Alison spotted them, virtuously waiting for the bus at the front curb. On the principle that any change in behavior in a four-and-a-half-year-old was grounds for suspicion, she went out to check and discovered that they had smuggled out the multi-folded remodeling plans.

"But it's show 'n' tell, *Mamacíta*! We want to show Miss Turtle—you told Daddy it shows where we're goin' to keep the ponies, an' my new room, an' Johnny's room, an'—"

"An' the room for James-or-Luisa," chimed in Johnny, "an' *all* our new house—"

"Well, you can't take them. I'm sorry, *niños*, but I need them. Look, you can each take a toy—Terry, why don't you take the big white pussy Aunt Angel gave you? Johnny—"

Fortunately the bus was late. She got them mollified in time and waved them off, and came back for another cup of coffee, told Mendoza about it. The cats were noisily crunching Friskies on the back porch and Cedric was slurping water from his big bowl.

"Um," said Mendoza. "I suppose we'd better look for a good parochial school over there. They'll be starting next year."

"Impossible as it seems," said Alison. She regarded him ironically; he was a little touchy about going back to the fold of the church. But the twins would get a much better basic education in nearly any parochial school. Her smile widened and he looked at her suspiciously.

"*¿Qué pasa?*"

"I was just thinking what my solidly Presbyterian father would say. Turning in his grave."

Máiri straightened from the dishwasher. "Och, no call to worry about it, *achara*. The man must know now what wrong opinions he had. I do believe I'll just slip out to the church and put up a prayer to the Holy Mother for that Shogart man."

"Between the two of you—" said Alison. "Are you going to work this morning, Luis?"

"I'm just leaving."

BUT MENDOZA didn't head the Ferrari down the Hollywood freeway toward the civic center. He turned the other way and drove over to Glendale, up to the house on Cumberland Road, and made a U-turn at the corner and came back past it. This was how she had left, that morning; and taking all things into consideration he thought they could forget any speculations about secret appointments. Everybody said Anita Chesney had been a plain honest woman, contented wife and mother. In all probability, she had simply been on her way to lunch with Felicia Russell in Pasadena; for one thing, she was expected.

The only small reservation in his mind, and it was a very small one, was the time she had left—eleven-fifteen. Intending to get there at twelve-thirty. Surely, a generous overestimation, unless she'd intended to stop somewhere along the way.

He stopped at the corner and looked at the County Guide, open on the seat beside him. Her quickest and easiest way was straight down Pacific to hit the freeway at the entrance just past Burchett. He started down that way rather slowly. It was all residential at the upper end, though Pacific was a minor main drag: middle-class houses, a couple of small apartments; then two blocks of businesses—a market, a beauty salon, a cleaners', doctor's office, stereo shop, dress shop, hardware store. All quite ordinary. At the freeway entrance, a handsome new Ramada Inn to one side. At this hour there was practically no traffic; there wouldn't be much at any time of day.

He slid up onto the freeway. The early-morning rush hour past, there was very little traffic on that either; he passed four cars down to where this Ventura freeway crossed above the Glendale freeway. The smooth broad expanse of concrete, nothing to either side but greenery on the banks, took him effortlessly bypassing east Glendale and Eagle Rock, up into Pasadena. She would have a couple of choices there. She could stay on the freeway up to the Fair Oaks exit, where only a few blocks down she could turn on Los Robles; but that would have taken her a little far north. It was likelier, Mendoza thought, that she had got off the freeway just into Pasadena, at Orange Grove Avenue, and gone through town on Colorado Boulevard. As he turned off there, he was back in the center of town and business again for the first time since getting on the freeway.

Here, Automobile Row: agencies on either side. A few blocks on, thickly crowded businesses: department stores, small shops, coffee shops—and crowds. Dozens of pedestrians thick along the sidewalks. This part of Colorado was narrow; Pasadena was one of the oldest towns in this area. And he had forgotten how conservative Pasadena was about traffic lights. They were timed for 20 m.p.h.—slower or faster, you got caught by every one, and there was one at every corner. He glanced at his watch: she hadn't overestimated the time.

The Ferrari was surrounded by pedestrians, and more cars than he had met on the way over. Traffic was congested. There was no way a would-be mugger could slip into a car, door carelessly unlocked, at some stoplight, without attracting instant attention. On a damp March day, possibly a little less traffic, fewer crowds; but it had been a weekday, it wouldn't have been much less crowded. An intelligent woman like Anita Chesney would have leaned on the horn, yelled, pretended to faint.

With a gun or knife on her? He caught the light at Marengo, and glanced to the side as he waited. He was in the right lane, as she would have been. There was a bus-stop bench there, not ten feet away, as there was at every corner. Four people waiting there; not one bench had been empty. A stream of pedestrians crossing two feet ahead of the Ferrari. No way, he thought. Only a lunatic would have tried it.

He was coming up to Los Robles, and flicked the turn signal, made the right turn. Here, more business: side-street business. Gas stations. A Japanese restaurant, expensive-looking, in an old tan brick building. A few large old houses in spacious grounds, dating from the era when fashionable—and rich—eastern ladies wintered here. Then the houses were smaller, newer, on ordinary-sized city lots. And just before he came to the San Marino City Limits, here was Felicia Russell's house on the right side of the street.

He slid to the curb and looked at the house. It was a very ordinary house for southern California, a small one-story stucco house painted a pinkish-beige with white trim, on a modest lot. There was a chain-link fence around the front yard, possibly also the back, and a well-manicured front yard with a patch of lawn, oleander bushes.

All down this broad street, with only one traffic light (near to business), only two stationary stop signs, there were houses and people. She wouldn't have had to make any stops, to give the would-be mugger a chance, except those; and she might have made the light at Green Street. It was a very wide street; put the mugger waiting on a curb, the lunatic mugger, he wouldn't have had time to get to a car stopped for a stationary sign; she'd simply have taken off. If she'd had any trouble with the car, there were people all around to help.

And most of the way on the freeway, no stops at all, little traffic.

After a moment he got out and went up to the house, pushed the doorbell. It chimed emptily at him; after five minutes he went back to the Ferrari and started the engine.

HACKETT WAS OFF TODAY; Lake had called him at home to tell him about Shogart. As they had all come in and heard the news, they had said about the same things. Poor old E. M., hope he makes it. Shogart hadn't been much liked by any of the men; he hadn't gone out of his way to be liked. But he was a good cop, and they were pulling for him.

Landers and Grace had been out most of the morning at Susan Horgan's apartment; the lab men weren't finished there, but they had made some deductions, dodging them. "I want to hear what Mendoza thinks," Landers said as they came into the office at eleven-thirty. "And I'll snatch half an hour after lunch to go see Rich. He knows Shogart better—he'll be damn sorry." Rich Conway was the only other holdover from the old Robbery office.

Mendoza had just come in; they found him playing with the cards, cigarette in mouth-corner. "We've got a detective-story mystery for you," said Grace.

"I've already got one," said Mendoza. But before they started to tell him about it, Higgins and Palliser came in; Higgins was looking slightly amused.

"We just got the autopsy on Swain, and it's a switch. She died of an O.D. of sleeping tablets, of all things. Well, I said there was no evidence of a struggle—you didn't see the photos, here they are—but there wasn't any suicide note. No estimate of time of death, of course—just ten to fifteen days. So do we read it she got remorseful after kicking lover-boy Riggs out?"

"Anything's possible, George," said Mendoza. He took the photographs idly.

"And there wasn't any used glass around, but she'd have had time to wash it out and put it away. Funny thing for a suicide to do, in a way, but she seemed to be a neat house-keeper. The only thing I don't like," said Higgins, "is that she was fully dressed. Most female suicides put on a fancy nightgown and makeup."

"But there's no hard and fast rule about it," said Palliser. "A few don't."

Mendoza put the photographs down. "What kind of sleeping tablets?"

"Nembutal."

"That's prescriptive. Did you come across the bottle?"

"We weren't looking for one, damn it. It wasn't out in the open anywhere, or come to think, in the medicine cabinet—I looked there, just poking around. She probably took all she had and pitched it out."

"I don't know," said Mendoza to the cards, "how a suiciding lady might feel—even a neat housekeeper—but I don't see her walking down the hall to the trash-chute or whatever equivalent that place has, to get rid of the bottle. Either just before or just after taking the stuff. It's probably in the wastebasket, but I think you'd better make sure."

Higgins eyed him, and a slow grin warmed his irregular craggy features. "How right you are. And how I came to forget one of the basic rules—"

"Come again," said Palliser.

Mendoza riffled the cards between his long hands. "You are an innocent upright young man, John. I've known a great many males who do themselves in without bothering to leave a note to say why. Either they don't care what anybody thinks, or they figure the reason is obvious. But in all my experience of human nature, *compadres*, I've never run across a woman who could resist leaving a note, quite often a long letter, explaining why. They just do it."

"At least," said Higgins, "there's a chance that Mrs. Lewis hasn't got around to cleaning the apartment yet. Or possibly the lab boys, being thorough, turned out the wastepaper-basket. But we'd better go look. And if it's not there—how do you read it, Luis? Riggs somehow slipped the dose into her?"

"I don't read it any way. All I say is that any woman about to kill herself is going to leave a note."

"Well, we'll have a look around." Higgins and Palliser went out.

Mendoza put the cards down, ran a hand through his hair. He had been to the hospital and seen Sylvia Shogart; she had a couple of the married children with her, was bearing up. The hospital was noncommittal about Shogart; he was still unconscious. "Well, so what have you got to show me?" he asked Landers.

"A mystery," said Landers, and presented it to him. They hadn't got any photos from the lab, but he drew a sketch of the apartment on the back of an envelope. Mendoza was intrigued; his long nose twitched at it.

"*¡Qué bello!* Now that is really a pretty little problem."

"In spades," said Landers. "We couldn't get hold of the married sister, a Mrs. Coulter, but we finally contacted the parents in Maricopa, and the sister's up there visiting while her husband's away on business. They're all coming down. But what they told us—and so did the other schoolteacher, and the apartment manager Kowalsky—is that Sue Horgan was scared to death of living in the big city since the crime rate's up so high. She was security-conscious plus. When she came back to that apartment, as soon as she was inside the door she put the chain on. Kowalsky had to use a hacksaw to get in, the chain was solid, and obviously it wasn't tampered with. She had extra locks on the window that just might be reached from the fire escape. She moved from the second to the third floor last year because she thought it was safer."

"And," said Grace, leaning back and lighting a cigarette, "nothing, but nothing, had been tampered with—um—security-wise, that is. Window locks all in place, including the extra bar on the sliding glass door onto the balcony. Chains up on both doors. Everything neat and clean, no apparent rummaging for loot. Also, we found—or rather Duke found—a little cache of money hidden away behind a picture of some pretty posies in a blue vase. Fifty bucks in tens."

"*¡Cómo no!*" said Mendoza. "Old maid schoolteachers. So there wasn't any burglar. The first place a burglar would look."

"Naturally. The only evidence of possible theft is her handbag—coin purse empty of paper money, and it's on the cards she'd have had some. See what the autopsy says, but Tom convinced me—she was knocked against the coffee table. Knocked right out, because there's no other evidence of a struggle there at all. Of course," said Grace, "there is the possibility that she'd just come in—having spent all her folding money on groceries—set the bag down, hooked the chain, and then had a seizure of some kind and fell against the table. She was only thirty-seven, but—''

''You don't think so?''

Grace sniffed. ''Like your reasoning on suicides. The way women operate. She had frozen stuff in that bag, she'd have taken it right out to the kitchen to put away. The coffee table's a good fifteen feet from the door. I can see her putting up the chain, and the next second picking up that bag of groceries. Even if the second after that she'd felt faint, had a fit, whatever, she'd have scattered those groceries when she fell. Since she didn't, I think—maybe—she was putting up the chain when—mmh—she heard a noise, or saw something—''

''To tell her she wasn't alone,'' said Landers.

''Somebody waiting for her,'' said Mendoza. He was interested and amused. ''I take it back about old maid teachers. She'd let somebody have a key? It was a personal motive?''

''I don't know whether she'd never been kissed or had ninety-nine boyfriends,'' said Landers. ''But even if somebody else had a key—or for some reason she hadn't put the groceries away when somebody she knew came and she let them in—even if there was a personal motive, will you tell me how in hell he got out of that place afterward and left those chains hooked and all the windows locked?''

''And I read somewhere the other day,'' said Grace sadly, ''that John Dickson Carr is dead. He might have offered a suggestion.''

LANDERS DROPPED INTO the hospital, the nurses ignoring visiting rules for cops, after lunch. He found Rich Conway sitting up and looking better. He'd dropped some weight; they'd just saved him from peritonitis. He grinned at Landers, sobered to hear about Shogart.

''That's a damn shame, old E. M. God, I hope he comes through all right. I know none of you took to him, and he can be a pain in the ass, but he's a good cop, Tom—a good old-fashioned cop.''

"I guess he proved that last night."

Conway nodded. His usually cynical gray eyes were grave. "I don't mind telling you," he said, "he taught me the hell of a lot, Tom. When I first made rank, under Goldberg. Goldberg's very easygoing, tends to overlook little lapses, but E. M. always kept after us, rules and regulations, do it right." After another minute he added, "Great family man, too—his wife'll be— Well, after thirty-five years, I guess he's just been putting in time, waiting to get out, take the pension, leave the thankless job to the rest of us. I just hope he doesn't have to get out the hard way."

"We'll keep you posted. How are you doing?"

"Better. They're letting me out of here on Saturday, but the doctor said better take another week before going back on the job."

"WELL, WELL, we can fix you up all right," said Dr. Rumbold cheerfully. "Just *anno domini* catching up, Mr. Hackett. It often happens in middle age that—"

"What the hell do you mean, middle age?" said Hackett. "I won't be forty until August."

"Um, early middle age, let's say. I don't think you'll have to get used to bifocals just yet. We'll make up these near-distance lenses for you and see. You had better try wearing them for all close work, but if you feel any discomfort in driving, we may have to consider bifocals later on."

Hackett, still feeling vaguely affronted by all this, picked out a frame at random, a rather squarish tortoiseshell frame, and was told he could have the glasses in a week.

Angel was out with Alison, looking at furniture for the new estate. At least she'd stopped talking about a bigger house since real-estate prices and taxes had started ballooning. Grateful for small mercies, Hackett thought.

God, he hoped old Shogart would make it. Grouchy old cuss, they'd all felt, and he sure as hell hadn't gone out of his way to make friends. He'd resented any change, resented the younger men; or was he just reserved, waiting for them to offer the casual friendship? But Hackett hoped he'd pull through, to retire from the job with time still left to him. Good old E. M., he thought almost sentimentally. And hadn't Luis always said, the man who jumped toward trouble instead of away, the born cop.

He had lunch at a Manning's coffee shop, and called in. There wasn't any change; Shogart was still unconscious. Back in the car, he said to himself, "Damn it, middle age. So I'm getting sentimental and senile."

He drove downtown and found a place to park on Vernon. In the middle of this block, five storefronts were taken up by a rather gaudy scarlet and blue sign that said *Kellerman's for Fun Music and Dancing*. This was an all-black area; there wasn't a white pedestrian on the street.

He walked up to the double-doored entrance, went in. The place was probably only just open; the crowds would start coming much later, around six.

There was, in fact, only one man in the place: the owner, Randolph Kellerman. He was wiping off the horseshoe-shaped bar at the left side of the central dance floor. He looked a little surprised to see Hackett, and then expressionless.

"We're not rightly open," he said. "Not until four. I just unlocked the front to let the boys sweep out."

"Yes," said Hackett. He hoisted himself onto a bar stool. "You know, Mr. Kellerman, I don't feel satisfied about this thing. Les Fulger and Jody Holt."

"What's wrong about it?" asked Kellerman.

"I don't know," said Hackett. They'd looked at Kellerman, casually; he was a good type. Fifty-five, a Navy career man, in twenty years; decent education, a family man

with five grown children and a wife he'd been married to for
thirty-five years.

He faced Hackett behind the bar, a big man but not fat,
his eyes watchful and shrewd; he was medium black, with a
pugnacious jaw and a long nose.

"That .32 shell we picked up," said Hackett.

Kellerman shook his head. "No comment, like they say.
I don't know where it could've come from. I only heard the
one shot, maybe two right together. I was on the phone to
the precinct right then, calling in the 415."

"I never thought to ask you," said Hackett, "but by any
chance do you keep a gun behind the bar—in case?"

Kellerman grinned. "In case of a robbery, or somebody
acting up? I don't have trouble here often, it's a family
place, neighborhood place, we get the decent people in. But
in case of heists, which can happen to anybody these days,
I surely do." His hand moved quickly, and he produced for
Hackett's inspection a workmanlike Police Positive .38,
fully loaded.

"Yes," said Hackett, and sighed.

Those witnesses—and Morrison's mocking accusation.
Jody Holt was just a stupid punk who'd got excited and
fired a gun, maybe not intending to kill, and was just telling a stupid lie to try to get out of punishment. Morrison
was likely quite right—not worth wasting time. Just an unlucky shot for Jody, but he'd held the gun.

Suddenly he thought, looking at Kellerman without seeing
him clearly, an unlucky shot? A very damned lucky shot it
had been—who fired at a man, a human target, without
meaning to hit him? A rank amateur with a gun, thirty feet
away—and a little gun, a .22. Quite a fluke of a shot that
had been.

FIVE

"WELL, NO, I haven't got round to cleaning the apartment." Mrs. Hilda Lewis faced Higgins and Palliser a little truculently, unapologetic. Firm in the knowledge that she was on the right side of the law—what the tenants did was none of her business as long as the rent was paid—she was willing to be frank. "Catch me!" she said with a little shudder. "That bed— We never had a death here all the time I been managing the place. I got a couple nigger women coming to clean on Monday—I haven't been near it. The trash? Well, there isn't one of those chutes you mean—they all take it down themselves, there's a couple big bins in the alley behind. Garbage truck along once a week, on Saturdays."

"We'd like the key to the apartment," said Higgins. The apartment had been sealed until the lab work was finished, but that was two days ago. She produced it without protest.

"I been thinking—all her things—not that I suppose she had much—I better just hand it over to the Goodwill, I don't suppose that Riggs'd want 'em."

Higgins and Palliser climbed stairs to the third-floor-back once belonging to Sylvia Swain. There wasn't any central air conditioning here, and the heat wave was building up. It was very hot and stuffy in the drab old apartment, and the faint sweet smell of death still hung over it.

They looked thoroughly for that little bottle. The lab didn't miss much if given specific orders; here they'd been strictly doing the routine, dusting for prints, taking photos. Higgins had talked to Marx, and the wastebasket had been checked: only one, in the living room; it had been half full of cigarette butts, used Kleenex, an empty nail-polish bottle. Now, they went looking in all the unlikeliest places, kitchen cupboards, pockets of clothes in the closet. Surprisingly, perhaps, she hadn't had many clothes; you could say, in her work she didn't need many. There was food spoiling in the refrigerator, a film of dust over everything.

"I don't," said Palliser, wrinkling his nose at the pervasive odor in the bedroom, "see her going down three flights to the alley at the back, just to get rid of the bottle. Before lying down to die."

"Not likely," agreed Higgins. He straightened from examining the two drawers in the bedside table, and met their reflections in the wall mirror opposite: tall, dark, rather handsome Palliser in a neat gray suit, himself just the ugly nondescript tough-faced cop. "It's funny—but sort of shapeless. No suicide note. Does that say homicide? The pro hookers are apt to run into the violent stuff, but a customer who fed her a dose of Nembutal? Funny isn't the word. It doesn't make sense."

"Very little," agreed Palliser, rubbing his nose.

"I'll tell you one thing," said Higgins, "which I thought at the time. Riggs was lying when he claimed he didn't know she was dead."

"I think we get hold of Riggs again and ask him some pointed questions," said Palliser. He looked around the drab little room and suddenly added, "Though why the hell we're making such a production of it I don't know, George. A four-bit broken-down hooker and a small-time punk like Riggs—what the hell?"

"Sometimes the job gets a little unrealistic," said Higgins. A faint breath of a breeze stirred the sleazy lace curtains, and just brought the hot fetid air of the dirty streets below closer. "Riggs left an address. Tomorrow's soon enough—it's after six."

WHEN PALLISER OPENED the driveway gate, the expectable solid object hit him in the chest immediately, but at the firm command, "Down!" subsided obediently to all fours. "You really are getting civilized," said Palliser, and Trina whined in gratification at his tone. Now over a year old, she just about had her full growth and was a very large German shepherd indeed. He hadn't had much luck with the book about obedience training, but he hadn't the time; Roberta seemed to be getting somewhere.

He went into the kitchen and said, "You know, she is a lot better. Congratulations." He hugged Roberta, bent to kiss her.

Her eyes were grave. "How's Shogart doing?"

"And where'd you hear about that?"

"It was on the morning news, naturally. How is he?"

"Well, he's still with us. On the critical list. We're hoping he makes it O.K. You're not fussing, Robin? Borrowing trouble? The civilians have about the same chance of running into violence these days as any cop."

"I know," she said. "No, it's all right. Dinner's almost ready. And don't you dare go in and wake the baby, I've just got him settled down."

TRAFFIC WAS THICK on the freeway, and it was later than usual when Higgins slid the Pontiac up the drive of the old house on Silver Lake Boulevard. The kitchen was empty when he went in, and the little black Scottie Brucie came skidding across the linoleum to greet him.

"George—" Mary hurried from the living room. "I was just deciding to start worrying—you always call if you'll be late. How's Shogart? Of course it was on the news."

"We'll hope he'll make it." They didn't mention it, but they were aware that Mary reacted to news of cops getting shot more than most cops' wives. Higgins hugged her casually and let her go. "I'm ready for dinner."

"In the oven." Her gray eyes smiled at him. "For once the kids are doing their homework early—you might call them. And don't disturb the baby."

WHEN HACKETT CAME IN he told Angel the latest news about Shogart automatically, as a matter of interest. Angel was a sensible female without a flighty imagination, not leaping to the conclusion that he was going to get shot up tomorrow just because another cop had. He told her about the glasses, and wandered into the living room to be set on by the children. He had to admire the gold star Mark had got for something in his class, and ride Sheila on his knee.

But at the back of his mind he was thinking about guns. A little .22. It took practice to shoot a reasonably good score with a handgun. Anybody, by luck or accident, could make the fluke shot; but it didn't happen very often.

Later, when he was getting undressed, he put the Police Positive .38 away carefully, as usual, in the locked steel box on the dresser, but he stood holding it awhile and thinking before he did.

GALEANO AND GLASSER were off on Friday. As Mendoza came in, a little late, Sergeant Lake said, "I checked the hospital. The nurse said his pulse is better but he's still unconscious. Hollywood called just now—Connolly. They want Shogart's gun."

"¿Qué?"

"They found some blood on the market door—not E. M.'s—and think he may have nicked the heister. Just in case, they want a sample for Ballistics. The hospital passed the gun to his wife, I gave Connolly the address."

"Bueno." But Mendoza hadn't got to his office before three civilians came in, looking nervous, and said they were Mr. and Mrs. Horgan and Mrs. Coulter. Landers and Grace were already in. Mendoza gathered them all into his office, found chairs, briskly introduced himself and his men.

"You'll be the one I talked to on the phone," said Horgan to Landers. He and his wife were looking bemused and bewildered; as it turned out, not even small-town people but farm people from outside Maricopa—Horgan a big man with a tanned face, huge hands, his wife dumpy and plain, both looking uncomfortable in dress-up town clothes. Alice Coulter had acquired town veneer; she was a thin woman in her forties, well-dressed.

Of course they asked how Susan Horgan had died. Landers explained the necessity for an autopsy, and without going into detail the possibility that there had been an intruder, a struggle. "Oh, dear," said Mrs. Coulter. "What she was always afraid of. But you don't really know?"

"Not yet," said Landers. "You understand, you can claim the body as soon as the autopsy is done. We'll let you know. We don't like to upset you at such a time, but we'd like to hear a little something about who her friends were here, any—er—associations she had, if you—"

"What for?" asked Horgan baldly. "If it was a burglar broke in, I don't suppose Sue knew him."

"Well, we don't know that yet, Mr. Horgan."

"You mean maybe somebody killed her deliberately?" He shook his head. "A burglar's bad enough. I can't see sense in the other thing."

Landers looked at him inquiringly, but Alice Coulter spoke up in a forthright tone. "Neither can I. It's a funny thing to say, I suppose, but nobody knew Sue well enough, I guess, to—to have any argument with her. She didn't really have any friends or—associates. Oh, she knew the other teachers, but not well."

"She was always what they call a loner," said Horgan, nodding. "Didn't make friends easy."

Grace said softly, "But she must have had a few acquaintances here, the time she'd lived and worked in L.A.?"

Alice Coulter frowned and looked down at her folded hands. "She had a pretty close friend who lived in the

apartment house. Sally Ford. They used to go out together
sometimes, to dinner or a show. But Sally moved away last
year, she works for a big insurance firm and all the staff was
transferred to Phoenix. Since then Sue—well, I suppose she
missed her. There wasn't anybody else close to her. I don't
know why you're asking anyway. That's just silly, that anyone would have a reason to—'' She shivered. "Poor Sue."

Mrs. Horgan began to cry gently. "I'm sorry, I just can't
help thinking, she never had much out of life. You and Bill
got out, married, had some kids—some grief too maybe but
at least you had something. Seems like Sue never had much
at all. Always holding back from making real good friends,
even at school. I used to be so sorry, tried to tell her you got
to reach out, be friendly—she was sort of pretty as a young
girl—''

Involuntarily Alice Coulter said a little snappishly, "It
was her own fault, Mother. Goodness knows when she was
first here I tried my best to introduce her to people I thought
she'd like. A few men too—but I might have known it was
a waste of time, she wasn't any different then than she'd ever
been. Ruth Thompson and Norma Keller both tried to be
friendly, asked her to dinner—but you know she was afraid
to drive after dark, she'd never go out at night. And the
men—well, I guess that was wishful thinking on my part, all
right. Even with her going to college at Santa Barbara, living awhile in town, she never got over being the shy little
farm girl. Always so tongue-tied with anything in pants, it
embarrassed them. Oh, for goodness sake, Mother, don't
look at me like that. You know it was so."

"She hadn't any men friends at all?" asked Mendoza.
"No close friends at all, since this Miss—Mrs. Ford had
moved away? Did she go out at all, to any social events?"

Mrs. Coulter transferred attention to him, appraising him
interestedly where he sat at his desk, hands making a steeple:
her eyes flickered on his elegant tailoring, the gold cuff

links, the heavy gold ring on his right hand, his sleek mustache.

"No, she hadn't—she didn't. Sally Ford was another one pretty much like her, reason they got on. I always said Sue'd have done better to stay in a small town—she never liked the city. She liked her job well enough, but even there she didn't get on— Well, it's all past and done, let it go."

"There was some friction with the other teachers?" asked Mendoza.

"Oh, friction—I don't know. She was always so quick to imagine people were talking about her, take them up wrong for no reason. It was last year, she said something about some of them being spiteful and gossiping. I don't know what about."

Horgan said abruptly, "Whatever happened, I don't suppose we could help you find out about it. One thing I better ask about, her car."

"Yes, sir," said Landers. "It's at the apartment, you can have it anytime, I can let you have the keys." The little red Datsun had been sitting quietly in its own slot to one side of the building, nothing significant in it. "We may want to examine the apartment some more, but as soon as we're finished with it, her personal effects will be released."

"We'd like to take her back for a funeral at home."

Mendoza explained the procedure for claiming the body; they nodded quietly at him. "We might as well stay with Alice till we can do that, then. I got a neighbor coming in to look after the stock till we get back."

"And what do we make of that?" said Grace when they had gone.

"Tempest in a teapot," said Landers. "What it boils down to, an old maid schoolteacher. What Horgan really meant, nobody'd ever felt strongly enough about her to want to kill her."

"Motives depend on who has them," said Mendoza. "I've got something on my own agenda later on, but I think

I'd like to take a look at Susan's apartment. Tom, it might just be worth interrupting a few of the teachers at their labors to hear any opinions they had, while Jase and I take a look at her security arrangements. We'll meet you at Federico's for lunch."

"It's your time to waste." Landers sounded disgusted. "After hearing all that, I don't think anybody did kill her. Going to all the trouble to fix up a locked room. She had a fit and fell against the table."

"The autopsy or lab report may give us some new idea."

WHEN LANDERS GOT to Federico's at twelve-thirty, Mendoza and Grace were already there, just sitting down at one of the tables in front. Sometimes, coincidentally, several of them would land here at the same time—unless they were far afield on the legwork, it was a favorite place. Nobody else from Robbery-Homicide was here now.

Landers sat down beside Grace and the waiter came up with coffee. "Pick up any spiteful gossip about Sue?" asked Grace.

"I'll tell you one thing," said Landers. "If Phil and I ever have a family—just for a couple of hours of talking to teachers, I'd say a public school is about the last place for any child to try for an education. There was just one I talked to seemed to be a normal sort of girl—good-looking too."

"What was un-normal about the rest? I thought teachers these days—" Grace stubbed out his cigarette.

"Oh, lost in the clouds," said Landers. "I only asked about Horgan's work, was she efficient, they talk about the whole child and Jungian theories of learning. I guess normal enough for teachers."

"The gossip," said Grace.

"Nobody would say anything except Poor Miss Horgan, and I didn't know enough to ask specific questions. Don't they discipline kids any more in school?—a couple of those classrooms, I couldn't hear myself think. The only thing I got, from this young one, Miss Wall, I don't think amounts to a damn. Something to do with a man teacher named Rasmussen. She just said, anything reasonably young in trousers, the unattached staff twittered over, and she had a vague idea that Horgan's nose was a little out of joint over him, sometime last year. Didn't know any ins and outs."

"Mmh," said Mendoza. "I'm bound to say, whatever else, she was efficient at arranging security. There's no way for a cockroach to get out of that place leaving the chains up and windows locked. What about Rasmussen—still at the school?"

"Nope. Transferred to a junior high school at the beginning of this semester. Do you think it's worth the time to look him up?"

"You never know what might turn up. That place," said Mendoza, "is a fortress, damn it. And yet, if you're reading it right, somebody was there. *¡Condenación!* If I could see any possible gimmick to explain that chain—"

"There isn't any," said Grace. "Well, more laborers in the vineyard of justice."

Higgins and Palliser came up and sat down. "I suppose you've heard Hollywood may have a lead on the heister. E. M.'s rallied a little, the hospital says." Higgins leaned back with a sigh. "You wouldn't believe what we've turned up, Luis. I've always said, you don't get rich at being a cop, but you sure as hell get an education in human nature."

"The vagaries of," said Palliser. He started to smile, caught Higgins' eye and they both laughed. "I don't suppose it's so funny at that, if it constitutes a motive for murder, but it was a little surprise, you can say."

THEY'D WANTED TO TALK to Leroy Riggs again, about that missing bottle, about a motive for Sylvia's suicide, about that quarrel. He had been asked to leave his address with Sergeant Lake, and he had left one. Lake produced it on demand; he was on a rigorous diet again and morose in consequence.

Higgins glanced at the slip and did a double take. "Who the hell is he trying to kid? The Beverly Hills Hotel? Riggs?"

"What?" said Palliser. "That's funny. But he seemed cooperative enough. Give him the benefit of the doubt, maybe he's got a job there, busboy or something."

"I suppose that could be." They drove out Wilshire, to that old, elegant and quite expensive hostelry, and at the desk Higgins showed the badge to a tailored personage who stiffened in disapproval of police officers intruding here. "Do you know if there's a Leroy Riggs employed here in any kind of job?"

"We have a good many employees, sir, I couldn't say offhand. Then the three restaurants are concessions and have their own staff." He paused and said after a moment, "What was that name again, sir?"

"Leroy Riggs. He's about five-seven, thin, blond hair, blue eyes—"

"Just a moment, sir. I think—" He reached for the thick register a little way up the mahogany counter. "Ah—excuse me, but it isn't a matter of *arrest*, is it?"

"Not at the moment."

"Ah. Well, here we are. I see they checked out yesterday," said the personage, with some satisfaction that there wasn't about to be any confrontation within the sacred premises. "Mr. and Mrs. Leroy J. Riggs, room eight-oh-four."

"What?" said Higgins in astonishment. Double rooms here might run to sixty dollars a day.

"There couldn't be two of him?" murmured Palliser.

"Registered as from Peoria, Illinois. They were with us, let me see, just over a month. They checked out yesterday, as I said."

"I'll be damned. I think," said Higgins, "we'd like to talk to anybody in the hotel who actually had contact with the Riggses. Maids, bellboys, whoever."

The clerk was annoyed, but resigned to cooperation with the law. Ten minutes later they were in the manager's office talking to a matronly, pleasant woman in a neat black and white uniform. She was thrilled and curious at being questioned by real-life policemen. Her name was Cora Moore.

"Yes, sir, that's him—not very tall, kind of wavy blond hair, a nice smile. Mr. Riggs. They were kind of ordinary people, not like some we get, at least I thought—my goodness, sir, I mean Sergeant, are they jewel thieves or something?"

"Not that we know of. What was Mrs. Riggs like?"

She pursed her lips. "Kind of ordinary. She was older than him, maybe thirty-two or -three. And not very pretty—kind of no color to her, she didn't know how to dress. She had some real expensive things, but not right for her, you know. Mousy blonde hair, she's a little thing only about five feet high, thin figure. Her name's Brenda. But she had nice eyes, real dark brown. And she was *nice*," said Cora Moore suddenly. "Real folks, you know what I mean. Some people with money, new money, treat you like dirt, thinking they're being grand the way rich people should. And some people used to a lot of money are real friendly and pleasant, but you get the feeling they're—" she smiled "—what my grandmother used to call gentry. Mrs. Riggs was just ordinary. Friendly as could be. And she was happy, and having a real good time. They hadn't been married long."

"Did she tell you that?"

"No, she'd be too shy, but you could tell. I had a pretty good idea she had the money. But that's all right, as long as it's tied up tight. All the better. He seemed like a nice young fellow, ordinary too—I mean it was like neither of them was used to a place like this. Kind of a pair of innocents, they were. That's why I was surprised, the police asking about them. Some of the characters here, I wouldn't be a bit surprised, but then—"

"Do you know where they were going when they left?"

"No, sir, I didn't hear anything."

"This is the damnedest rigmarole," said Higgins when they'd thanked her and come out to the lobby. "Mr. and Mrs. Riggs! Peoria! Nice eyes!"

"Well, it says this and that, doesn't it?" said Palliser, stroking his nose as he made deductions. "Shame to spoil the honeymoon, but this could explain Sylvia. Riggs somehow wormed his way into this girl's life, and she sounds like an innocent—Sylvia was making trouble, probably wanted a cut, and he had to get rid of her—she could queer the whole deal for him."

"I see it, I see it," said Higgins querulously. "I'd just like to see some way of proving it."

"At the least we want to question him again, and a lot harder. Let's see if the garage knows what they were driving."

Downstairs in the underground garage a uniformed attendant was also interested to talk to cops. Mr. and Mrs. Riggs? Yes, they'd had two cars. Mrs. Riggs was driving a new two-door Buick, emerald green; it was a rental car from Hertz. Mr. Riggs—a subtle note of disapproval—had several times come in in a ten-year-old gray Dodge with two dented fenders and a broken back window.

"Well, that's the old heap registered to him," said Palliser. "What we got from D.M.V. a couple of days ago. There's no telling where they've got to, but we'd better put out an A.P.B. on both cars just in case."

In any case, it looked more now as if they had a possible Murder One on Riggs, if there was some way to show how he could have got the Nembutal into Sylvia. The garage had the plate number of the Buick, and they had Riggs'; they went back to headquarters and put out the A.P.B.'s.

THE RAPIST-KILLER, Jack Thatcher, was being indicted this morning, and Hackett went to cover that, put in the police evidence briefly. It was over in fifteen minutes; the arraignment, next week or the week after, would be fuller. The judge appointed a lawyer for him, and he was taken back to jail.

Hackett came back to headquarters and went down to R. and I. Phil Landers—she really was a cute one, with her short-cropped flaxen hair and freckled nose—was busy over some mug-books with a scared-looking female civilian and Captain DuBois of Bunco. She came back to the desk presently, noticed Hackett, and said, "What can we do for you, Sergeant?"

"I want a session with one of your projection machines and some microfilm. It's a juvenile pedigree—Jody Holt, it'll be seven or eight years back." No police department of any size would have the space to store ordinary records more than a year back; beyond that, it was all down on microfilm, the only way to examine it with a table magnifier.

"Can do." He followed her back to a vacant small office; she brought him the little projector, and after a longer wait the strips of microfilm.

For the next thirty minutes he had a rather illuminating look at Jody Holt's record. They couldn't print the j.d.'s, but these days some of the most horrendous of violent crimes got committed by the juveniles, and records were kept. On occasion, it could be grimly frustrating to look at those records—the juvenile given probation time after monotonous time, until he graduated into legal adulthood and became at least eligible for some punishment.

Jody's record didn't read that way. When the first strip of film flashed on, Hackett felt a little unexpected chill up the spine as he saw the sprawling signature of the man who had written the report, in the old Robbery office. E. M. Shogart.

Jody was sixteen when he was arrested for armed robbery, along with another sixteen-year-old named Arnold Gleason. It was a stupid effort; they'd held up a drugstore in their home territory and the druggist knew Gleason by sight. He said it was Gleason who had the gun. The gun, an old Colt .45, had belonged to Gleason's father. They both got probation.

About two years later, Jody had been caught burglarizing the cash register of the gas station where he worked parttime. Those reports were written up by a man Hackett didn't know in Juvenile. The money had been returned, Jody had lost his job, and he'd got probation again.

He'd never had any narco counts. That was all the record.

"Well," said Hackett. It wasn't exactly the record of a vicious little punk apt to graduate to mayhem and murder.

He drove down to the jail on Alameda and asked to see Jody. When the warder brought him into the little room, he looked surprised to see Hackett. "Oh, I thought maybe you was my new lawyer."

"You asked for one?"

Jody nodded. "Mr. Morrison just said he'd tell the judge and I'd get one. But anyways, they said the trial'll be a ways off yet."

"Probably," said Hackett. Entitled to speedy justice, that was a laugh, with the backlog in the courts. Jody might wait a couple of months for his trial, and he hadn't made bail. "I've been looking back at your record, Jody, and it's not a very bad one." There were degrees in these things, even armed robbery. "That first time, when you and Gleason held up the drugstore—he was the one had the gun, wasn't he? Did you ever handle it?"

"No, sir. Arn wouldn't let me." Jody took the offered cigarette, bent to the lighter, and said to the floor, "That Arn dude. Ma said, bad company. He sure was, I guess. I— liked him a lot then—we was in school together—I'd do whatever he said. After that time, my dad said I wasn't never to speak to him again. And I never. You know what happened to Arn." He really thought Hackett did, because it had been so important to Jody.

"No, I don't. What?"

"He got himself killed. He got on the H and he went to robbing, get enough bread to pay the supplier, see. One night he tried to heist a bar, and the barkeep, he shot him dead. He was only twenty."

"I see," said Hackett. "You never went in for the narco bit, Jody? Not the grass?"

"No, *sir*." For the first time since Hackett had known him, Jody suddenly grinned, showing even, very white teeth. "I seen some of what that can do to you. I don't reckon I've got such a great big old brain to start, I need all of it there is, Mr. Hackett."

Hackett grinned too. "What about the gas station thing?"

Jody sighed. "It was crazy. It was just after my dad died, he had a heart attack. Ma was awful hard up for money, the funeral and all. She was the only one workin' regular, and I just had that part-time job. I had some crazy idea, you know, help out more than I was—but a'course it wasn't no way to do it."

"No. You know, there's something nobody ever asked you, though I suppose you'd have told us. That night Fulger got shot —did *you* see anybody with a gun?"

Surprised, Jody said, "No, I never. Why?"

"Well, damn it, there was another gun floating around that night, you know. One besides the gun that killed Fulger."

"How d'you know that?"

"We found a .32 shell casing in Kellerman's," said Hackett absently, and knew he shouldn't have said it. Jody would pass it on to his lawyer, and it might be an issue at the trial. It was completely irrelevant to the shooting, but juries had quirks. But if it confused a jury enough to let Jody off, Hackett wouldn't lose any sleep, at that.

"But how'd you know there was two guns?"

"The .32 was an automatic," said Hackett. "The gun that killed Fulger was a revolver. Ballistics can identify individual guns almost the way the lab men lift fingerprints, you see."

"Oh," said Jody.

Hackett looked at him. "You don't know much about guns, do you?"

"I don't know nothing about them, Mr. Hackett."

"Jody, did you ever in your life actually fire a gun?"

He raised his head slowly and looked at Hackett. After a long dragging minute he said deliberately, "I'll tell you true. Just once in my life I fired a gun. And as the Lord's my witness, Mr. Hackett, it wasn't the gun that killed Les Fulger."

ALISON SAID, "I see, thank you." She banged the phone down crossly. "Honestly!" she said to Máiri. "Honestly!"

"That one won't come either, then."

"And I thought I had such a bright idea!" Most of the supermarkets now had bulletin boards somewhere outside, with the free advertising—babysitting, cute kittens free, used refrigerator $25, 1960 Dodge for parts, and so on. This morning Alison, with some difficulty squeezing James-or-Luisa behind the steering wheel of the Facel-Vega, had made a pilgrimage to six markets, studied all the ads, and found four persons, calling themselves handymen—fix small appliances, fix anything, repairs all kinds. She had just finished talking to all four.

Only the first had been unconsciously rude. A rough male voice had said incredulously, "What? Fix a kids' swing? The brackets loose—my God, lady, anybody could fix that in five minutes, if your husband's got two hands—"

Annoyed, Alison had hung up and only then realized she should have said she didn't have a husband, was all alone, and played on his sympathy. The second one asked where she lived and said he couldn't come so far for such a small job. The third one said he had jobs ahead that would keep him busy for weeks, call him next month.

The one she'd just talked to had said, in a high youthful voice, "Oh, gee, didn't I take down that card? I should've. Look, usually I could come, whatever you got, but right now I got year-end exams to study for, I'm sorry."

"Honestly!" said Alison.

"Don't get in a pother," said Máiri. "It's no good for the bairn."

"Well, I will admit," said Alison moodily, "I've got just a touch of cold feet, Máiri. Such a big job—so many things to do—it's costing thousands and thousands. The fence. The blacktop road from the gate. And there'll be landscaping. And the worst of it is *afterwards*. Somebody to take care of it all—mow the lawn and so on. And those blessed ponies. And all the housework—do you know that house has nine thousand five hundred square feet? How I ever got into this—"

"Och, well," said Máiri comfortably, "it'll all work out if the Lord intends it."

LANDERS, HALF CONVINCED it was a waste of time, drove over to Montrose, to the junior high school where, so Miss Wall had informed him, this Rasmussen was now teaching. He asked for him at the registrar's office without showing the badge.

"Mr. Rasmussen?" said the spectacled female clerk. "I'm sorry, he's not here today."

"Well, where is he? It's rather urgent that I talk to him."

"He'll be back on Monday."

"Where is he, do you know?" He brought the badge out with that, and she uttered a frightened squeak.

"Oooh, what's it about? Police—"

"I just want to talk to him. Is he off sick, or what?"

"No, sir. His mother just died, and he's gone up to San Francisco for the funeral. He'll be back on Monday."

"Oh. Well, thanks." Landers didn't really think that Bernard Rasmussen had anything relevant to tell them.

Of course, when they got the autopsy report it might say that Susan Horgan had had a stroke or heart attack, and the head blow was irrelevant. That would simplify matters a good deal. Locked room cases were just dandy between book covers. In real life, on the job, he could do without them.

MENDOZA EMERGED from Glendale Police Headquarters at five-thirty, his eyes feeling tired, and got out the keys as he came up to the long black Ferrari. The dusty pavement reflected smelly heat; it must be ninety-five over here. And he felt that he'd wasted the day.

Not altogether. What Higgins and Palliser had turned up on that hooker—he grinned. Maybe a reason he stayed on the job, even after his grandfather died and all the loot came to light, was his fascinated interest in the endless surprises of human nature.

He'd got delayed coming over here by getting Jane Doe identified—that teenaged O.D. Carey of Missing Persons had brought in a distraught mother just after Mendoza got back from lunch. She'd been on a trip, hadn't known her daughter was missing. They'd been about to authorize a city-paid burial.

He yawned, sliding under the wheel. He'd spent the rest of the day here looking at microfilmed reports—the reports Costello had written, four years and three months ago, and since, on Anita Chesney. Costello had given him the bare gist of the case; he had thought that the day-to-day reports made at the time might show some significant detail, just to hint at some possible lead.

He hadn't got through all of them yet. Costello, though a sloppy typist, was a thorough and energetic detective. He had gone through all the motions and then some. But in the last two hours Mendoza hadn't weeded out any suggestive wheat from the chaff. Husband stated A. C. probably wearing two-piece green nylon dress, black raincoat, black shoes. Southern Pacific ticket agent William Nieland statement on file attached states sold coach-fare ticket Chicago to woman substantially conforming description A. C. approximately one-forty day of first missing report. Correspondence CPD attached.

There might still be a kernel of suggestion somewhere in those records. All the information, the results of investigation, written down at the time, just after Anita Chesney hadn't come home. He would go on and look at what was left, the follow-up reports before the thing petered out and got put into Pending, unsolved and unsolvable cases.

Which it probably would be again. The only difference between Mendoza now and Costello then was that Mendoza had a body.

He switched on the ignition and started home.

THE WORD FROM the hospital was that Shogart was stable, whatever that meant. "It's funny," said Schenke, "how we all used to growl about him—the day watch too, before he transferred—and now here we are praying and pulling for him, hoping he'll make it O.K. Well, damn it, he is a cop, and a good one."

"And from our side of the desk, Bob, I guess that says it all. When the chips are down—" Piggott was supposed to be off on Friday night, but he'd come in because they were shorthanded with Shogart missing.

It was quiet; they didn't have a call up to ten-thirty. Of course that didn't say it was quiet out on the street: the usual things would be going on to make business for the squad cars. "Wait for tomorrow night," said Schenke.

At ten-fifty the desk relayed a call from a squad car: a heist on the street, and the Traffic men were bringing in the victims.

Patrolmen Moss and Wainwright brought them up to Robbery-Homicide at eleven-ten, a tall gray-haired handsome fellow in a tuxedo, a well-preserved blonde in expensive evening dress, mink stole. Mr. and Mrs. Rodney Parton. They were indignant and angry.

"I know the crime rate's up, but a lighted public parking lot outside a lighted building, for God's sake—"

"I don't care about any of the rest of it," wailed the blonde, "but the Medal! It's priceless but I don't suppose a fence'd give anything—"

"Calm down, Paula. I can give you some idea of what the bastard looked like, there was pretty good light—about my height, five-eleven, slim build, I guess more dark than light—he got about fifty bucks from me and my watch, and Paula's diamond ring—"

"And the Medal!"

"Now let's take it in order, sir." Piggott got out his notebook.

They had been to a concert at the Dorothy Chandler Pavilion on Grand Avenue. And when they came out—well, there hadn't been a very large audience, not too many people around, they were late coming out because Paula had misplaced her cigarette case, thought she'd dropped it in the lobby at intermission, they'd looked and found it—just as they got to the car, there was a man with a gun. "A public parking lot!" said Parton. "You don't expect—it was a little way off from the nearest cars, but—"

"Yes, sir. Fifty dollars in cash, and the jewelry. Do you think you'd recognize his picture, if we showed you some?"

"Mug-shots," said Parton. "God, I don't know, it all happened so fast—"

"The Medal!" Paula Parton was sobbing now. "It'd be worth—I don't know what."

"A medal, Mrs. Parton?"

"Yes. The *Titanic* medal." They looked at her uncomprehendingly, and she hiccuped, gained more control, and said, "You know the *Titanic*. The *Carpathia* came and rescued the survivors, and Mrs. Brown—Mrs. J. J. Brown—had these medals made for all the *Carpathia*'s crew. My grandfather was a steward on the *Carpathia*, and I had the Medal from him. It's bronze, but it's in a fourteen-karat frame, on a gold chain—I suppose he thought it was valuable, I mean in money— Valuable! I wouldn't take a million dollars for it!"

"Now, Paula," said Parton helplessly.

SIX

THE *TITANIC* MEDAL made Mendoza's morning. He came in on Saturday to find Hackett and Grace chuckling over it, and was entranced. "We ought to get this and the other jewelry on the pawnbrokers' list," said Hackett.

"I'll see to it—it had better be a detailed description."

Lake was off on Saturday, Sergeant Farrell sitting at the switchboard. The word was that Shogart had been briefly conscious, and barring complications they thought he'd make it. Landers was off too. Mendoza was still discussing last night's new heists—there had been a later one at a bar on Third—with Hackett, and Palliser had just come in, when Grace marched into the office and said, "Well, now we know. And if you have any ideas, I'd appreciate it." He thrust a manila envelope at Mendoza.

It was the autopsy report on Susan Horgan. Evidently it had been a straightforward job; and it said that she had died of a depressed skull fracture apparently occasioned when she had been attacked and fallen against some hard object: the surgeon suggested a sharp-cornered table, a refrigerator, a bedroom dresser. There was a bruise that had broken the skin on her right cheek, coincidental in time with the fracture to the left temple. Estimated time of death, last Saturday to Monday morning.

"We know she was alive on Sunday, Kowalsky saw her go out about five o'clock. But the rest of it—"

"Not really a surprise," said Mendoza. "You deduced it. But how in hell—"

"Just tell me!" said Grace savagely. "Tell me how somebody attacked her and got out of that apartment leaving everything locked and chained up! It's an impossibility—you said it yourself! There's also a lab report, which gives us more of the same." He added that to the other, and Mendoza looked at it.

The lab had picked up a lot of Susan Horgan's prints in the apartment, as expectable: only two other latents. That in itself was funny; however clean a place was, there were usually extraneous prints around left by visitors, sometimes weeks before; but they knew that Susan Horgan hadn't had any visitors as a rule. The two latents picked up had been on top of the chiffonier in the bedroom. They weren't in LAPD's records, had been sent to the FBI in case they were known. And that was all the lab had to say.

"I give up on this one," said Grace, "and what Tom's going to say—I suppose I'd better do a follow-up report."

"That's funny," said Hackett thoughtfully, "but there's got to be an answer. Some simple explanation."

"So you go look at that apartment and find it, *amigo*."

"I mean, it doesn't match. A spur of the moment thing like knocking her across the puss, and then creating a locked room. There must be—"

"I had got there too, but I've seen the place. Damn it—" Mendoza got up with Piggott's notes in his hand. "I've got things on my mind. You go and look at Horgan's place, you'll see what we mean." Galeano came in with more manila envelopes, looking resigned.

"Look," he said. "I've now got a lab report and an autopsy on Hanley, and it's a handful of nothing. They couldn't get anything off the piece of two-by-four. I didn't really expect it. There were a lot of smudges on the cash register, was all. All the autopsy says, he was hit on the head and died of it, he had a thin skull and not much force was needed. I'm inclined to think it's very possible this Chip Bishop did it, he was seen going in there about half an hour before Hanley was found, but there'll never be any way to prove it."

"Claro que no," said Mendoza. "How many of that kind do we waste time on? If we worried about that kind, we'd all have high blood pressure. Shove the damned thing in Pending, Nick, and go and help the other boys hunting the heisters. I've got a little errand." He took up his hat and went out through the detective office.

Galeano, muttering, sat down at his desk to write a final report on Hanley. Grace had a triplicate form rolled into his typewriter but wasn't typing, hunched over that lab report smoking and swearing to himself. Higgins had been typing a report, stopped to light a cigarette.

"I swear to God!" said Grace. "Any day give me the stupid heisters—at least now and then they leave us prints or get recognized in mug-books."

"Piggott said that Rodney Parton was coming in to look at mug-shots," said Hackett. "There's got to be some simple little explanation of the locked room, Jase. Ordinary people don't go to such infinite pains to set up that kind of thing."

"That is an extremely helpful observation, I must say," said Grace acidly.

Higgins took a drag on his cigarette, laid it in the ashtray, and regarded his typewriter gloomily. "Stymied, are you, Jase? So am I, on this Riggs. Even when we pick him up, there's not one damned bit of evidence for a murder charge, only strong grounds for suspicion, and what with the damn fool things females can do, the D.A. wouldn't consider any charge. Unless we leaned on him enough to get an admittall—"

"Bricks without straw," said Galeano from the next desk, and suddenly laughed. "The job gets frustrating sometimes. Look at it philosophically, a lot of the victims aren't so lily pure, though I'm sorry not to nab somebody for old Hanley. We all picked the job—it's our own funeral."

Grace was flicking a disposable lighter vainly, after a moment swore, groped in his pocket and found a book of matches. "No handle, my God—nobody interested enough in the woman to have any reason to murder her, let alone set up the elaborate locked room, and there's no way for anybody to have done that anyway—"

"That's why I say," said Hackett, "that it was accidental somehow." Grace just looked at him, hunched over and began to type again.

Suddenly Higgins sat straight up and let out a bellow. They all jumped and looked at him. "Funerals!" said Higgins. "Funerals—" He leaped up and made for the door. They stared after him.

MENDOZA HAD A COPY of the book at home, but there were bookstores nearer. He seemed to remember that one of the big chains had opened a new one in that underground Broadway shopping mall; he tried there first, and of course it wasn't open yet, but he could see lights and people inside, and rapped on the glass and held up the badge. Grudgingly, a fat woman unlocked the door and told him they didn't open until nine-thirty, even for the police, and what did he want? Just to look at a book, well, he could have waited until opening time like normal people, but now he was here—

They had one copy in—the new, much-illustrated edition of the classic *A Night to Remember*. He leafed through it quickly, found what he was looking for—the photograph of that bronze medal presented to all the *Carpathia*'s crew— and made a detailed sketch of it. He'd often wondered idly what had happened to all of those: probably a number of them jumbled into Grandma's button bag or Grandpa's top drawer—hopefully some of them still floating around were appreciated as the historical mementos they were. He hoped they could recover Mrs. Parton's. A street heister wouldn't know a pro fence, but a pawnbroker would probably give him something for the fourteen-karat frame and chain.

He wanted to get back to Glendale and finish going through those records sometime today. He went back to the office and found Bainbridge waiting for him, with Hackett sitting in his desk chair squinting at a report.

"Well, there's your autopsy report," said Bainbridge, gesturing with his cigar. "And it gives you damn all, Luis. There's no indication how the woman died—no evidence of shooting or knifing. If she was strangled, or poisoned, or even died of a heart attack, there wouldn't be anything to see now anyway. There's not enough of the stomach left, any of the organs, to run tests. And of course it's impossible to say exactly when she died, the day she disappeared or six months later."

"Damn it, we have to go by probabilities. Nobody held her hostage for six months."

"Sure, sure, probably she died that day or within a short time, but I couldn't swear to it. I'll say again, you were just lucky to get the body identified positively, it's more than you might have expected."

"*Ya lo creo,*" said Mendoza resignedly. "What about the clothes?"

"What clothes? A few shredded pieces of cloth. Not enough for the lab even to look at," said Bainbridge, puffing.

"We couldn't expect it," said Hackett, putting down the report. "*Finis.* There's no lead at either end—where she began or where she ended."

"We can have a look for that Jones couple, the Smith girl, Talmadge—"

"Oh, don't be silly, Luis. Sure they knew the house was empty, and so did everybody else that lived on that street or a couple of blocks around. And the transient population of an area like that, everybody renting, my God, it'd be impossible to track down even just the people living on that dead-end street at the time. And so what if we did? Just as an academic exercise, think about it. Suppose we collected 'em all, maybe two, three hundred people, just what connection would there be? *¡Nado absolutamente!*''

"You tell me nothing, Arturo."

"As far as I can see," said Bainbridge, getting up and brushing cigar ash off his comfortable paunch, "it's just one of those things to provide food for thought on long winter evenings. Or for your memoirs. Exercise in imagination—what did happen to the woman, how'd she get there? And echo answers how. You'll never find out because there's just no way to tackle it."

"For God's sake don't say that to him," said Hackett. "He'll work it into the ground, Doctor, from now till Christmas."

"*¡Diez millones de demonios!*" said Mendoza. "There's got to be a handle somewhere."

"Let me know if you ever get hold of one," said Bainbridge. "I'm curious too." He bustled out.

Palliser looked in and said, "How about earning your keep, Art? Jase and Nick are on reports, and I've got a possible heister to lean on."

Hackett went out, and Mendoza, looking at his watch to find a good part of the morning gone, set to work and drafted the little list to add to the hot list for all pawnbrokers, copying the sketch of the medal carefully—he thought it would reproduce. He gave it to Farrell to send down to Communications and had his hat in hand ready to leave when Lieutenant Carey of Missing Persons came in.

"Something a little annoying, Mendoza. You know that suicide a week ago yesterday? Man found shot in the cheap hotel room on Temple? There wasn't any I.D., and you passed the description on to my office. Well, we just got him identified—he was listed as missing from Azusa, his name was Edgar Mundy—but Azusa took their own sweet time sending in the description and prints. They checked out yesterday, and this morning I've got his wife on the phone wanting to claim the body, and damn it, the city buried him yesterday.''

"Awkward. Where do I come in?''

"Well, damn it, I'm up to here in paperwork,'' said Carey. "And it's your office handles the corpses, after all. You can call her or write her and explain there'll have to be an exhumation order. Here's the name and address.''

"¡Condenación!'' said Mendoza; but least said soonest mended. He sat down again, put through the long-distance call to Azusa, and spent fifteen minutes on the phone with a tearful female who had to tell him how despondent Edgar had been lately, not being able to get a job, and what with the ulcers not eating properly, but she'd never dreamed he meant to kill himself, she'd just been worried out of her senses when he'd gone off like that, but now she knew he had, of course she wanted him buried in the family plot. Mendoza was patient, finally got a chance to talk, explained about the exhumation order, at last got rid of her.

It was getting on for eleven o'clock. He took up his hat again and was just passing Sergeant Farrell at the switchboard when Farrell let out a yell of unseemly mirth into his phone. "What? Well, the boys do get handed some fairly crazy things now and then, but that's got to be the craziest in a month of Sundays! O.K., we'll get somebody on it. What's the address again?''

Fatally, Mendoza paused. "Something funny, Rory?''

"Oh, my!'' said Farrell. "That was a squad—Zimmerman and Foster. Somebody has left a body in a Goodwill salvage bin. The collector nearly had a heart attack when he came across it just now, among all the old clothes.''

"¡Me gusta mucho!'' said Mendoza, awed. "And they say, nothing new under the sun. This I have got to look at. Where is it?''

HIGGINS' CONSCIOUS MIND hadn't dredged up the memory until Galeano spoke the word, and then the coin dropped and he made the connection. And he could have phoned, but he knew the morgue: half the time not enough people on duty, or undressing corpses in a back room.

Probably, he calculated by the autopsy report, Sylvia Swain's body would have been due for release on Thursday sometime.

At the morgue, the one clerk in the outer office said disinterestedly, "Swain? Just a minute," and rummaged in the files. "Yeah, a fellow came in Thursday and wanted to claim the body. We didn't have any authorization yet, I told him he could sign the papers and tell us what to do with it. He did. We got the release on it yesterday and notified the undertaker they could pick it up."

"Which one? Let's see the duplicate claim." As he'd expected, it was signed by Leroy Riggs.

"King and Anderson, over in Pasadena. They sent a hearse for it yesterday afternoon."

"O.K., thanks," said Higgins. A damned peculiar thing, he thought. He hadn't given it much thought when Riggs came out with that, taken it for granted he was putting on a little act; now he wondered. He was just curious enough to follow this up. He drove down to the Stack, got on the Pasadena freeway and half an hour later was talking to Mr. Charles Anderson of King and Anderson Morticians.

"Oh, yes. We had specific instructions." Anderson was appropriately cadaverous, tall and solemn. He looked somewhat bewildered at Higgins' badge. "May I ask what the police interest is, Sergeant?"

"I don't know that there is any directly. What were the instructions, and from whom?"

"Why, a Mr. Riggs spoke to me on Thursday—late Thursday afternoon. He explained that a family connection of his was in the city morgue—all he said was, and of course as a tactful man, I hope, I didn't ask any questions, was that it was a sad story but of course he wanted her to have a decent funeral. He asked about rates, and—"

"Just a minute. He came here?"

"No, he was on the phone. I quoted him some figures, said perhaps he'd better come in, choose a casket and so forth, but he said he couldn't do that, he was leaving the city. It was rather unusual," said Anderson, "but in my experience people are a trifle queer in the presence of death, Sergeant. It was all quite straightforward. He asked if a thousand dollars would be sufficient to cover a—er, a decent funeral was how he put it, and I said it could be done for that. You see, he didn't want a service, a minister or any ceremony. Just, he said, a nice casket and some flowers."

Higgins was sure Riggs would have said coffin. "And I suppose she's buried now."

"Well, um, when we brought the body in, it was in a condition that made it somewhat mandatory to expedite burial," said Anderson, neatly euphemistic.

"I believe you," said Higgins.

"She was buried this morning, quite a nice plot in Rose Hills. I accompanied the casket myself—it seemed strange not to have any service, I felt it was the least I could do."

"Yes. How were you paid?"

"Mr. Riggs sent a cashier's check on a local bank. It arrived by special delivery yesterday morning."

"I will be damned," said Higgins. "Didn't you think it was a little peculiar, Mr. Anderson?"

Anderson looked at him gravely. "Some queer things happen in this business sometimes. We render services for payment received, Sergeant."

Higgins, however, thought it was a little peculiar. Not that Riggs should have arranged the funeral: that could have been a sop to his conscience. A lot of people were superstitious about such things. But where in hell had he got the money? So far as they knew he'd been living on Sylvia except when he had the casual little underpaid jobs, some of them part-time. Granted, he now seemed to have hooked up with this innocent female who had some money, and by what that hotel maid said, she was paying the bills while they lived high, wide and handsome. You could imagine her paying bills for his new clothes, the hotel bills, and so on; conceivably she even supplied him with ready cash. But also going by the maid, Brenda was sold on him as an upright young man; she thought they were married, at least. And it was a little difficult, in any case, to imagine any girl reacting with calm sympathy to the plea, "Just let me have a thousand bucks, honey, I've got to arrange a decent funeral for my ex-girl friend in the city morgue."

He pulled himself together and laughed. Of course, Riggs could have, would have, told some plausible tale. But he still thought it was a funny thing for Riggs to have done. And it didn't offer any help in locating him: they'd hope the A.P.B.'s would do that.

A GOOD MANY public places had the Goodwill bins handy for the convenience of the charitable public disposing of unwanted items, chiefly old clothes. This one was at one side of a big public parking lot on Third Street.

Mendoza had collected Galeano to join him, and he said now, flicking on the left-turn signal, "We might have expected a crowd."

"Nine days' wonder, all right."

There were two squad cars there, three uniformed men dealing efficiently with a curious crowd getting bigger every minute. This was a business area: two big markets within this block, a tall office building, blocks of stores. The parking lot was crowded with cars. Mendoza parked in a yellow zone and they walked into the lot. The lab truck was on the way.

The Traffic men greeted them with relief. "This is the damnedest thing I ever saw," said one of them. "I thought first we'd have to call the paramedics for the poor old guy, but I guess he's coming out of it." Up there against the side of the office building, the fourth uniformed man was bending over a half-recumbent figure; beside him was a woman in a nurse's uniform. "She's the one called in. A Mrs. Snell. She works in a doctor's office in the building, was just coming out to the lot when he yelled, and she kind of took charge."

They went over there first. The man propped up against the building was elderly, scrawny, neatly dressed in ancient clean denim overalls. He was very pale, but his eyes were open and he was sitting up sipping a paper cup of water held to his lips by the efficient Mrs. Snell.

"You feeling better now, sir?" asked the Traffic man.

"Oh, my God," he said in a faint voice. "My God. A terrible shock that was. Me thinking I'd got a break, get this good job with the Goodwill. Nice easy job—just go round pick up the old clothes. My God."

They went to look at the body. It wasn't immediately visible. The Goodwill bin, like all of them, was about five feet square, with a generous-sized square hole in its front. Stenciled brightly on both sides of it was the legend, *Thank You For Your Contribution!* Mendoza chuckled at that, bending down to peer in, and one of the Traffic men offered a flashlight. "My week for finding bodies in strange places," said Mendoza, and switched it on.

In order to empty the bin, the collector would unlock the entire front of the thing, which was hinged and folded down. This one was open, the entire front resting on the ground. Mendoza bent down and looked in.

There was a miscellaneous heap of contributions in there, mostly clothes, he thought, but the body was right on top. It was the body of a woman in some shapeless dark garment: not a young woman—her hair was gray. That was about all he could see. He handed the flash to Galeano and went back to the salvage collector. The big blue-painted truck with the Goodwill sign was parked out there in a loading zone along the alley behind the office building.

"You'll be all right now," Mrs. Snell was saying. "Would you like some more water?"

"Thank you, ma'am, I guess I'm O.K."

"Are you feeling well enough to answer a few questions?" Mendoza squatted down beside him and offered him a cigarette.

"Thanks, don't smoke no more—since the heart attack. Yeah, sure. My name's O'Brien. Joe."

"Mendoza. How often do these boxes get emptied?"

"Should be checked every week or so. Depends if we got enough drivers. I only worked for the Goodwill a couple of months now, but that's the routine. They hire—I guess you know—handicapped guys. Can't work full-time, or with one leg, or something. My God. I just unlocked the thing and it opened down and I bent over and reached in—my God, I get hold of a leg. I yelled—well, anybody would—"

"When was this one emptied last, do you know?"

"I checked it out last Saturday. Wasn't much in it but I cleaned it out. There wouldn't have been a truck by since."

"Thanks," said Mendoza. The lab truck was just pulling up.

Marx and Horder took one look and exchanged a disgusted glance. "You are finding them these days," said Horder. "I suppose you realize there'll be no way at all to tell if any of that stuff in there is connected with the corpse."

"Sé. Just look at what's immediately under her."

They took some flash shots, and finally got the body out. A little moan of excitement went up from the crowd in the background. "Well, at least this one hasn't been dead long," said Galeano.

The corpse was that of an old woman, at least in her sixties: rather an ugly old woman, with a shrunken-looking face which was explained when they found she hadn't a tooth in her head. She had sparse gray hair; there was a single livid bruise on one side of her forehead. She was wearing a black nylon dress, cotton stockings, heavy black oxfords.

"I don't think," said Marx, "that any of this belongs with her. Right under her, just a heap of old clothes, all size forty-two, and she wouldn't take more than a twelve. What do you think?"

"Yes," said Mendoza. His mouth twitched. "Funerals are so expensive these days. What shall we do with Mother, boys? Oh, just drop her off at the nearest Goodwill box. ¡Porvida! What people will think of next—yes, probably you're right." He glanced at the crowd. "I wonder if I've just said something profound." He went back to the Traffic men and Galeano. "Look, it's just possible that she hails from around here somewhere, that somebody might recognize her. As a regular customer at one of the markets, say. Let's canvass that crowd, get hold of the market employees, all the business people around here, and let them take a look at her."

That took quite a while, but in the end about a hundred people, one by one, filed past to look at the body on the stretcher, with revulsion, morbid interest, even pity. Nobody knew who she was.

"O.K., you'd better send her in," said Mendoza. The morgue wagon had been waiting quite a while.

It was three o'clock, neither of them had had any lunch, and the day was sliding rapidly away. "I'll pull rank on you, Nick. You can go back and write the report."

"Sure," said Galeano amiably.

SINCE LAST MONTH Landers and Phil had both had Saturdays off, which was a nice change. Not that they usually went anywhere, but it was nice to be able to if they wanted.

This morning Phil got at the usual chores, changing the bed, mopping the kitchen and bathroom floors. He helped her carry everything down to the laundry room. He'd called in to ask about Shogart, and Farrell had passed on the bit

about the *Titanic* medal as of idle interest. It reminded
Landers of that book he'd read years ago, about the *Titanic*; he thought he'd like to reread that sometime.

Phil had library books due, so that afternoon they went
to the library. Looking in the card catalog, Landers went
hunting that book and discovered there was a new edition
of it out, with a lot of photographs. He brought it home and
settled down with it while Phil started dinner.

AFTER DINNER, in the still-bright sunlight of daylight sav-
ing time, Mendoza wandered out to the backyard, Cedric at
his heels, and looked somewhat helplessly at the moribund
swing.

"My apologies, *amada*. I'm a broken reed when it comes
to handicrafts."

"I know," said Alison. "It seems funny in a way, when
you're so handy at manipulating a deck of cards. I was
hoping to get it fixed this week, it's the last week of nursery
school and they'll be at loose ends."

"I suppose if it's that urgent," said Mendoza doubtfully, "I could ask George or Henry. They built that dark-
room for Steve Dwyer."

"Oh, you can't take up their spare time. I'll find *somebody*," said Alison.

SATURDAY NIGHT TURNED OUT just about as usual, the
busiest night in the week. It was, of course, a lot busier for
Traffic than Robbery-Homicide. There were two more
heists, a liquor store and a gas station, and a brawl in a bar
on Temple with a man knifed dead. That posed some difficulty: the knifer didn't know a word of English. Finally
Piggott and Schenke were reduced to looking around the
building for somebody who spoke Spanish, to read him his
rights. They found a young fellow named Ortiz sitting on a
Traffic switchboard downstairs, and he obliged them on his
coffee break.

At least they were pretty sure that Shogart would make it.

They went off at 2 A.M., leaving all the new business for the day watch.

THEORETICALLY MENDOZA WAS supposed to be off on Sunday; generally he looked in to see what was going on. When he got to the office at nine-thirty, Hackett had already had an interview with the knifer and was typing a report, head reared back like a striking cobra to get far enough from the keyboard.

Everybody else but Landers and Grace was out chasing the heisters. Landers and Grace were muttering over the autopsy report, which Landers had just seen.

"I've been back over that place, Tom, and if there's any way I can't see it." Grace was brushing his mustache in frustration. "But there it is in black and white, somebody hit her. There in the living room."

"Look," said Landers, "there are things we are equipped to do, Jase. But I don't know anything about magic. There is just no way to go hunting an X who can dematerialize and walk thought walls."

Grace said morosely to Mendoza, "Maybe we ought to exchange jobs. You getting anywhere on your cold trail?"

"Not far," said Mendoza. He looked at the night reports. The hospital was sounding more cheerful about Shogart; he ought to call his wife. He waited until a decent ten o'clock to do so; she sounded tired, grateful, numb.

"Of course they say it'll be quite a time before he's really all right. They only got one bullet out, when he's stronger they'll operate again. Has Hollywood picked up the man yet?"

"Not yet. We're all very relieved and happy, Mrs. Shogart."

"Yes. I know Emil would appreciate how good you've all been, Lieutenant."

Mendoza wandered out to the communal office again. He meant to get back to Glendale sometime today. He wondered if anything had showed up on the old woman in the Goodwill bin; yesterday he'd passed on her description to Carey's office, in case somebody missed her.

Glasser had come in from somewhere and was talking about the locked room with Landers, who was sounding impassioned.

Wanda Larsen, who was also supposed to be off on Sunday, came in briskly and said, "Would somebody like to back me up looking for a heister?"

"What are you doing here?" said Glasser.

"Overtime," said Wanda crisply. "You know, that pharmacist was so sure of that first mug-shot he picked, and the second one was exactly the same type—I've been looking at some. Looking for the same types. I've picked three who might fit. I'd go to look at them myself, but the rules and regulations—"

"You and your target scores," said Glasser. "I'd written that one off, but I'll bite." They went out together.

Mendoza stood gazing into space absently, and suddenly said, "Truax. I'd forgotten that. No, of course it'd be a waste of time to go chasing all those tenants—if by some impossible chance they could be connected, no way to prove it now. Or any of the other people on that street. I thought that before, start from the other end. Her end."

"The Chesney woman." Grace looked up from studying photographs of the Horgan apartment. "Who's Truax?"

"The cleaning woman she had. Nellie Truax. But how to find her—I don't know if she came from an employment agency or where. And what the hell she could give me I don't know."

"Well, she wouldn't sleep at an employment agency. You know my simple mind—let's take a look at the phone book."

"*Mea culpa*. Art's always telling me I like things too complicated."

She wasn't in the Central book. There was an N. Truax in the West L.A. book, but Mendoza shook his head at it. In the Valley book they found her, big as life: Nellie Truax, an address in Eagle Rock.

"Well, I was heading in that general direction," said Mendoza. "We'll see if she's the right one."

SHE WAS THE RIGHT ONE. She looked at Mendoza and the badge, on her front porch this hot Sunday morning, and said, "Well, I never had the police after me yet. What's it about, sir?"

"Did you used to work for Mrs. Anita Chesney?"

"That I did. It's—that? That poor lady?" She held open the screen door. "You'd best come in, sir." It was a very little house, a white frame bungalow on a narrow street, but its front yard was a blaze of bright flowers. The living room directly inside the front door was filled with old-fashioned furniture, a shabby old Oriental carpet, but everything was neat and polished and clean.

She sat down and looked at him. "After all this time." She was a plump little light-brown woman with bright eyes like a bird's. "Why, sir?"

Mendoza told her. "That just don't seem possible," she said, staring. "After all these years. In all my life that was the queerest thing I ever knew to happen. And to happen to such nice people, too. She was the nicest lady I ever worked for. She'd work right along with me, many's the time, and sit down to lunch all friendly. We never could make out what could have happened—and Mr. Chesney, that poor man, he didn't think the police were really looking for her, really interested."

"They were. There just wasn't anything to find. Do you know what happened to Mr. Chesney?"

She nodded slowly. "The poor man. Oh, I know how he felt. The police never asked me any questions, but I heard him talking about what they asked him. Real bitter he was, and I could see why—if you'll excuse me, sir. They loved each other—they were a real happy couple. And the children nice, polite children, well raised."

"You went on working there, after Mrs. Chesney was gone?"

"Yes, sir. They had to have somebody keep the place up a bit—Ann, the girl, was still in school. I went in twice a week, cleaned up, did the laundry, all the general work. Until Mr. Chesney killed himself, poor man, and after, a while, till the place was sold. Mr. Willard, he arranged everything, about the will, and the money for the children. And so now we know she was dead all along. It's the queerest thing."

"You weren't there the day she left?"

"No, I'd been the day before. If the police ever had asked me questions, I could have told them it was foolish, thinking she'd gone off somewhere of her own accord. She was all busy about a dinner party she was giving the next week, I was coming in special to help. Twelve people she was having, and I said I'd make my lemon meringue pies, which I do pretty good—she was always crazy about them, and Mr. Chesney too."

"The day before—did she say anything to you about her plans for the next day?"

"Only, she was going to lunch with this old friend of hers. She said—we were doing out the good china to have it ready, that was a Thursday and the party was going to be on Tuesday—she said she'd have to get the tank filled in her car."

"Yes." That little detail had showed up in the reports; Chesney had said she had told him she'd got the tank filled the afternoon before, so she wouldn't have to stop that morning.

"Mr. Chesney wondered afterward if that's when she had the tire changed. He went on and on about it, first he'd think one way and then another. I suppose we'll never know."

"The tire?" said Mendoza.

"Come to think, I suppose the police never heard about that. Let's see, it was early March when she—she went—and they never found her car for two-three days, and then the police kept it to look at it. It was all of a couple of weeks before Mr. Chesney got it back. And by then, he was so downright heartsick and sore, and so mad at the police, he didn't even look at it. Put it in the garage and it sat there. It wasn't until, let's see, that June when the boy turned sixteen, Mr. Chesney had kind of pulled himself together and one day he said Bryan might as well have it to learn on. And that's when he found the tire had been changed."

"*¡Cómo!*" said Mendoza softly. "He didn't tell C—the police about it?"

"Bryan thought he ought to. He just said, a waste of time, they didn't believe anything he said anyway. I'd hear them talking, you know—I stayed to get their dinner, days I was there. The way I said, he went on about it—sometimes he thought she'd had trouble with the tire that day, but you can't see how that could have made her disappear like that. And sometimes he thought it had been before— 'But she'd have mentioned it,' he always said, 'she'd have said something about it.' Poor man."

"Well, thanks very much," said Mendoza. "You've given me something to think about, Mrs. Truax."

"I guess you've done the same for me, sir. Time passes by, and you forget this and that. I hadn't thought of Mrs. Chesney, the rest of the family, in quite some time. She was such a nice lady. They were all nice. Well, at least she'll be at rest now, and him too, we can hope. I hope you can find out what happened, sir, but—after all this time—I don't suppose you will."

HE FOUND BRYAN CHESNEY alone in the apartment, study-ing for exams. He let Mendoza in rather unwillingly, stiffly polite. Mendoza asked him about the tire, and Bryan said, surprised, "Where'd you hear about that? Oh, the cleaning woman. I guess we never realized—talking in front of her—Well." He jingled the coins in his pocket; he hadn't asked Mendoza to sit down. "I thought Dad ought to have told the police, but by then he was fed up with them. And I don't suppose it meant anything, anyway."

"What about the tire?"

Bryan sighed. "They were all Goodyears, to start. Then Mother picked up a nail or something and ruined one. Dad got a good buy on a Goodrich, for a new spare. And—af-ter Mother went—it was a while before Dad looked at the car, after we got it back. Then, when he did, the spare was on—the Goodrich. On the left front. At first he was all ex-cited, it must mean something. If it had happened before, she'd have mentioned having a flat. Oh, the other tire was in the trunk—it had a piece of wire in it, the tube was punc-tured."

"You don't say," said Mendoza. "What did you think?"

"I don't know," said Bryan. "I don't know what it could mean. The other tire wasn't fixed. If she'd had the tire changed at a gas station she'd have left it, wouldn't she?" He was silent for a moment and then said, "After—after Dad died and the probate was through, Uncle Alan got the Dodge registered to me. But I—never felt very good about driving that car. No way. As soon as I could, I turned it in on a good used job, a Ford. Not as good a car really—but I never liked driving the Dodge."

SEVEN

MENDOZA TOOK HIMSELF out to lunch at the cheerful, bright little coffee shop at Brand and Glenoaks where they'd first heard the story of Anita Chesney from Costello. Over a grilled cheese sandwich and three cups of coffee he considered that tire.

For about 99 percent sure, she'd had that flat tire the same day—the day she went. In the casual give and take of family life, if she'd had it before she'd probably have mentioned it. Equally positive, she hadn't had it on the freeway. There had been an A.P.B. on that car. If she had had a flat on the freeway, she'd have had to walk to one of the emergency phones spaced at intervals, to call the Highway Patrol, and they'd have had it on record.

There was more to be deduced. Generally speaking, when you had a flat tire, you left it to be repaired. She hadn't. Didn't that say, with some degree of certainty, that the flat hadn't happened on the Glendale side of the freeway? Either in Glendale, before she got on the freeway, or in Pasadena after she got off, she wouldn't have had to walk three blocks to a gas station. In Glendale, she'd have been likely to leave the tire. In Pasadena, she might quite likely have said, Don't bother. It was on the cards that the Chesneys, like most people, had regularly patronized the same gas station; she'd have intended to leave the tire there, closer to home, for repair.

He thought of the terrain there, through Pasadena after she'd left the freeway, and said to his cup of coffee, *"¡Imposible!"* Between the freeway exit and within six blocks of Felicia Russell's house there might be forty gas stations. Few of them might have the same employees, fifty-one months later; there'd be no record of a casual transaction like that.

In any case—as Chesney had probably concluded—the flat tire said nothing at all about her disappearance. She hadn't been kidnapped or murdered at any one of fifty gas stations at noon, either in Glendale or Pasadena.

"Claro que esto es según se mire," he said to himself, fished in his pocket for a tip, paid his bill and drove down to Glendale headquarters. He spent the next hour looking at microfilmed reports, all the rest of them, and didn't spot anything suggestive. Costello had done a lot of solid detective work on it, and nothing had showed. Nothing raised the least glimmer of an idea in Mendoza's mind either.

RODNEY PARTON CAME IN to look at mug-shots; Galeano took him down to R. and I., and he looked, but didn't make any.

The third possible heister for the pharmacy job was Alfred Shaw; he was on P.A. for armed robbery, looked like the first one the pharmacist had picked out, and was listed at an address on Council Street. Glasser and Wanda landed there at three-fifty; it was a rambling old house with a sign in a front window, *Rooms by week $12.* A slatternly woman answered the door, looked at the badge with resignation, and said, "Oh, him. Third on the right down the hall."

Glasser rapped at that door; it swung open cautiously. "Mr. Shaw?" He showed the badge. "We've got some questions to ask you about a holdup at the Grandview Pharmacy, a week ago Friday night."

Shaw was hulking, hairy, dark, with a drooping mustache; he had on a sleeveless T-shirt and shorts. A little old-fashioned electric fan stirred the air in the small hot room. "Jeez, where you been?" asked Shaw. "I thought you'd be on me in two-three days."

"What?" said Glasser.

"Jeez, I let that guy get a real good look at me. I been expectin' you all week. You know how it is," said Shaw plaintively. "Kind of strange, after you been in the joint a while. The P.A. guy got me a job, but it's not so much, pumpin' gas eight hours a day. I just got to thinkin'. I got a couple real good pals back in Folsom. I figured it's better back in the joint."

Glasser burst out laughing. "Well, one for the books. Sorry to keep you waiting, Alfred. I guess we goofed on this one."

"Been expectin' you all week. That guy got a good look at me, and I thought sure—"

They took him in and booked him, and back at the office started the machinery on the warrant. "You do have ideas," said Glasser to Wanda. "You and your street experience."

Wanda was looking a little subdued. "At least I'm finding out it doesn't always work out according to the books."

"It's your day off. Go home."

Just before five o'clock Lake put through a call from the Hollywood precinct. "I thought you'd like to know that we've got him," said Connolly to Hackett. "No dogged detective work—one of our street snitches blew the whistle on him. Your man winged him, but it was superficial. One Tyler Sanford, pedigree from here to there—a big habit to support, and he's only four months out of Folsom on P.A. I just hope a judge puts him away for a long stretch, but no bets."

"Congratulations," said Hackett. "I don't know if you heard—Shogart's probably going to be O.K. More surgery, and it'll be a while, but he'll make it."

"I called the hospital. Congratulations all round," said Connolly.

Hackett passed on the news to the men in—Grace, Landers, Higgins. "All's well that ends well. I wonder if we'll get a replacement for E. M."

"Don't hold your breath," said Higgins. "You know the force is shorthanded all round."

"I'm getting old and tired, boys," said Hackett. "They do say, time starts going faster as you age. It doesn't seem all that long since they sent you to us as a replacement, Jase—"

"Yeah," said Higgins heavily. "For Bert." For a moment they were silent, he and Hackett and Landers thinking of Bert Dwyer dead on the marble floor of the bank. Then Higgins turned away and Hackett lit a cigarette, Grace bent over his typewriter. Landers went down the hall for coffee. Time passed on all right, reflected Hackett, and that was a while ago; cause and effect, or just blind chance, new things had grown out of Dwyer's death, out of Grace's coming to join the team. Hackett looked at his typewriter and thought with a sudden little smile about two of the new things. Margaret Emily Higgins and Celia Ann Grace.

It didn't look as if Mendoza was coming back. Hackett scrawled a note for him about Sanford, in case he did, and went home a little early.

ON MONDAY MORNING, with Palliser off, there was only one new piece of business left them by the night watch. A squad car had spotted a body about midnight, in an alley cutting through Second Street alongside an old fifth-rate hotel. It was the body of an elderly man; he had forty cents and an old straight-ward key on him, and on a hunch Piggott had routed out the night clerk at the hotel, who had identified him as a John Smith registered there for the last couple of weeks. Piggott had sealed the room; his report said it looked like a natural death, probably acute alcoholism.

The routine was always there to be done. Higgins, wondering why those A.P.B.'s hadn't turned up Riggs, went over to the hotel. John Smith hadn't left much behind him. There was a much-worn leather suitcase which held a frayed gray suit, two dirty shirts, some underwear, and in the pocket at one side an old letter. The postmark was Milwaukee, the date seven years back, with a return address for a Gladys Donovan. It said, in an even round hand, "Dear Uncle Robert, I am sorry for your bad luck, but after talking with Jack we have decided we can't ask you here on account of the children. I hope you understand. It really would not work out as I could not forget how you treated Aunt Min."

Funny the things people kept, thought Higgins. He came back to the office and got on to the Milwaukee police, in case there was any family to pay for a funeral. Then he went to show the letter to Mendoza.

Mendoza was slouched back in his desk chair, talking on the phone. "Well, that's a step in the right direction. Carey hasn't had a word on her. I know, I know. Just get to it, and let me know when you identify it." He swiveled around, putting the phone down, and said, "Horder. They've come across a cleaners' tag in the dress the old woman was wearing, the one in the Goodwill bin. Maybe a shortcut to identifying her." He heard about John Smith. "*Extraño*, yes. The vagaries of human nature—Jase and Tom in? I've given a little spare thought to the locked room, and I may have come up with an answer."

"That'll lower Tom's blood pressure." When Higgins went to find them, Galeano had just brought in a new suspect, so he joined up to lean on that one.

"I hoped you might see something in your crystal ball about Horgan," said Landers as he and Grace came into Mendoza's office. "What's the brainstorm?"

"Something—mmh—ridiculously simple. It just occurs to me, there are all sorts of cases on record where somebody sustained a serious head injury and went on walking around for five or ten minutes before falling down. How does it strike you, that she got attacked outside—in the hall, say—and managed to get into the apartment, put the chain up, before she fell against the coffee table?"

They looked at each other. "I suppose it could be," said Grace doubtfully. "But who or what attacked her?"

Mendoza shrugged, reached for the lighter and pulled the trigger; the revolver barrel belched flame. "Your guess is as good as mine. Daylight burglar trying to break into her place or one of the other apartments. I just say it's possible. In fact, it strikes me as the only possible solution."

Landers massaged his jaw thoughtfully. "Well, it's an answer. It doesn't send us anywhere, but thanks for the idea—anything rational better than X dematerializing. We might ask the doctor."

They both thought enough of the idea that they went out to find the surgeon who'd done the autopsy, and ran him to ground at the morgue, and put the question to him. He was one of Bainbridge's bright young men straight from internship; he said, "Which corpse? Oh, yes, I remember. Well, I should think it was a pretty damn long chance that she was conscious at all after the blow. It's remotely possible. Funny things happen with head wounds. But if I were you I wouldn't build a case on it."

They went back to the apartment to see Kowalsky, have a look at apartment doors for any sign of attempted break-in. Kowalsky, surprised, said they hadn't had a burglar since last year, but with the crime rate up— Nobody had complained about pry-marks on doors, but if they were right about this, it could be Miss Horgan had surprised somebody before he got far. "I've got her sister here just now, of course the rent's paid up through this month but I suppose she'll be coming to clear things out. But listen, a burglar—it was broad daylight. I saw Miss Horgan go off in her car about five that Sunday afternoon, and she'd have been back long before dark, she never drove at night. No, I didn't see her come back, but—and I guess we don't know it was Sunday she got killed, at that."

It was likely, because of her not showing up for work on Monday, but even that was up in the air. They went upstairs to look for any marks, and met Alice Coulter just coming out of the apartment. She said, "Oh—have you found out any more about it? Oh. I've just come to get her best dress. For the funeral. Mother and Dad saw the undertaker Saturday and the—the body's being sent home. I'll come back later and pack everything up."

"We never asked you," said Grace, "and I suppose you'd know—to take a look around, see if anything's missing."

"I did look, naturally," she said rather sharply. "Just now. There's nothing gone that I can see. She hadn't anything very valuable, jewelry or anything." She looked down at the big brown paper bag she was holding and without warning her eyes overflowed with sudden tears; she dropped the bag and fumbled for a handkerchief in her handbag. "This is j-just silly," she said, mopping her face. "Not as if Sue and I were ever very close—but it just, all of a sudden, struck me. The way she was so nervous of burglars, such a scaredy-cat about everything. It's just like Job in the Bible."

"What's that, Mrs. Coulter?" asked Landers.

" 'That which I feared most has come upon me,' you know. I—you don't want me for anything, do you? We're all driving up home today—the funeral's on Wednesday." She turned off down the hall with the paper bag.

There wasn't any evidence of an attempted break-in on any of the doors on this floor. "Well, there wouldn't necessarily be any traces," said Landers.

"And if that's the answer we'll never prove it," agreed Grace. "We'd be occupied more constructively helping to hunt the heisters."

They went back to the office, got the names of some possibles, and went out looking.

Galeano brought in one of the suspects just before noon, and he and Hackett had an unprofitable session with him. When they let him go and came out to the detective office they were both starving. "Oh, Art," said Lake. "There was a call from the jail. That Jody Holt's asking to see you."

"Oh? Well, he can wait till after lunch," said Hackett. "Come on, Nick." Mendoza was already gone; presumably they'd meet him at Federico's.

They didn't. And Hackett was up to two-twenty again, but the hell with it; he ordered the steak sandwich with all the trimmings.

HE WAS FEELING BETTER when he sat waiting for a warder to bring Jody to the bare little interrogation room. Jody came in, the warder shut the glass-paneled door and remained watchful outside. Hackett said, "Well, what's on your mind, Jody?"

Jody sat down. He looked a little scared and a little grim. "I want to tell you something, Mr. Hackett. I want to tell you the truth. It was what you said—the other day—about guns. I told you, I don't know nothing about them. I don't. I never knew you—the police—could tell guns apart, the way you said. I never knew that. Mr. Hackett, I told you all a lie. I-I-I did have a gun that night."

"Oh," said Hackett.

"It was just an accident I did. I got no interest in guns. But you know I'd been outta work, and things was pretty tight at home. There was this dude owed me some money— fifteen bucks I loaned him about six months back. He met me on the street that same day, I was on the way to the employment office downtown, he says he's got no money but he'd give me this gun instead, it was worth something, maybe more than fifteen bucks. He said his uncle had just died, it'd been his, and he hadn't no use for it, this dude I mean." All this was coming out in a little rush. Hackett sat still, listening. "I hadn't no use for it either, but he said I could sell it to a pawnshop. I took it. I—could I have a cigarette?"

Hackett gave him one, lit it. "Thanks. I didn't know if it was loaded, neither did he, and I didn't know how to find out. I meant, take it to the pawnshop on my way home, but I hadda wait at the office, and it kind of looked as if I might get took on at the bus company, only they got all the drivers they had jobs for before they got to me. So, time I got off the bus on my way home, the pawnshop was closed. And you see, my sister Bea, she'd brought her young ones for Ma to watch while we all went out to Kellerman's, and I thought, best not leave the thing in the house. So I still had it on me."

"You don't know what kind of gun it was?"

"No, sir. Just a little black gun, sort of square. I had it. And—and—" Jody's Adam's apple bobbed nervously. "Time all that ruction started with Les Fulger draggin' Kathy away, well, there was a lot of noise, and George tried to stop him, and got knocked down, and the girls were hollering, and I guess I was excited too, he hadn't any call treat Kathy that way, and I took that gun outta my pocket. I don't know what I meant to do, honest, I guess I had some notion maybe I could scare him with it. But it went off right then—like to scared me to death, I didn't touch the trigger, I don't think—the girls were ahead of me, they never saw it, and all the noise, I guess nobody heard—it was just a little crack like. Scared me to death—sort of brought me to my senses, and I put it back in my pocket. Quick. And then— then the police came—and said Les was shot dead—and the Lord's my witness, Mr. Hackett. I know I hadn't killed him, but I had that gun—"

"Do you have any idea where the bullet might have gone, when it went off?"

"I dunno. I was just takin' it out of my pocket, it was sort of pointed down at the floor, I guess. Mr. Hackett, I thought sure if the police knew I had a gun, they'd say I did it! I—I just wanted shut of it. I didn't think anybody'd seen it, all the excitement."

"But if it wasn't the gun that killed Fulger, we'd know that."

"That's why I'm tellin' you. You said the police could tell—it was a different gun. So maybe that'd prove—I didn't do it."

"What did you do with the gun?" asked Hackett.

"I got up in the middle of the night and buried it in our backyard," said Jody. "Right beside Ma's pink hibiscus bush. Pretty deep."

"I see," said Hackett.

"What—what you goin' to do about it?"

"Why, we're going to dig it up," said Hackett, "and have a look at it. And if it isn't the gun that killed Fulger, well, it doesn't seem very likely that you were carrying two guns that night, Jody. And this explains why those people said they saw you with a gun, which might let you off the hook."

"I—kind of figured it might give me a better chance, anyway," said Jody.

"WELL, of all the damn fool things to do," said Galeano. "You'd think any idiot would know all guns aren't alike. Are you reading it that that was the .32 automatic that left the casing?"

"That's what it's got to be. It's logical in a way. You know how hair-trigger some automatics can be—and evidently whoever'd handled it last had left one up the barrel. That was the damn fool thing, but they will do it. It was just damn lucky nobody did get shot with it—the pal who handed it over to Jody seems to have been another simpleton."

"I suppose if we do find it we can trace it to the uncle."

"I suppose." Hackett pulled the Barracuda up to the curb. The Holts lived on Forty-fifth Place; it was an old narrow street with modest frame houses on either side, on standard fifty-foot lots. Most of the houses were neatly kept up, the front patches of lawn showing a little brown now in the heat.

Mrs. Holt opened the door and looked at them in silence. "Mrs. Holt, we haven't got a search warrant," said Hackett, "but I hope you'll let us come in. You've got my word that Jody asked us to come and find something for him. Something important."

"Well, you always struck me as an honest man, Mr. Hackett." She looked bewildered. "I guess you can come in. What are you looking for, for Jody?"

Hackett just said, "It's in the backyard." He and Galeano went out there, through a neat kitchen; she trailed them mutely. "Have you got a trowel?" The hibiscus bush, covered with pink blossoms, was at one side of the yard, near the fence. Hackett squatted and began to dig. Five minutes later he uncovered it and sat back on his heels.

"Where'd that come from?" she asked, frightened. "It's another thing to make Jody look bad, a gun—"

Hackett looked up at her. "No, Mrs. Holt. I rather think it might save him."

They slid it into an evidence bag and took it back downtown, dropped it off at S.I.D. Upstairs, they found Mendoza back and told him about it. "It's an old S. and W. automatic. In the morning we're going to have a damn good look around Kellerman's and hope to find that slug. We couldn't handle the gun until it's been printed, but I'll just bet you there's a full load minus one in it, Luis. And that's got to get Jody off the hook. I told you, I always felt there was something fishy about the thing."

"So you did," said Mendoza. He was looking annoyed, amused and slightly angry all at once.

"Where've you been all afternoon?"

"Out on the cold trail. Sit down and hear the latest news." Mendoza snapped the pearl-handled revolver.

In the outer office, Higgins could be heard asking what the new one looked like, and Landers' voice said disgustedly, "Another queer one—another mystery, for God's sake! And I'm damned if I'll start a report now, it's nearly quitting time."

"Don't tell me you've turned up something new on that," said Hackett, sitting down.

Mendoza laughed shortly. *"¡Sin mujeres y sin vientos, tendríamos menos tormentos—* Women!"

HE REALLY SHOULD, he'd decided, talk to Felicia Russell, not that he expected her to give him anything new. He'd called this morning, to be sure of finding her home; a rather deep voice had crisply confirmed an appointment at one-thirty.

For no logical reason but to satisfy his own curiosity, he had started back at Pacific Avenue and noted all the gas stations along the way, down to the Burchett freeway entrance, past the Orange Grove exit in Pasadena, down to Felicia Russell's home on Los Robles.

He introduced himself over the shrill yapping of a small black poodle. "Quiet, darling," said Mrs. Russell. "Do come in and sit down, Lieutenant." The poodle sniffed at his ankles. Mendoza was not enamored of poodles; if Alison had had to saddle them with a dog he preferred Cedric any day. He sat down on a tapestry-upholstered chair and looked at Felicia Russell.

She was nice to look at; not young, but still a pretty woman, a discreet blonde, good figure, smartly dressed in a blue knit pantsuit, white sandals. She said in her deep voice, "I suppose I mustn't offer you a drink?" There was central air conditioning on in here. It was a cool, rather dim living room, quietly furnished. "Of course I know what this is about. I was never so—surprised, I guess, is the only word—when Alan Willard called to tell me, and then Ann. It—brought it all back. And so she's been dead all this while—and we still don't know anything."

"Not a great deal. And I don't suppose you can tell me much I don't know."

She had a trick of suddenly widening her eyes and then lowering the lids modestly. "You don't mean to tell me you're trying to find out anything now? I don't see how anybody could. I suppose, in spite of what John Chesney thought, there was a competent police investigation at the time. But really—and I said that to the police sergeant who came to see me—once they'd found out there wasn't an accident, Nita wasn't in a hospital—well, there wasn't anywhere else to go, was there?"

"Why do you say that, Mrs. Russell?"

"Oh—" impatiently "—female logic, call it. Nita wouldn't have left home voluntarily—like that—just taking off. She wouldn't have left, period. I saw that while everybody else was clinging to the hope of—oh, amnesia, or kidnapping. Silly. It had to be something—violent and sudden."

"Did you have any theory about it?"

She shook her head. "It was just—unimaginable. Wild. There isn't a word for it. Excuse me, do you mind if I have a drink?" When she came back from the kitchen with a long glass, he saw that despite her cool voice her hands were shaking.

"You were fond of Mrs. Chesney."

She set the glass down a little clumsily. "She was—my oldest friend. We'd grown up together. We knew each other—inside out. I expect we were opposites—Nita was always quiet, liked all the domestic things, keeping house, cooking—catering to a man, the kids. I'm not—maybe that efficient—or tolerant. Probably not as successful as a female, Lieutenant. I thought John Chesney was a damned fatuous bore. Obviously she didn't—she adored him, and the kids. Without being sloppy about it." She picked up the glass and drank. "He didn't think much of me. Any woman who's got a man ought to stay married to him."

"Not that it's any of my business," said Mendoza sardonically, "but what pays the rent and groceries?"

She gave him a quick smile. "Oh, after the first shock I used some common sense. I didn't marry him for his money, though it was nice he had it, but when I found out he was spending it on three other women at once, I figured he owed me my keep first. Which was another reason Chesney didn't like me. Rapacious female."

"How did Anita feel?"

"I told you, Nita and I understood each other. Live and let live." She was stroking the poodle absently where it nestled against her on the couch. "We're getting away from Nita, aren't we? I can't tell you anything, of course. About it. Anything you don't know. Just, I expected her, she didn't come, I called the house, got no answer, finally got hold of Ann."

"Yes," said Mendoza. Like trying to lay hold of a ghost, finding any trail back to Anita Chesney that damp March day.

"I talked to her the day before, you know," said Felicia, a little dreamily. "She called to ask if she could borrow some extra shrimp-servers for her dinner party. We'd planned to go shopping after lunch, but the weather turned threatening, we decided just to stay in and talk. I'd made a chicken creole casserole and biscuits, and Hollandaise sauce for the asparagus." She finished her drink. "It must be the worst thing in the world, Lieutenant, simply *not to know* what's happened. The way that was—is. You can stand anything, however bad it is, if you just know the truth. Not to know— it's unbearable. I think that's really why Chesney killed himself." A pause. "Nita, just driving off like that—into the blue. Waving at the neighbors at eleven-fifteen that morning—" She smiled, a little amused at some memory. "Of course she needn't have left so early, except for her secret way over."

"What?" said Mendoza.

"She was scared of the freeways. She didn't like heights, and you know since they've re-routed the Pasadena freeway, it goes way up and around, and no guard rails. She hated it. And she liked to shop in Pasadena, it wasn't just coming to see me. And she was ashamed of being scared, too. She'd never have confessed it to John, but she figured out all sorts of ways to stay off freeways, and she'd found what she called a wonderful secret way into Pasadena."

"Which was?" Mendoza suddenly felt the little cold thrill up the spine that always told him he was about to reach in blind and draw an ace from the pack.

"I'll show you—" She rummaged in the magazine rack beside the couch, and produced a County Guide. "Nobody would ever think it was there, we're all so used to roaming around on freeways—I said there wasn't any way to Pasadena from Glendale except on the freeway, unless you went all round Robin Hood's barn—so she showed me." She laid the guide on his lap, open to page 26, and her long polished nail pointed the route. "Here, where Colorado Boulevard in Eagle Rock turns into the freeway, you just keep going straight and you hit La Loma Road. It's a funny twisty little street, but easy to drive—nothing ever on it, she said—and you just follow it around till you come to Arroyo Boulevard, and just a short block up you turn right on California and you're in the middle of Pasadena."

"I will be damned," said Mendoza. "I will be— She followed surface streets all the way to Eagle Rock, as far as Colorado goes before turning into the freeway?"

"That's right."

"You give me something to think about," said Mendoza.

"But that couldn't have anything to do with—"

"I wonder," he said, and put the County Guide down.

"Oh, that's silly."

"What else did she say to you on the phone that day?"

"Small talk. About the shrimp-servers, and how much rain we were getting, and some deal John was making, it was going to mean quite a lot of money—" She shook her head. "All of that was a reason too, you see. Why I knew right away it was—something wild. Unexpected. Violent. Because—she didn't know she was going."

It was, he thought, a curious way to put it, and yet graphic. No, taking off so lightheartedly that morning, Anita Chesney hadn't known she was going—anywhere but to Pasadena, by her secret way, and home again.

At FIVE O'CLOCK that afternoon Landers said to Grace in exasperation, "Out of the frying pan into the fire. Locked rooms, and now this!"

They'd been chased out to Budlong Avenue a couple of hours before, to an unspecified call that just promised a body. When they got there they found confusion and uproar, and for a while couldn't make any sense out of the situation.

There were two squad cars on the scene and a paramedic truck. The action was at a garage behind a pink stucco house in the middle of the block. There were curious neighbors out, one of the Traffic men keeping them out of the way. In the garage the paramedics were working on a man lying flat on the floor behind an old Ford sedan. As Landers and Grace came up, they left off their efforts and one of them said, "*Terminar*. Sorry, he's gone. I thought there was just a chance, but no go."

The trunk of the Ford was open and there were two more bodies in it, heaped together gracelessly, two females. "They're both long gone," said the other paramedic. "We didn't even try, after one look. Three or four hours at least."

Landers and Grace could see that, and see why. The uppermost face was a bright pink, as was that of the man on the garage floor. All the corpses had died of carbon monoxide poisoning.

There was a young woman about twenty sitting on the step of the back porch sobbing violently.

"What goes on?" Landers asked the Traffic men.

"Search me. We got the call about forty minutes ago, from the girl there. She didn't really go to pieces till we got here. Her name's Linda Dunlap, and she goes to L.A.C.C. Lives here with her mother and younger sister. Edna and Amy Dunlap. That's them in the trunk. She got home, they weren't here, and then she hears the car engine in the garage, so she went to look. Had the sense to turn off the ignition and open the door, and called us, and the fire department."

"And who's Number Three?"

"She doesn't know," said the other Traffic man. "The paramedics have been working on him, we haven't looked for an I.D."

"My God," said Landers. "Well, let's have a look. We'll want a lab truck." By the time Grace had called in for that and come to join him, the paramedics had gone away and Landers was searching the dead man. He was an elderly man in a stained white jumpsuit that had *Ernie's Garage* sewn on the breast pocket in red thread.

There was a wallet in his hip pocket, and in it a driver's license for Carl Webster. The address was on this block, across the street by the number.

It would be a while before they could talk to the girl; they waited until the lab truck came, with Duke and Scarne in it, and then walked up the block. The house was another small stucco place painted tan. The woman who came to the door was in her sixties, a little plump, gray-haired, placid-faced.

She stared at the badge in Grace's hand. "Does a Carl Webster live here, ma'am?"

"Why, yes, he's my husband. Police?" She looked across the street, down to where the squad cars stood. "Why, what's going on? I've been out in the backyard, I thought I heard a siren a while ago, but you're always hearing—"

"We're sorry to tell you that Mr. Webster's, er, had an accident," said Landers. "We'll have to ask you to come and identify him."

"Identify—why, Carl'll be at work like always, he doesn't get home till six—I'm sure I don't know what this is all about—" She was flurried and a little indignant. They waited while she took off her apron, and started back across the street. "That's the Dunlap house," she said. "We don't know them, just the name. What's happened?"

"Well, we're not quite sure, Mrs. Webster." Landers began to feel that possibly they should get a female officer down here.

She took one look at the dead man, said, "Carl!" and began to cry slow, difficult tears, but she didn't lose control. "What's happened? What's he doing here? We don't know these people. He went off to work this morning same as usual—and he's dead. He's dead." Turning, she got a glimpse past Scarne of the bodies in the trunk, and let out a loud gasp, and said faintly, "I got to sit down. I got to—*what's happened*?"

They wished they knew. They put her in one of the squad cars and Landers called in to ask if Wanda could come down. She got there in twenty minutes and was efficient, getting both women into the house out of sight of the bodies. But five minutes later she came out and said, "You'd better have a look in here. I've got them in the living room, nothing seems to have happened there."

Quite evidently there had been violence committed in the house. They looked, and brought the lab men in to take pictures. In the kitchen, used breakfast dishes (from the remnants of toast and scrambled eggs) were broken on the floor: a throw rug was in a heap where a hall led down, and in a back bedroom all the clothes were dragged off the bed and there was blood on the rug there. Farther down the hall toward the front bedroom, there was a bloodstained hammer on the floor.

"My God, what went on here?" said Grace. "And why didn't somebody hear it?"

They left Scarne and Duke taking pictures and went into the living room. Mrs. Webster was sitting bolt upright in an armchair staring straight ahead, with a shocked, bewildered expression. Linda Dunlap was still sobbing now and then, but talking to Wanda rationally.

"We won't bother you too much right now, Linda, but we'd like just a few answers if you're up to it," Wanda was saying.

"I don't know—what happened—just can't imagine—to see them like that—" She hiccuped. "Oh, I'll try. You've got to find out—what happened. Everything just like always—when I left. At eight-twenty—for my nine o'clock class. Except Mother didn't go to work—had one of her migraines, she was in bed—Amy was having breakfast, I got it for her—"

"Didn't your sister go to school?"

Linda sobbed convulsively. "She—was—was retarded. Just like—five-year-old kid—but so sweet, such a sweet kid, so happy and so pretty—her beautiful gold hair—"

"Just take it easy. You left about eight-twenty. Driving?"

"Yes. My VW. Everything— But when I came home, nobody there—I heard the car running— Mother's, in the garage—I— How did they get there, in the trunk? Some old man there, I didn't know him—"

Wanda shook her head at Landers and Grace. They turned to Mrs. Webster, and found she was staring at Linda. "He was only sixty-two, not old," she said with an effort. "What was Carl doing here?" But she seemed to have focused, foolishly, on the one word. She said, "Old? You don't ever feel old, you got your health—young folk don't know—but times, you get lonely, and Carl a widower and me with no chick nor child— What happened to Carl?"

Watching the bodies being loaded into the morgue-wagon, Grace said, "That was a good question."

Which was when Landers said, "Out of the frying pan—My father had hopes I'd follow in his footsteps and be a veterinarian. Why didn't I, Jase?"

RICH CONWAY lived in a bachelor apartment in Holly-wood, so when he'd finally decided there was something wrong with him that required outside help, and called the paramedics, a week ago Thursday night, they'd rushed him to Hollywood Receiving Hospital.

He'd never been known as backward with the girls, and this afternoon when the shift changed and the plain little nurse with the nice hazel eyes came on, he got her to bring a wheelchair. If it had been the same floor he'd have made it on his own—they'd let him up the last couple of days—but it was another wing, higher up, on the other side of the building.

"I can't leave you more than ten minutes, Mr. Conway. He's not supposed to have any visitors but his wife."

It was a two-bed room, and the curtains drawn around the bed nearest the door. She pushed the wheelchair up to the side of the bed and left. It was dim in the little cubicle. Shogart lay flat in the bed, the sheet folded down to show his bare chest with the sparse gray hair, the big bandage. There was a tube attached to his left arm and a drip-bottle on a stand. Conway reached out and touched the big flaccid hand on the sheet.

"E. M. Hey, E. M., it's Rich."

The eyelids flickered and slowly opened. "You're doing fine," said Conway. "Did anybody tell you, you winged him, E. M.? They got him."

A faint smile stretched Shogart's mouth. "Thought—I did."

"That's right. You're doing great. You can't keep a good man down." Conway pressed the hand, but Shogart had drifted away into sleep again.

EIGHT

"WE APPRECIATE this very much, Mr. Kellerman." Hackett had called him yesterday afternoon to ask him to let them into the place sometime this morning.

Kellerman shrugged. "No trouble." His eyes were curious on Hackett and Palliser.

"They were sitting at this table, right?" said Hackett. "Do the tables get moved around much?"

"Some. They're pretty heavy."

"That casing was twelve feet toward the door, you said, which way up—other side of the table? Tell me about where." Palliser was measuring with a folding rule. Hackett had borrowed a metal detector from the lab; he stood beside the table with it.

"Say Jody got up, took a few steps like this. The ruction's under way and Fulger's dragged Kathy out. All right, he gets out the gun and it goes off—generally toward the floor, probably some to the right." He lifted the metal detector.

"What gun?" said Kellerman.

The detector passed slowly over the old scarred plank floor. Nothing. "Could have ricocheted," said Palliser. This big old place was dim in the morning, too big with only three people there in the high-ceilinged hall. Palliser switched on a flashlight and sent the beam back into corners. The table that made a starting point was in the first row against the front wall. The detector moved slowly along the baseboard, out, back, in, out.

"Jackpot!" said Hackett. "Gimme the light." He knelt and the beam focused on the small black mark there on the baseboard, hardly noticeable among the scars and stains of years. Hackett got out his knife and probed, while Palliser held the flash. "Here we are." He sat back on his heels and held it up: a scarcely damaged slug, buried two inches in the age-softened wood. "Jody's passport out of jail."

"What the hell's that?" said Kellerman. Still squinting at the bullet, Hackett explained economically. "You don't say," said Kellerman. "So that was why all the witnesses— I'll be damned."

"One gun," said Hackett, "canceling out another. And very nice too."

They took the slug back and dropped it off at S.I.D., asked for a comparison test of slugs out of the .32 automatic.

Upstairs, they found Mendoza on the telephone; when he put it down Hackett told him about the slug. "It'll match, and that's got to be grounds for dismissing the charge—explains away those witnesses. Damn it, if he'd known the first thing about guns and come out with this when we first talked to him—" Belatedly Hackett was annoyed at Jody. "And of course this leaves the shooting all up in the air."

Mendoza put out his cigarette. "Human nature is what makes the job for us, Art. That was the Milwaukee boys I was talking to. They can't find a listing for a Gladys Donovan anywhere in the city or suburbs. It looks as if the L.A. taxpayers will be paying for the old drunk's funeral."

"Yes?" said Hackett. "Well, I'd better get on to the D.A.'s office and set up a date with one of the assistants to discuss getting Jody out of jail. And I wonder who did shoot Fulger. The size of that crowd, and I suppose there were other people there who knew him and had some reason—"

"John can do that," said Mendoza. He stood up and absently pulled down his cuffs, straightened his tie; his suit this morning was a poem in silver gray Dacron, his tie muted silver and blue stripes. "I just want an opinion, Arturo, that

my crystal ball is still operating. I'll take you on a little ride.
John, you go talk to the D.A. Come on, Art.''

"Where?" asked Hackett.

"Ghost chasing," said Mendoza. "I don't think I'm
being too subtle, but you'll tell me."

Palliser watched them out—the boss having a hunch
again—and went out to his desk to contact the D.A.'s office.

ABOUT ELEVEN O'CLOCK that Tuesday morning a 415 call
went down and Henderson and Murillo got sent out on it.
It was Adams Boulevard, and when they got there a little
crowd had collected. An excited fat black woman in a red
pantsuit called to them as they got out of the squad car, "In
here, officers!—I called the ambulance, she looks awful
bad—"

It was a little independent variety store, a lot of five-and-
dime stuff, an old place. In front of the counter an old black
woman was lying bloody on the floor. "What happened
here?" asked Murillo. The ambulance came screeching up,
skidded to a halt outside.

"My husband's got them—pair of young devils—what
the world coming to, just kids, my Lord, and Mis' Tucker
she just about gets by here, this little old store—we heard her
yelling, and Roy went runnin' to see—"

The old woman wasn't good, losing a lot of blood; the
ambulance attendants bundled her off. Henderson and
Murillo went next door to a little radio and appliance store
and found a big fellow waiting for them, hanging grimly on
to two little kids.

"I grabbed 'em for you," he said. "Take my hand off 'em
they're gone, and I don't know either of 'em—just no-good
little punks. They was at the register in Mis' Tucker's when
I run in—there's the money they took," and he nodded at
the counter. "Told my wife to call you."

The kids were just two black kids, twelve, thirteen, not very big. They wouldn't say anything, squirmed and looked sullen. "The old lady didn't look too good," said Murillo. "Do we call Juvenile or Robbery-Homicide?"

They decided Robbery-Homicide could ring Juvenile in if it seemed indicated, so they called in, and waited.

Galeano and Higgins had just come back from talking to more possibles on the perennial heists, without finding any reason to bring them in for further questioning. They went out again into hundred-degree heat resignedly, and listened to what Henderson and Murillo had to say before going into the appliance store. "They're just little kids," said Murillo, "but the woman was cut up pretty bad."

They went in and showed the badges. "I'm Roy Page," said the big man behind the counter. "My wife and I heard her yelling, Mis' Tucker, and caught these two—I sure hope she ain't hurt bad—"

Galeano looked, and said, "Tommy Hooper." Small dark knowledge moved in his mind.

"You know 'em? I never laid eyes on the young devils."

"One of them," said Galeano. "What about it, Tommy? You like to tell us what happened here?"

He gave them a look of pure fierce resentment. "She hadda go yellin'! They hadda come messin' in! We only wanted the bread."

"Oh, my God," said Higgins tiredly. They could both foresee all the red tape on this. "How come you know this one?"

"Hanley," said Galeano briefly. He turned to the other boy. "What's your name and where do you live?"

"You go to hell, fuzz."

Galeano walked up the block to the Hooper apartment, and found Mrs. Hooper among the bedlam of small children. "Tommy? He's at school," she said.

"Well, I'm afraid not. He's in some bad trouble, Mrs. Hooper. You'll have to come down to headquarters with him—"

"But how'm I goin' to leave the kids? What's he done? Tommy's never been in any trouble—what you mean?"

She was some help. When she looked at the other kid there, before they all left for Parker Center, she said, "That's Ronny Hopewell. He's in school with Tommy. What they been up to?" She knew where the Hopewells lived, a couple of blocks away, and Higgins went up there to find the mother.

They took them all back to the office and called Juvenile, and a female officer came down to sit in. The mothers seemed more surprised than upset at first, and kept saying the kids had never been in any trouble.

"Suppose we hear what happened, Tommy," said Galeano. The detective office was empty of other men; they brought chairs from Landers' desk, Grace's, Palliser's.

"I guess you know what happened," said Tommy in a sullen low voice. "Ever'body hadda come messin' in. Ole lady Tucker yellin' like that."

"Which one of you had the knife?" Silence. "Whose idea was it?" Silence.

"So what about Mr. Hanley, Tommy?" asked Galeano. "Was that you too? Was Ron with you?"

Tommy said, "I never had no knife. Ron had the knife."

"You Goddamn snitch—no call tell 'em that, Goddamn—" The other boy fell on him, gouging and kicking; Higgins hoisted them apart, one in each big hand, and the phone on Hackett's desk buzzed. Galeano made a long arm to reach it.

"Robbery-Homicide, Detective Galeano."

"This is the emergency desk, Central Receiving. We were asked to inform you that the patient Tucker was pronounced D.O.A."

"Thanks," said Galeano, and turned back to the scene around Higgins' desk. The mothers were loud on protests now, Higgins sounding patient and still holding the squirming kids.

Kids! thought Galeano. He was a patient man himself; but suddenly he barked, "Shut *up*, all of you! Shut *up*!"

They looked at him, the noise cut off as if with a knife. He leaned on his desk and said deliberately. "The Tucker woman's dead. So is Mr. Hanley. Was Ron in on that too, Tommy? Which one of you killed these people?"

"I never—I dint know nothin' about ole Hanley till—it was Tommy, but he said the ole man batted him one, he said easier if there're two of us—"

"You snitch yourself, Goddamn snitch! I never meant to kill nobody, she hadn't no call try to hit us—"

Higgins gave each of them a casual shake. "Oh, my Lord!" said Mrs. Hooper in a thin wail. "Oh, my Lord— what Dave'll say—"

"Why, Tommy?" asked Galeano. "You needed money for something?"

The thin black boy gave them a resentful look, grown-ups never understanding. "Let's see what's on you," said Higgins, and delved into pockets. Nothing on Ron but twenty cents and a candy bar; in Tommy's pockets a dollar bill and a little box holding one loose-rolled cigarette. "One joint, hah? How long have you been on the grass, Tommy?"

"None o' your business." But he was only thirteen and not as tough or unafraid as he would be later on. His mother was rocking to and fro in a silent paroxysm of grief. He gave her one miserable look. "It's a dollar a joint an' I never get no chance at bread—two bucks outta her purse last week's all—an' she—an' she—sent me get that beer, he open the thing give me some change, I see all the bread inside, I think—I found that piece o' wood in the alley, come back an' hit him, dint go kill him, but he knocked me down— he called me names, an' I just hit him again hard as I could—'' He transferred his burning resentment to Ron Hopewell. "An' I give Ron half the bread too! He said ole Mis' Tucker, she so ole an' lame can't put up no fight, but she hadda go yellin'—''

"Oh, Lord, oh, my Lord—''

The Juvenile officer sighed and recrossed her knees the other way.

Galeano felt very tired suddenly. They saw a lot of blood and dirt on this job, and it was scarcely the first time he'd seen a kid start off this wrong this young; but sometimes you felt tired; you wondered what the answer was, if there was any.

There was a good deal of red tape on it. They took the boys down to Juvenile Hall, and rounded up the male parents and explained procedures, explained rights. Hooper was just morose; Hopewell was belligerent, accusing the fuzz of railroading his kid. There'd be reports to get out on it, probably several sessions with some assistant D.A., and what it would come down to was a charge of involuntary manslaughter and probation.

It was three-thirty before it was over, temporarily. He hadn't had time for lunch. Higgins was still upstairs talking to somebody in Juvenile, and instead of starting the first report on it Galeano went out and drove through the baking streets to the restaurant on Wilshire.

In the middle of the afternoon it was nearly empty; there wasn't another customer at Marta's station. He was empty, but not really hungry; he told her to bring him a chocolate malt. "Would they fire you if you sat down and talked to me?"

She smiled. "There is no one else to serve. I don't think so." She watched him spoon up the whipped cream. "There is something wrong, Nick?"

"Nah," said Galeano. "The job." He told her about Tommy.

"That," she said soberly, "is very terrible. Did you always want to be a policeman?"

"Well, I thought it'd be an interesting job. Most of the time it's just routine. Sometimes too interesting."

"And sometimes dangerous—like the officer who is shot the other day. But I think it's—" she hesitated for the word "—also a job where you do much good, Nick. You are—serving to make justice."

"I sometimes wonder," said Galeano. But he felt better; he looked across to her serious dark eyes, her wide mouth with its hint of smile. "One way to look at it. Hey, you've got a night off again tomorrow night. You like to try that Castaway place again?"

MENDOZA SLID THE FERRARI into the curb. "From here on," he said to Hackett. "It's the only possible place. I don't know what, or why, or how. But it was here."

"You always had an imagination," said Hackett.

"I didn't need one on this." Mendoza had showed him the terrain, from the top of Pacific Avenue all the way through town—Glendale and Eagle Rock—the busy streets, the crowds; just now they had passed that place where busy Colorado Boulevard veered off up the Ventura freeway. Instead of going with it, he drove straight across the intersection, across Figueroa where it cut in slantwise, and they were suddenly climbing a little rise on a narrow curving street. He cut the motor then. "From here on. I had a look yesterday, after I'd heard about it. Now you look at it." He started the engine again and drove on slowly.

From being in the middle of town, suddenly they were on a quiet secluded street. A hill rose first to one side, then the other, just gentle rises. First, to the left, were smallish houses, older, but on wide lots; and this was an old street, trees high and full and casting deep shadows of shade, obscuring the houses set back from the street. To the right, they passed an iron fence and a very large house set back from the street on perhaps half an acre. To the left, little winding streets led off; there were houses down there but hardly to be seen behind trees. And now the houses on this street were far apart. The Ferrari wound to the left, climbing, and to the right, descending, past fences thickly grown with ivy, past tall trees, that made it difficult to see the houses behind them. As the car slowed for dips, they heard the whirr of a power mower off to the right, but a tall hedge obscured the gardener. The little streets wandered off to the left, Sequoia Drive, Juniper Drive, Glenholly; no house on them near this street; and on this street the wide frontages, the hedges and fences.

Here Avenue Sixty-four crossed, but here it was a shadow of its busy business self down in South Pasadena. Just a narrow street crossing; and beyond, the Ferrari still sliding gently along La Loma Road, there were even fewer houses. Only one street going down to the left, one to the right a little way beyond; and here, the houses set back even farther down long curving drives, the trees even thicker, the hedges as tall. Most of the way since they had got onto La Loma, they had been in deep shade. The Ferrari moved on round a curve to the left, and another street jogged down: San Rafael Avenue. It was a street like this, narrow, empty. To the left a steep bank fell away—down there was a little wilderness area, thick trees and underbrush. Mendoza swung the wheel left, and they were on a new street; a bare half block up he turned right.

This was California Boulevard, a secondary main drag of the city of Pasadena. Quite suddenly they were once again right in the middle of town. Large old houses lined the street here; to the immediate right was a square block of park, modestly crowded on this hot summer day.

"That's a queer little section all right," said Hackett. They hadn't passed a single car all the way, coming or going.

"All along the rest of her way, people," said Mendoza. He swung the Ferrari into a side street and parked.

"Crowds. Gas stations. Along La Loma, no. Like a quiet country road. It was about this time of day—on a week-day—and you see what it's like."

"About the only people who'd be driving it, the ones who live there. Workmen coming in, delivery trucks now and then—"

"*¡Muy poco!* And people using it as a shortcut. But damn few people would know it's there, Art."

"All right. I see it. This is the way she came, and every-where else she was in the middle of crowds. Only along there, a lonely empty stretch. There are still people there, in those houses."

"And all the trees and fences and hedges. People in houses aren't looking out of the windows all the while at cars passing—and up there they couldn't see the road from most of the houses."

"Just which way is your mind working, *amigo*?"

"I don't know," said Mendoza slowly. "All I see, Art, is that it was along that stretch of the way, no traffic, no crowds, that she must have run into—whatever she did run into. However. Whatever. There's no way to guess. But there was the flat tire. If she had a flat along that lonely road, what would she do? All dressed up for lunch, and she prob-ably didn't know how to change it. What?"

"Well," said Hackett, "probably she'd go to one of the houses, ask to use the phone, call for help."

"*Pues sí,*" said Mendoza. He started the engine, made a U-turn and headed back; turned off California onto Ar-royo Boulevard and back to La Loma. The Ferrari crept along. "Most of these places are older, expensive houses. I shouldn't think they'd change hands often. Should think most of them are still occupied by the people who lived here then."

"Grasping at straws," said Hackett. They passed, on the right, a long low gray ranch house seventy feet back from the road, beyond a picket fence covered with climbing roses.

A fat man in green shorts and no shirt was clipping an ever-green hedge at one side of the drive. "Do you think she went up to one of these places, asking to use the phone, and got mugged by the householder? One of these classy places?"

"*¡Qué va!*" said Mendoza. "No. No. I don't know what I'm thinking." He was silent all the way down and around the street, and where the busy roar of the intersection opened up before them, he backed and turned the long car, started slowly back up La Loma. "It's a fascinating little backwater, you know. You'd never guess it's here."

"And she could certainly have met the casual mugger here, and nobody around any the wiser. But you'll never find out now."

"I don't know," said Mendoza. He was cruising along, looking left and right, as if he hoped to see the accusing ghost of Anita Chesney wave him down at the spot marked X. "I don't know. Suppose she had that flat tire here. Meant to go to one of the houses, use the phone. And before she did, a good Samaritan came along. Suppose she went to a house, and called, and came out to wait for help to arrive. They didn't belong to an auto club, she'd have called the nearest gas station willing to send help. And while she was waiting, somebody came along— The householder wouldn't be keeping an eye on her, and if the truck came and didn't find her, they'd assume she'd been rescued, just head back for the station—no big deal."

"You can suppose anything you want to, you'll never prove it," said Hackett.

The Ferrari slowed to a stop. Mendoza leaned back and lit a cigarette. "Four years and three months. All I'm tell-ing you—¡ya lo sé!—whatever happened, happened along this road."

"Excuse me." They both looked up. They were parked opposite the gray ranch house, and the fat fellow in shorts had walked across the street, shears in hand. He looked at them curiously. "Can I help you find an address? Noticed you driving back and forth."

Mendoza produced the badge, and he looked more interested. "Don't know there's ever been any police trouble up here. Not even wild parties. What's it about?"

"Have you lived here long, sir?"

"Padgett—Andrew Padgett. Seventeen years."

"Do you ever remember someone having car trouble, asking to use a phone, call for help, along here?"

He ruminated. "Don't think so. Ordinary thing to happen, of course, and you're sure a ways from a phone. I could ask my wife—she's home more, when she's not running around to club meetings like now—me and the colored maid home alone right now. I don't remember anything like that, but if it happened in the daytime, well, I've only been retired six months."

"You know, Luis," said Hackett, "there's some more current business on hand back at the office."

"Too true." Mendoza nodded at Padgett, used his driveway to turn the car, and headed back. This time, passing, they saw the power mower being wielded by a naked-chested young Negro on the strip of parking. Farther down, they passed a little telephone truck coming up.

THE GRACES got to the County Adoption Agency downtown early that Tuesday morning. They'd had some experience of the red tape before, and were resigned to it. At least, unlike some fussy people who came here, they weren't demanding any particular sex or age. Anything up to six months, said Virginia, and a boy would be nice but she wouldn't mind another girl, if one as nice as Celia showed up.

"There isn't one as nice as Celia," said Grace. "Nice in a different way is all."

"Well, you know what I mean, Jase."

"Let's hope the people in here know what we mean."

LANDERS AND PALLISER had teamed up to try to make some
sense out of the Webster-Dunlap thing. They'd seen Mrs.
Webster, talked to Linda Dunlap, the neighbors on both
sides of the Dunlap house. They'd gone to Ernie's Garage
on Vermont and talked to Ernie about Webster. He was astonished and grieved to hear about Webster.

"Gee, that's a shame. He called in sick yesterday, so I
supposed he was still under the weather. First time he ever
was since I hired him. I kind of took a chance, man his age,
but he was a damn good mechanic, reliable."

"How long had he worked here?"

"Well, lessee. About four years. Yeah, that's right. He
said he'd just come out here from North Dakota—but I
never bothered to write for references. He was a real nice
guy, Carl—I'm damn sorry to hear he's dead. Was it a heart
attack or what?—you didn't say—and come to think, why
are the police—"

He had told his wife, whom he'd married two years ago,
that he was a widower from Chicago.

They came into the office at four-thirty and tossed a coin
to see who'd write the report; Palliser lost, but before he
started it they went in to catch Mendoza up on this one. He
was swiveled around in his desk chair talking to Hackett. He
listened to what they'd got and said, "Funny. Shapeless."

"What the lab may turn up I don't know," said Landers, "but the whole thing—"

"Well, good, I hoped you'd be here," said Horder from
the door. He came in and laid a brown paper parcel on
Mendoza's desk; his square bulldog face wore a pleased
expression. "Two birds with one stone. Here's your Goodwill lady, Lieutenant. That is, her dress. We pinned down
the cleaners for you. It's the Rite-Way Cleaners on Fountain in Hollywood. They may be able to identify the dress—
you can take it from there. Now—" he looked at Landers
"—about this funny one yesterday. It was a pretty straightforward job—you'll get a formal report—but I can pass on

this and that. It looks as if this Webster just walked in and attacked the two women. Probably yesterday morning. That hammer had his prints all over it. I couldn't say which one he went for first—''

"The girl," said Landers. "Linda Dunlap said her mother was still in bed when she left."

"Oh. Well, he went in the back. His prints are on the screen door."

"Probably not locked," said Palliser.

"No, he just walked in."

"His wife told us what he was driving—a four-year-old Chevy—and we found it parked on the street behind. There's a vacant house there, backs up to the Dunlaps'. He could have walked through the backyards."

"Likely. We can guess maybe he went for the girl, and she yelled, and the mother came rushing up to see what was happening, and he knocked her out. You'll get a better idea from the autopsy reports, but both the corpses had head wounds, I could see that. Now, his prints are also plastered all over the trunk of the car in the garage. It looks as if he bundled them into the trunk, started the engine and shut the garage door. And why in hell the neighbors didn't hear or see anything—''

"Neighbors on both sides all work," said Landers briefly. "It could be they didn't make enough noise to carry any farther. And the big garage door was down when Linda left. He could have carried them out and in the side door one at a time. But what a crazy—''

"It gets crazier," said Horder. "You heard what the paramedics said. It looks as if he stayed in that house, or went away and came back, and went out to the garage to see if they were dead. He'd closed the trunk, I think—there's a palm print in the middle of it. So he opened it to see if they were dead, but the damn fool forgot the engine was still running. He lingered a minute too long, and passed out himself."

"Crazy, I said," said Landers. "Suddenly going berserk like that. All the neighbors on their side of the street said he was a very nice fellow, quiet, they stayed home most of the time. His employer said he was a reliable worker. There's not a thing against him. And all of a sudden he goes and murders two people. He didn't even drink, they were both teetotallers."

Mendoza stroked his mustache. "Mmh, yes. Just one little thing, Tom. He told his employer he was from North Dakota, and told his wife it was Chicago."

"Whereas he was really from Hoboken? He met her in church, by the way," said Landers. "The Methodist church."

"Really. I just think it might be a useful gesture to send his prints to the Feds and see if they know him. I take it they're not on file with us."

"Well, of course not—first thing we looked for."

"Yes, well, let's see what the Feds say about him."

THE RITE-WAY CLEANERS was more or less on Mendoza's way home; he went a few blocks out of his way, found a parking slot, and walked back there carrying the brown paper parcel. At the door he was brought up by the neat sign inside: *On vacation open again the 11th.*

"*Caray,*" he said, annoyed. However, it couldn't be helped. He drove on home.

In one way daylight savings time was a blessing; after their usual boisterous welcome, the twins chased back to the rear yard with Cedric, and Mendoza had the leisure for a drink before dinner—pouring another for their alcoholic cat El Señor—and some civilized conversation with his wife.

Later on, inevitably, he read Grimm to them before bedtime, and presently came back to the living room where Alison, as close to the floor as James-or-Luisa let her go, was poring over her remodeling plans.

"But, damn it, you know that's got to be the answer," he said, standing in the middle of the room.

Alison, who had heard about La Loma Road over dinner, sat up and looked at him. "Oh, yes, I think so too, Luis. The only place she could have been—waylaid and murdered. But—"

"We don't even know that she was murdered."

"Of course she was. But she wasn't the only one who knew about La Loma Road. Just as you said, delivery trucks and gardeners and workmen."

"Who don't usually go in for mugging."

"I had another thought. College kids. Pasadena College isn't so far away. A couple of them, maybe out for a joyride, and high on something—"

"¿Por qué? But on second thought, how right you are, and anything—from the pot to coke—destroying normal inhibitions. I could see that. But if," said Mendoza, staring at her unseeingly, "she was mugged at all—for her cash, for that spectacular diamond ring—why in hell didn't they steal the car? Why didn't that ring show up at some pawnbroker's? And why in God's name Sixty-second Place?"

"Toda obra importanta requiere trabago," said Alison sententiously. "Important work needs labor."

"Helpful," said Mendoza. He wandered out. Later, when she went down the hall to the bedroom, she looked in the door of the den; he was sitting at the desk, cigarette in the corner of his mouth, practicing the crooked deals.

ONLY ONE PIECE of business came up for the night watch, but it occupied some time. They got the call at midnight: a homicide over on Hoover. It was an old court, three duplexes to each side with a strip of brown lawn down the center, and there were people out, two squad cars, a good deal of confusion.

"It's the last one on the left," said a uniformed man. "You'll be interested."

They were. There was a dead man on the living room floor, a fat young man naked except for shorts. He'd been shot in the chest. The old place was in a shambles, but some of that was due to careless housekeeping: dirty clothes lying around, dirty dishes in the sink, beer cans. The drawers pulled out and dumped, clothes yanked off hangers in the closet, looked more like a burglar. And some of the contents of the drawers— "The devil pretty busy these days," said Piggott sadly. There were a dozen brand-new hypodermic needles, about a thousand empty capsules: in a box under the bed, about a hundred made-up joints of marijuana.

There wasn't any other dope in the place, H or coke or the uppers and downers.

"Either he was expecting a new supply," said Schenke, "or our boy cleaned him out."

"Would he have had time, Bob, after he shot him? That probably brought the neighbors out in a hurry. Hot night, all the windows open."

"True," said Schenke. "Let's talk to them and see."

The nearest neighbor lived in the other side of the duplex. "Well, for God's sake—a'course I know his name," he said. His own was Leo Henninger, and he'd put away a few beers but was a long way from being drunk. "His name was Gordon De Soto, he's lived here a couple years, just a young guy, my God, this guy comes right in and shoots him—Rena and me just sittin' here watchin' TV and all of a sudden there's a helluva ruction next door and shots—my God, and we see him run right past—I told Rena to get cops and went to look—"

"Did you know De Soto very well?"

"Nah, he just lived here. Nice young guy, friendly."

"He have many people coming to see him?"

"Yeah, he had a lot of friends. Coming and going all the time."

"I bet," said Schenke. "Could you describe the man you saw run past?"

"I can do better than that for you," said Henninger. "I said there was the helluva ruction. Shouting and cussing. I heard De Soto yell, 'Stop it, Monty, don't do it, Monty—' and then there's the shots—"

Everybody else had heard the shots, but nobody had anything else useful to tell.

The lab truck came; Piggott and Schenke were already back inside the stuffy old four-room apartment poking around. In the bedroom, on top of the box of hypos, was a dime-store notepad, and at the risk of annoying the lab men Schenke had a look through it.

"I thought maybe, when it was with his supply, it might present a handle," he said proudly. "For once maybe we guess the end of a thing instead of just starting it off for the day watch. Have a look, Matt."

Piggott looked over his shoulder. "Very nice." There was a list of names in the book, page after page, just names and amounts of money entered opposite them. "De Soto the street supplier. Getting his stuff from somebody a little higher up. These were his accounts, and it'd be strictly cash."

They looked at the names; there were about forty different ones, repeated over and over. On the second page appeared *Monty Lopez*; it recurred on nearly every page.

"The boys will appreciate this," said Schenke.

"The devil usually takes care of his own, but he does slip up now and then," said Piggott seriously.

THE DAY WATCH did not especially appreciate being handed a new one, even with X's name on a platter. It all made more paperwork.

Landers was catching Grace up on Webster-Dunlap—they ought to get a kickback from the Feds on those prints sometime today or tomorrow—and Galeano and Palliser had been summoned up to Juvenile for some red tape on those kids yesterday, when a messenger brought in an autopsy report.

Mendoza looked at it absently. Hackett had had an appointment with an assistant D.A. and it was Higgins' day off; he hadn't anybody to talk at. He wanted to tell Higgins about La Loma Road; Higgins' solid common sense sometimes produced an idea.

It was the autopsy on the lady in the Goodwill bin. Well-nourished female aged approximately sixty-five; accustomed to wearing false teeth, which were missing. He deciphered the technical terms automatically; she'd had a bang on the head and died of it. A fairly hefty bang. And that cleaners' wouldn't be open until tomorrow.

They hadn't heard a thing from any pawnbroker about the *Titanic* medal.

That spectacular diamond ring, he thought. Aside from the cash, the car, the only thing of great value Anita had had with her. What had happened to it?

Four years and three months. He didn't know enough about it to know whether or not whatever X was involved here might have known a pro fence. The ring could have been broken into its component parts long ago.

Oh, yes? Also, X might have had some rudimentary cunning. Aware of the pawnbroker's hot list, he might have hung on to that ring—a couple of months, six months, longer?—hoping the heat would be off. One thing, it wasn't an anonymous solitaire; it was a very individual piece, and he thought that any pawnbroker who had ever laid eyes on it would remember it. It would, of course, have come off the hot list eventually; within six months at least. If every stolen item unrecovered was left on that list indefinitely, it would outweigh the *Congressional Record* in a short time.

"*¿Dónde estamos ahora?*" he said to himself. "It's an idea." He sat down and drafted a description of that ring, to be sent to every pawnbroker in the county with a special note: have you ever seen it at any time in the last four years?

It would probably produce nothing. It was a chance.

THE ASSISTANT D.A. was interested in Jody's gun. The ballistics report had come in before Hackett left the office: the slug from Kellerman's had been fired by the automatic Jody had buried. "Well, there you are," said the assistant D.A. "It's grounds for dismissing the charge all right. Explains away all those witnesses, which is really all we had. And—er—may I say, Sergeant Hackett, it was a commendable piece of police work. After all, you had the case tied up—you needn't have spent more time on it."

"I always felt there was something funny about it, was all. I'll be glad to see him get off, basically he's a solid citizen."

"But as to who did kill the man—" The assistant D.A. shrugged. "Well, one of those things all up in the air."

"That's about it."

"I'll get the paperwork started. You can tell him he'll be let loose sometime today."

"Good." As Hackett got out of the elevator on the ground floor of the Hall of Justice, he saw Reg Morrison in a little group of men just coming in the door. For a moment he hesitated, tempted to go and tell him about that; and then he let it go, and went out to the parking lot. Morrison probably wouldn't give a damn. But if Morrison was really, honestly concerned for his clients, not just with building up his own ego and the fast buck, he might have been sympathetic enough with Jody that all this would have come out before the arraignment.

At the office, Lake told him Mendoza had gone out. Looking, he said, absentminded. Hackett could guess where he'd gone. Grasping at straws. Roaming back and forth on La Loma Road—even, for God's sake, fifty-one months later, asking the householders, Do you remember a woman coming—

His instinct was quite right, of course. Luis always had the gut feelings about these things. That was the only place. But after all this time, they'd never find out what, why, or how.

At one o'clock that Wednesday, a squad car called in on the A.P.B. on Leroy Riggs. They'd spotted the plate number of that old Dodge in a used-car lot on La Cienega.

"Well, at long last," said Hackett. "And my God, it's George's day off again. It can't be helped—I'll call him, Jimmy—he'll want to sit in on this."

NINE

THE SALESMAN at the lot on La Cienega was surprised. "Police—and those two?" he said. "What the hell have they done? Oh, well, excuse me, ought to know better than to ask the fuzz their business. Sure I can tell you. They walked in here last Friday, turned in that old clunker on a new Sportabout. Quite a deal. The old clunker's barely worth a hundred, which is what we gave 'em, and they came back in an hour with a certified check for the rest of it. Forty-five hundred and something."

"So I don't suppose," said Higgins, "you've got an address for them?"

"Sure I got an address. There's a warranty on the car, you know—the company's got to keep records. I'll look it up for you."

The address was Beverly Place in West Hollywood. "This is a waste of time," said Hackett, switching on the Barracuda's engine, "because there'll never be any proof. Unless he comes apart and admits it, which I doubt he's about to do."

It was a small new apartment building, brick and redwood, lush tropical greenery in raised beds. They had the apartment number; it was at the rear on the ground floor, the door overlooking a big kidney-shaped sparkling swimming pool. Higgins rapped at the door sharply; in a moment it opened and Leroy Riggs looked at them.

"Well, Mr. Riggs," said Higgins, leering at him, very much the tough cop ("At least we can try to scare him a little," he'd said to Hackett), "we finally catch up to you."

"Oh, hell," said Riggs unhappily. "Listen, I don't want you guys to upset Brenda, see. She's out shopping. I don't know what more you want to ask me, but you just come in and get it over, and go away before she—"

"Yes, we understand you've found a nice cozy spot for yourself, rich bride," said Hackett. They went in and Riggs shut the door. It was a handsome new place, nothing elegant, just a good apartment with modern comfortable furnishings. "And Sylvia was going to throw a monkey wrench into the works, wasn't she? She wanted a cut of the take, or maybe she'd tell your innocent girl friend this and that about you—was that it?"

"What?" said Riggs.

"How did you get Sylvia to take the Nembutal? Farewell drink together—only she didn't know it was farewell?"

"What are you—talking about?" Riggs stared at them, slack-mouthed. He was a little handsome with his wavy-blond hair, nattily turned out in well-tailored sports clothes. "I thought—some red tape maybe—you wanted—"

"Come on," said Higgins, looming at him. "She was standing out for a cut of the loot, and you weren't about to divvy—we weren't born yesterday, Leroy."

"I—" said Riggs. "I— *You think I hurt Sylvia?*" There was naked pain and astonishment in his voice. "You think—"

"She didn't leave a suicide note," said Hackett.

He looked at them, blinking, for half a minute, and then he said, "Yes, she did. You don't understand about it at all, I don't know if I can make you. I've got to try, I suppose." He sat down on the stark blocky modern couch and looked at the floor. "I don't know if cops would understand."

"Well, you can try us," said Hackett.

Riggs didn't say anything for a while, and then he took a long painful breath. "I guess I can see what you might think—about Sylvia and me. But the funny thing is, it wasn't so. There never was any sex stuff between us. You

asked me—if we'd been together—five years, and I said yes.
It was more like ten, there—other places. Sylvia and I met
up when I was a green kid about seventeen. You know how
they say, misery loves company? I guess that was Sylvia and
me. We felt sorry for each other. She was awful good to me,
you know. We had, you know, a lot of the same kind of
memories together—I don't remember my mother, my old
man was a hell of a lush, and both her folks were too—she
was out hustling when she was sixteen, get enough to eat.
Same as me making a buck where I could, and who's particular how. We—kind of took to each other." He looked up
at the two big tough cops watching him, and said quietly,
"She was kind of like my big sister. Even a mother. Sure I
know what she was. It was how she got the rent paid. She
gave me a roof and meals, I was down on my luck, and
plenty of times I paid the rent and bought the groceries when
she was broke. I thought one hell of a lot of Sylvia. Maybe
she wasn't much from where you sit, a five-buck hooker
past her best days, but she'd been good to me, like I was her
kid brother. Do you dig that at all?"

"It's your story. Go on," said Hackett. He and Higgins
had sat down on the matching armchairs opposite the
couch.

"I was damned sorry I couldn't go to the funeral," said
Riggs. "But I guess she'd understand about that. Well, I
know she would. I—I told Brenda she was an old friend of
my mother's, sick and alone and killed herself—reason she
was at the city morgue—I sort of felt obligated, and Brenda
gave me the thousand. Hell, Sylvia'd have said, Good for
you, boy, only she'd probably have said I was nuts spending it on her funeral." Suddenly Riggs laughed. He sat up
and lit a cigarette. "You thought I hurt Sylvia some way! I'd
have cut off my right hand. The first time I saw her I hadn't
had a meal in four days, Dad had drunk up the welfare
check. I was a green kid, nobody'd give me a job. We got

talking on a bus. She bought me a meal, and she only had six bucks on her and the rent due."

He drew a long breath. "Look, it's funny how things happen. I got a part-time job at Hertz's about six months ago. How I met Brenda. Brenda Little. She was just a steno back in Peoria, Illinois, orphan working girl—she's older than me, thirty-three—when this uncle died and left her a lot of loot, about a million. She came out here on a trip, first time she'd ever been anywhere, and I rented her a car. She was having fun and not having fun, see, all alone—a real simple girl, kind of innocent. I don't mean stupid. She didn't like the first car, brought it back for another, we got talking, and I could see she'd be a real pushover—nobody ever paid any attention to her before, and I said to myself, maybe this is where Leroy comes in for a real soft deal. And I was right. Brother, was I right."

He put out the cigarette, lit another. "She's not a stupid girl, Brenda. She isn't dumb, she knew I probably wouldn't have gone out of my way, except for the loot. And no fooling around if it wasn't serious, see. She knew I liked the money, but it was nice for her to have a man around—I can put up a pretty good front. And then—then I started to like her. She's a good kid, Brenda, a nice girl. I—I don't know but what I'd have married her even without the money. We got married over in Vegas about six weeks ago, and went to stay at that fancy hotel—

"Sure Sylvia knew. She was all for it. She thought it was the greatest thing ever happened for me. She just said, You be good to the girl, don't go half-assin' around and turn her off, and you got a meal ticket the rest of your life, a real sweet deal, she said. I—that last time I saw her, we said goodbye. Oh, Brenda likes California all right for a vacation, we got the new car and we're going to drive up the coast—she said that hotel was too expensive so we got the apartment so she can cook for us—but she wants to go back east to live."

"Sylvia," said Higgins. "The last time?"

He swallowed and looked away from them. "Before we were married. She said—how great it was for me—and drop her a line once in a while, let her know how it was going, but she wouldn't write back because it'd look funny. But she'd been down, I could see—no luck picking up johns, and she hadn't been feeling good. So—after we got back from Vegas and were at that hotel—Brenda was out shopping, getting her hair done, and I thought I'd just drop in, see Sylvia, slip her a few bucks. She was dead. There in the bedroom. She left me a letter. I guess she knew I'd come by again."

Slowly, reluctantly, he got out his billfold and took a folded page from it. "It was to me," he said. "I didn't care about anybody else seeing it."

Hackett unfolded it: a sheet torn from a cheap lined tablet, the writing in ballpoint large and sprawling.

"Roy honey, you shouldn't feel bad about this. It isn't on account of you because I couldn't be happier you got in such a good spot and all the money and you say you really like the girl too. You be happy and have a good life here on in. You know I been tired and seems like too much trouble just keep on the rat race. It's best I get out now and I'll be glad have a rest. Sylvia."

"She was dead," said Riggs softly. "It was my letter, so I took it, and the bottle of pills—there weren't many left— I don't know why, except I wanted it to look—like she'd just died, not—not done anything. But I couldn't just leave her there. I went and told the Lewis bitch we were moving out, so she'd go up and find Sylvia right away. But she didn't. Just left her there all alone."

"We'll have to have this letter, you know," said Hackett, "for the report—the inquest." The inquest had been adjourned pending more investigation. "If you want it back—"

"No, I guess not," said Riggs. "I told you, before, I didn't know she was dead. I just wanted to keep Brenda out of it—" He smiled faintly. "She's a nice girl, but I guess she wouldn't understand about Sylvia. But that's the way it all was. Do you believe that?"

"I don't think we've got any choice," said Hackett gently. They left him still sitting on the couch, head down. At the curb beside the Barracuda, he said to Higgins, "You never do know about people, do you, George? As much human nature as we've seen in too long at this job, they can still surprise you."

"There's Brenda," said Higgins. She parked the new Sportabout at the curb and got out, took a big sack of groceries from the back. She was a little thing, mousy and too thin, with a plain freckled snub-nosed face, but she looked cheerful and happy, trotting by them toward the apartment near the pool.

"Well, good luck to them," said Hackett. "Or rather to her—maybe she'll need it."

WHAT WITH FIVE ANIMALS in the house, either Alison or Máiri had occasion to visit the Los Feliz Small Animal Clinic on a fairly regular basis. If Sheba's allergies weren't acting up again, El Señor would tangle with a neighborhood tom or Bast would find something long-dead and get a stomach upset. On this occasion it was nothing more serious than a rabies shot for Cedric, and Máiri offered to take him.

"No, I don't mind, you've got those curtains to do, and it won't take an hour," said Alison. She found Cedric's leash and he galumphed into the car happily, taking up three-quarters of the front seat.

When they got there, and she found a parking place on the street and led him into the little waiting room, mercifully it wasn't crowded. There was a woman with a shivering collie, and a man with a picnic basket on his lap. Alison sat down in the chair next to him after announcing their arrival to the receptionist, and Cedric nosed interestedly at the basket. "Down," said Alison. There was a loud hiss from the basket. Cedric whined.

"He likes cats," said Alison in apology.

The man smiled. He was about fifty, with a humorous, lined, weathered face: a tall lanky man in comfortable old clothes, open-necked shirt, gray pants. "Quite a bit of dog you've got there. Old English sheepdog—a nice fellow." The basket hissed again. "Nothing much wrong with him, looks like."

"He's just in for a shot." You always got talking to people at the vet's. "Yours doesn't sound too bad, the way she's cussing Cedric."

"He," said the man. "Mother always does like a cat around. I'd let you see him—he's quite a fellow, coal black—but he'd be up the wall. Name's Nicodemus. Got in a little fight and needs a few stitches."

"Poor boy. They will do it."

The collie shivered and whined and rattled his collar.

"Yes," said the man ruminatively, "I can turn my hand to most anything but best leave that to a doctor." Outside traffic whizzed noisily by. The receptionist said, "Mrs. Gray, you may come in now," and the woman with the collie got up and took the trembling dog into the recesses of the hospital, leaving Alison and Cedric alone with the man and the picnic basket.

He sighed and shuffled his feet. "Fellow like yours needs a lot of exercise."

"He should get more than he does, but we'll be moving to a new place where he'll have lots more room. Four acres, which should be enough," said Alison.

"That so?" He looked interested. "Around here? Oh." The basket emitted a raucous wail and he patted it. "You hold on to your patience. We're thinking of getting out of town somewhere too—mistake to come here. It might sound fine, money coming every month and no work, but you might as well be dead. Mother says the city sidewalks make her feet hurt, and I don't know what to do with myself all day." He was talking to himself, not garrulous or intrusive.

Alison was always immensely interested in people and what made them tick. "You're from the country?"

"Up in Trinity County. Big new dam being built up there, and the government took our spread without an aye, yes or no—paid decent money for it, but still— Anyway, our daughter Jane lives here with her husband, and it sounded fine, retire and take it easy. Only neither of us like town much. You miss the space."

"What did you have, wheat or something?"

"Cattle, miss—ma'am," he corrected himself, his eyes twinkling. He was an easy, comfortable sort of man, rather slow-spoken.

"Oh," said Alison. "I suppose you'd know something about ponies."

He looked surprised. "Know something about most kinds of stock, sure." As if conscious that she might think he'd been talking too much, he fell silent. Cedric whined at the basket and the basket wailed.

"I suppose," said Alison, "you could fix a swing, couldn't you? The brackets came loose, and I can't get anybody at all, nobody'll come to do such a little job."

He looked surprised again, but laughed. "Farmer has to turn his hand to anything. I expect I could."

"I don't want you to think—" said Alison hurriedly.

"Matter of fact, I've been thinking of maybe setting up to do odd jobs for people, give myself something to do." He smiled reassuringly at her, a nice slow smile.

"I've been at my wit's end," said Alison. "My husband can't drive a nail straight, you see."

"Well, there are some like that. Good at other things."

"I suppose," said Alison, "you and your wife would like to have another ranch someday."

He looked a little wistful, sighed. "Don't know that I'd take on another big herd, that big a spread. It'd be nice to

have a smaller place, where Mother could have a garden
again. Since we been here, I just dunno what people find to
do in town.''

Alison looked at him with something like awe. There
really was something like Fate about it, she thought. Here
in this very waiting room, over four years ago, when she'd
also been at her wit's end with the twins keeping them awake
all night, she'd unexpectedly found Máiri MacTaggart; and
now Fate obligingly answered her need again.

"Mr. Kearney," said the receptionist, "you may come in
now." He got up.

"Er—Mr. Kearney," said Alison, "would you come to fix
the swing? I'll write down the address for you—"

"Be glad to, ma'am." He took the slip of paper. "This
afternoon be all right?"

"Fine," said Alison. Mr. Kearney took the basket inside, and she thought, undoubtedly Fate. The man to take
care of the ponies, and the landscaping. And she felt mor-
ally sure that Mother would turn out to be a dear, an in-
valuable ally in the house. The conviction was based, of
course, on the picnic basket; only a real cat person, a thoroughly nice and reliable human being, would—lacking a cat
carrier—pop a black tomcat into a picnic basket for a trip
to the vet. I wonder what her name is, thought Alison.

LANDERS AND GRACE had inherited the new homicide by
default, awaiting the autopsies on Webster-Dunlap, and had
been out most of the day looking for Monty Lopez. He appeared in their records, with a small pedigree of narco possession, B. and E. The address given was Huntly Drive, not
far from the civic center. They found his mother there,
bleary-eyed and smelling strongly of muscatel; she said she
didn't know where he was, and couldn't suggest anywhere
to look.

There wasn't a car registered to him, which made it largely
a futile gesture to put out an A.P.B. They would, of course,

spread the word among their various street informants, and somebody might blow the whistle on him eventually. He had held a job, the last time he was on parole, at a gas station on Flower Street; they talked to the owner and he said that punk he hadn't seen in six months and didn't want to.

They landed back at the office at three-thirty, feeling limp from trailing around in the heat. Landers sat down and loosened his tie. Grace said plaintively, "Why isn't there a machine that dispenses iced coffee?" As they'd come in past the row of interrogation rooms, it seemed that two were in use: somebody questioning heist suspects. Nobody was in the office except Hackett, who was typing a report with his head reared back.

"You been accomplishing anything?" he asked, stopping to light a cigarette.

"Killing time," said Landers. "Just killing time."

Mendoza came out of his office, asked the same question and got the same answer. "I just had a buzz from the desk. There's a Fed on the way up."

"About what?" Hackett bent to the typewriter again.

"We'll find out." A minute later a tall gray-haired man came in past Lake and looked around the office.

"Mendoza? Williams. You sent some prints back to Washington. Where'd you pick them up? We're interested."

"There, you see, Tom, the day isn't wasted after all. You'd all better come in and sit down." They adjourned to Mendoza's office, Hackett trailing along out of curiosity. "One Carl Webster," said Mendoza. "You know him?"

"We do. Only his name isn't Webster. Where'd you get the prints?"

"From a corpse," said Landers. "Who is he?"

"Well, I'm glad to hear he's dead. As far as we know, his right name was Kent. There's a record on him as long as your arm, and every entry reads the same way. Rape with violence. He's served a little time in nine states, and skipped out from under charges in more. It's kind of a confused trail, going back nearly forty years. At the moment he's wanted, from ten years back, in New York and Atlanta."

"I will be damned!" said Landers, astonished. "All we turned up, he was living a quiet ordinary existence, working a regular job."

Williams nodded. "That was the pattern. Back to forty years ago. He was married twice, and both times the wife left him after he was arrested and charged. He'd go along for a while, looking as ordinary as you please, everybody thinking of him as good old Joe Doakes—I couldn't count the different names he used—and then the urge would set him off again. Not just the luscious young things—kids too. He got by with a second-degree murder charge in Ohio, killed a seven-year-old after raping her. That was in the forties."

"Well, if that's not a little surprise," said Grace mildly. "We'd been thinking the old fellow had a brainstorm and just went berserk. You know, Tom, that says a little something, doesn't it?"

"The sixteen-year-old," nodded Landers. "We said, crazy, just walk in and attack them, but maybe we can read it different with this background."

"He's accounted for another one?" asked Williams.

"Two—and himself. That kid—retarded, the sister said, but pretty. Like a kid. Maybe just the kind to rouse the old urge in Webster, after he'd spent about four quiet blameless years here—and married another wife. The mother works, but we heard that a woman came in days to look after the kid, usually drove up in front about eight. Say he's noticed the kid, got the urge, and can we say that he noticed the woman didn't come. As a matter of fact she'd been in a little accident on her way, called the Dunlaps and said she couldn't make it, but he wouldn't know. He thought the kid was home alone, didn't know the mother had stayed home from work. He left for work at the usual time, went around the block, and got in through the back. Attacked the kid, and the mother came running—he was caught again. He'd have to shut both of them up." They told Williams the rest of the story, and he laughed grimly.

"Delayed retribution! Well, good riddance, I'm just damned sorry to hear he took those two with him. And what a hell of a shock for the poor innocent widow he'd married. At least we can take him off the books." He looked around. "They keeping you boys busy lately?"

"Tolerably," said Grace. He looked at Landers. "This means a final report on it. I did the last one."

"I won't argue with you. Chance to stay in, in the air conditioning."

"I TELL YOU, it's Fate," said Alison.

Mendoza regarded his household with some misgiving. He had found everybody out in the backyard, the twins madly swinging on the reconstructed swing, Cedric making little rushes at it and barking loudly; the cats spotted about under bushes except for El Señor, who was sitting regally upright on the back porch. Máiri was cutting roses from the bushes along the back of the house.

"You go so fast, *enamorada*. You don't know anything about this fellow—"

"Yes, we do. His name's Ken Kearney, and he was a cattle farmer. He can turn his hand to anything and he knows about ponies. His wife wants a garden again, and they have a black cat. He's really a darling man, Luis. A very nice man. He fixed the swing in about ten minutes, and the twins love him. He's good with children—they've got three grandchildren of their own."

"So you've decided, in about five minutes, that they're going to be our new live-in help."

"They'd be just right, I should think. That old winery building is huge—we could make a nice apartment for them, so they'd be on their own. Of course they might not want to live in, but it'd be more like a farm for them up there, the space and the view—"

"The one thing that's on my mind," said Máiri, adding a rose to her basket, "is that cat, *achara*. El Señor isna going to take kindly to him."

"There'll be scads of room for them both," said Alison recklessly.

Mendoza regarded Máiri suspiciously. "You made up your mind in five minutes too?"

"Och, he's a comfortable sort of body. Easy and honest as day."

"And suppose his wife is a shrew?"

"She couldn't be," said Alison. "At any rate, I'm going to see them tomorrow, and sort of sound them out. They can come and see the place, and hear what we'll be doing. We'll just see, that's all. But it really seems like Fate—and of course you'll have to meet them too—"

"Gracias," said Mendoza. "I'll do that, and make up my own mind, *por favor."*

THERE WAS ANOTHER HEIST at a liquor store on Wednesday night. Predictably, the A.P.B. hadn't turned up Monty Lopez. "If he took off with De Soto's supply," said Landers, "he might show up as an O.D. in some back alley."

"Piggott thought De Soto was waiting for new goods," Grace reminded him. They only hoped he'd turn up some time, to clear that off the books. Meanwhile, there were always heisters to hunt for.

And today that Rite-Way Cleaners should be open for business again. Mendoza and Higgins landed there at ninethirty.

Beyond the door it was a small square place with a counter cutting it in half. A loud bell on the door announced their entrance and a little bald man appeared from the back room. "Yes?"

Mendoza produced the badge and the brown paper parcel. "We'd be interested to know if you can identify this for us. It's got your tag on it. Do you remember the customer?"

"Oh, dear. We have so many items coming in—" He spread out the black dress on the counter, examining it fussily. "Yes, that's our tag all right. Just a minute, perhaps my wife—Myra! I don't recall this personally, but—"

Myra was a haggard-looking blonde. She looked at the dress, felt the material and said, "It was a dye job. I remember it. Don't remember the name, but I can look it up— we don't have many dye jobs now, and I don't think it was so long ago, it'll be in this year's accounts." She went away, came back. "Yeah—it was a Mrs. Agnes McKeever. Hawthorn Avenue."

"Thanks so much," said Mendoza. The pair watched them out incuriously.

Hawthorn Avenue was a little street up from Fountain, here in the heart of old Hollywood. Unlike some, it had escaped the bulldozers where old single houses had made way for the jerry built new garden apartments. Along its narrow width were small frame and stucco houses, most of them neatly kept up. The one they wanted was more than adequately landscaped: the lawn in front was lushly, richly green, and standard rose trees lined the front walk. Darkly crisp evergreen shrubs made a contrast against the spanking white paint of the house. The lawn continued around on both sides. There was an oscillating sprinkler going at one side of the walk. The house was a bungalow with a wide front porch all across its width.

Higgins pushed the doorbell. The sound of the falling water was cool and grateful in the already humid, hot morning. The front door was open behind a screen door.

A man appeared behind the screen. "Yes?"

"Mr. McKeever?"

"That's me."

"Mr. McKeever," said Mendoza, "where is your wife?" He showed McKeever the badge.

The man stood looking at them for a moment. He said, "Is it any of your business?"

"It shouldn't be too difficult to find people who know her, to identify the body. You'd better let us in, you know."

After another long minute he unlatched the screen door. "I'd best turn off that sprinkler." He came out to the porch, a not-very-big man, with remnants of red hair turning gray; he had a long nose and a long clean-shaven upper lip and freckles. Higgins made a move, and he said testily, "I'm not goin' anywhere. Just to turn off the sprinkler. I'll be right back. We might as well talk inside, it's a sight cooler." He went down the steps, shut off the faucet, and came back slowly. They went in, to a dim living room with stiff old-fashioned furniture precisely placed.

McKeever sat down and planted his hands on the knees of his shabby stained work pants. "So you found her," he said. "How'd you know who she was?"

"There was a cleaners' tag in her dress," said Mendoza.

"Luis, you'd better tell the man his rights," said Higgins.

"I know my rights. I never thought of that," said McKeever. There was mild regret in his tone. "I didn't know but what she might be traced by her teeth, so I took them out. Never crossed my mind about her clothes."

"Would you like to tell us about it? Why you killed her? Or did you?"

"Wasn't anybody else here, was there? I won't say I'm not sorry you found it, because I'm damn sorry. Fixing to have some peace and quiet from now on. Not that I meant to do it, because I didn't. But once it was done—" He sighed and sat back in the chair and brought out a pipe. He didn't fill it or light it, just held it. "I guess I can take my time, telling you. Not to try and excuse myself—it wasn't a right thing to do. But there was what you might call mitigating circumstances. I was married to Aggie for forty years, and she was a right pretty girl. Awful warning. Makes you think of the old saying, handsome is as handsome does." He sucked at the pipe. "Women, they get a man broke in while he's still feeling romantic about 'em. Before I knew it she had me broke to harness. Couldn't smoke in the house, couldn't put my feet up on the couch, couldn't take a little drink or I was bound straight for hell, couldn't miss church on Sunday, don't do this and don't do that.

"She was pretty strict with Ellie too—that was our daughter—but Ellie grew up all right. Favored me over Aggie. But getting older, Aggie just got more and more hidebound. Nothing ever suited her, people or the weather or me or Ellie or the neighbors. First thing really riled me—I mean more than she'd ever riled me before—she takes a fit against this fellow Ellie got engaged to. Nice fellow, in regular work. Matter o' fact it was me introduced her to Bill—I drove a city bus a good long time, and he was one of the dispatchers. Aggie takes it into her head he's a no-good bum because he likes a beer now and then and don't go to church. Wouldn't have him in the house. Oh, I went to see them. They got married, lived over on Fountain, Ellie was always glad to see me, and Bill was a right nice fellow.

"But it was nag, nag, grouse, grouse, bitch, bitch, day in day out. I like to work in the yard—you see how nice I got it. And she was forever complaining about how much I pay for fertilizer, tracking in mud, smell of the manure, and so on. By that time, I'd got so I didn't hardly hear her no more, in one ear and out the other, you could say. And then Ellie and Bill got killed."

His mouth sagged a little. He looked at the pipe. "They never had any kids. And they got killed together on the freeway, last January. Coming home from a movie. Drunk going the wrong way on an off-ramp.

"After that I didn't have anyplace to go. Been retired a couple years, and not much money. I put in my time workin' on the yard, but it seemed like whatever I did she just got worse.

"You know something funny? That dress she had on, she had it dyed special to wear to Ellie's funeral. Hadn't talked to her own daughter in fifteen years, but she had to have a black dress for the funeral, show respect. That's funny.

"Anyways, come to last Friday night. I'd been out at my compost heap—it was just getting dark, I come into the garage to put away my tools, and she's there takin' a load of laundry out of the dryer. She starts in again, bitch, bitch about the smell of fertilizer, I'm all the time in dirty clothes in the yard, leave her alone, and before I knew what I was doing—I had the shovel in my hand—I told her to shut up, and I biffed her one. A good one—it's a heavy shovel. And when I saw she was dead, I didn't feel anything particular about it except it was a good job done, and I could have some peace and smoke my pipe in the house." He reflected. "After I'd taken her away, I stopped on the way home and got a six-pack of beer. Enjoyed it too. Tasted mighty good, a hot night and all."

"Mr. McKeever," said Mendoza with genuine interest, "what made you think of the Goodwill bin?"

McKeever smiled, a slow, strangely satisfied smile. "Well, I'll tell you," he said. "There'd been a throwaway paper in the mail just that day. From the Goodwill. And it said, all those items you no longer need or want, please let us have them. And of all the things I didn't need or want any more, Aggie was tops on the list."

Mendoza and Higgins both laughed involuntarily. "And you hoped she'd never be identified. How were you going to explain it?"

"I don't expect the neighbors would miss her. She'd quarreled with 'em all. Thought I'd say she was visiting back east, and then say she'd died. I guess I was foolish, think I could get away with it."

"We'll have to take you in," said Higgins.

McKeever nodded and put away his pipe. "I only wish I knew somebody, come and take care of my yard. A few days' neglect in this weather and it'll go to rack and ruin."

THE GLASSES FELT QUEER and stiff on Hackett's face, but they certainly did make printing jump out at him clear and sharp. Dr. Rumbold fussed about getting them fitted just right, and was finally satisfied. He presented Hackett with a slightly staggering bill, and Hackett made out a check, got up and nearly fell flat on his face.

"Only for close work," said Dr. Rumbold, coughing.

Hackett put the glasses away in their case and went home. Angel was dusting in the front room, and hearing him come in the back hurried out dust-cloth in hand. "Let's see what you look like. Why, Art, they really make you look very distinguished! Man of distinction—a real V.I.P. I like the frames." She surveyed him from all sides. "You look like a college professor."

"When you say that, smile," said Hackett. Sheila came trotting into the kitchen and he bent to pick her up. "How's Daddy's Sheila?"

Sheila gave the glasses one horrified look, burst into screams and struggled away. "Oh, dear," said Angel.

"You'll say more than that," said Hackett, "when I tell you what they cost."

THERE WAS ANOTHER HEIST at a liquor store just before midnight. Piggott and Schenke got statements from the owner and a clerk, got a description, and came back to type a report. The victims would be in in the morning to look at mug-shots.

"We ought," said Schenke, "to find out when E. M. can have visitors, and go to see him. Take him some cigarettes or something. You know, Matt, it's a damn funny thing, but now we know he'll be O.K.—and be retiring early—I'd really like to see the old boy, kind of—like they say—wish him Godspeed."

Piggott grinned. "We'd better do that. Well, he's not such a bad fellow, Bob—and he was a good cop. But it's a good deal more peaceful without that radio of his, isn't it?"

"You are so damn right," said Schenke feelingly.

FRIDAY, with Glasser and Galeano off, saw the office shorthanded in other ways. An inquest on Agnes Mc-Keever was scheduled for ten o'clock; now they knew more about her, fuller evidence would be offered, and Higgins would cover that. An inquest on the Dunlaps—there would be a different one for Carl Webster now—was scheduled for ten in another court, and Palliser would be there.

Mendoza came in briefly, looked at the night report, and went out. Hackett shook his head after him, muttered, "Grasping at straws," and got out the glasses to look at Piggott's report.

"Well, very handsome," said Landers. "They make you look distinguished. Very V.I.P."

"Just like a college professor," said Grace. "No, I mean it as a compliment. Do they help?"

Hackett looked up from the report and saw Grace as a brown blurred outline. "Um, for close work. I guess I'll get used to them. But it's a damn nuisance putting them on and taking them off."

Higgins came in for the first time since Hackett had arrived; he'd taken the liquor-store owner and his clerk down to R. and I. to look at mug-shots. "Hey," he said, "they're not bad, Art. Very distinguished. You look like a—"

"College professor," said Hackett rather crossly. "Thanks so much." There was still a report to get out on Riggs; he sat down to do it, and found the typing was much easier, everything nice and clear at that distance. He just had to remember to take the damned things off before he got up, or he'd lose his balance.

About ten o'clock Lake put through a call for him. It was Mrs. Holt.

"Mr. Hackett," she said a little hesitantly, "we just thought we'd ask you. We're having a little party here tonight, for Jody. Just to—kind of celebrate. And we surely take it kindly, you being the reason he's out of trouble, if you'd stop by and have a little glass of wine with us."

"That's very nice of you, Mrs. Holt, I'd like to do that, thanks very much."

"You surely must have brought us good luck, you know. He got a call from the bus company just this morning, he's got a full-time job driving for them."

"That's good news, I'm glad to hear it."

"Maybe about eight o'clock, then, we'll see you. It's just some friends and family."

"Thanks, Mrs. Holt."

Five minutes later Lake buzzed him. He was the only one in. "A 211 down—the Traffic men nabbed him, they're bringing him in."

"Well, pleasant change," said Hackett.

Fifteen minutes later he took charge of the heister from Henderson and Murillo. The heister had tried to hold up a bar just as it opened. "You can thank the barkeep," said Henderson. "He's an ex-Marine about six-five, and he just belted the gun out of our boy's hand and grabbed him."

"Three cheers for the Marines," said Hackett. The heister was about twenty-two, middle-sized, dark and hairy. He stood there staring at them moodily, hands cuffed in front of him.

"There's no I.D. on him. He wouldn't give a name."

"We can always book him as John Doe."

"My name's Lopez," said the heister sullenly.

"Well, well, not Monty?" said Hackett. He did answer the description; Hackett hadn't seen his mug-shot. Murillo handed over a Colt .32 revolver. "Won't it be interesting to see if Ballistics matches this up with the slug out of Gordon De Soto. What about it, Lopez?''

Lopez didn't say another word. Hackett read him his rights, questioned him awhile without hearing anything, and ferried him down to the jail on Alameda to book him in.

The warder told him to empty his pockets; the cuffs were off then, and he brought out a pack of cigarettes, a handful of change, a knife, and unexpectedly, what looked like a necklace.

''What's that?'' Hackett picked it up.

Lopez said wearily, ''I couldn't get nothing for it. The pawnbroker said it was junk.''

It was the *Titanic* medal.

TEN

THE HOLTS' PARTY was just beginning to sparkle. Hackett had purposefully come early, aware that he'd been invited out of pure politeness and would constitute a skeleton at the feast. He'd congratulated Jody on the new job, had ice cream and cake pressed on him, drunk a glass of wine with Gloria and her mother, and after he finished the second glass in his hand, he'd shake hands all round, wish everybody luck, and leave; and without his slightly inhibiting presence the party would begin to swing.

The Linkers had come in a little late, and joined the family group at first. Hackett had just finished the second glass of wine and was looking for his hostess to make the ceremonial farewells, when Bea Linker said, "Oh, Mr. Hackett," and he turned. "It's nice you could come. You know, I want to apologize to you."

"What for, Mrs. Linker?"

"Well, I thought Ma and Gloria were foolish, ask you to help Jody." Her eyes were grave on him. "I didn't think a cop would listen, after he'd arrested somebody and didn't have to."

"Well, we're supposed to be concerned with the truth of a case, not just an arrest," said Hackett soberly. "Quite a lot of us are."

"Anyway, I'm glad I was wrong, and we do thank you for what you did for Jody." She looked across the little crowd, people having a good time. "I don't suppose we'll ever know the right of it. Who really did do it. Well, the Lord knows nobody'll miss Les Fulger. It's a puzzle why a nice girl like

Kathy ever married him. But it's a shame such a thing had to happen at Mr. Kellerman's place.''

"Pretty popular place.''

"Oh, yes! But what I meant was, Mr. Kellerman's such a nice man. And a real good man, he does a lot of good that people don't all know about. Saw most of the neighborhood kids grow up, around here, and he's always doing things for people—nickels and dimes for the kids, and helping out people down on their luck, so long as they aren't lazy, like that. He thought the world of Kathy, you know—it was him argued her into finishing high school and taking that business course. He's helped other kids too, found out about that scholarship for Rudy Woods and lent Ben Blake the money for music lessons."

"That so?" said Hackett.

"Well—" she sighed "—spilled milk like they say. Whatever happened, Kathy's well rid of Les, and thanks to the Lord—and you—Jody's all right." She smiled at him. "We're grateful for it." She drifted off to join the little crowd around Jody and Mrs. Holt.

Hackett regarded his empty wineglass thoughtfully, set it down on the dining-room table, and started making his way toward his hostess, thanked her, wished them all good luck, and took his leave.

ON SATURDAY MORNING, with Lake off and Farrell sitting on the switchboard, Landers off, and another overnight heist, Grace and Higgins went over to the jail to question Monty Lopez. They didn't get much out of him; for one thing, he was jumpy and restless because he needed a fix. They asked him about De Soto. He said thickly, "That son of a bitch, he never give anything unless the bread's in his hand—I tole him I'd get it—"

"Is that why you killed him, Monty?"

"I never kill nobody. I hadda little fight with him—I remember that. Wouldn't give me no stuff. But all I could find was one lousy deck of H—"

That wouldn't feed his habit long. "You remember heisting some people on the street, Monty? You didn't get much there either."

He just shook his head. His eyes were bleary. "Listen, I got to have something. You tell them to get me something—H or coke, I don't—I'm gettin' the shakes, I got to have—"

They wouldn't get any more from him, and it didn't really matter; Ballistics had pinpointed the gun found on him as the one which killed De Soto. And of course they had the *Titanic* medal. As evidence, they'd have to hang on to it for a while, but Hackett had called Mrs. Parton and told her about it, and she'd been tearfully grateful to know it was safe.

There was an inquest scheduled on De Soto on Monday morning. McKeever would be indicted on Tuesday. Meanwhile, there were the heisters to look for.

The hospital had announced yesterday that Shogart could have visitors, one at a time and five minutes only. As the men could make time, they all dropped in to see him, took him the cigarettes, candy, for later on. He grinned at them weakly, pleased at their coming.

That heister, Tyler Sanford, had been indicted on Friday; it was to be hoped he'd get handed a stiff term in the joint, but nobody either at Hollywood division or Central was taking any bets on that.

Landers dropped in to see Shogart on Saturday afternoon. He'd never worked much with him even when Shogart was on day watch; he knew Shogart had put some backs up, but he'd never felt much about him one way or the other. Now, as a cop, he was just grateful that Shogart wasn't going to add another name to the Honor Roll in the lobby at Parker Center.

He'd brought him some chocolates; Shogart had a sweet tooth. "How're you doing? You know we were all pulling for you, E. M." Shogart nodded slowly.

"Thanks. Going to be—O.K."

"Sure you are," said Landers heartily. "You'll be out of here in no time."

When the nurse chased him out, he went down to the apartment on Norton Avenue to see their other invalid, and found him peacefully propped up on the couch with a paperback. "Oh, I'm fine," said Conway. "Be back to the rat race on Monday. What's on hand besides all the heists, anything interesting?"

"Not very," said Landers, "once you get them unraveled. Phil said I was to bring you home for dinner."

"I'll take you up," said Conway promptly. "She's a pretty good cook. I was just wondering what TV dinner I'd stick in."

"So when are you going to find a nice girl of your own to cook for you?"

Conway grinned and said, "Don't rush me. A lot of nice girls around—maybe I'll settle on one someday."

EXACTLY AS ALISON HAD KNOWN it would turn out, she liked Mrs. Kearney on sight. Her name was Kate, and she was a plump little robin of a woman with bright brown hair and merry eyes.

"Well, really, Mrs. Mendoza, you don't know the first thing about us," she said, amused and interested. "I don't know—we'd been thinking about getting a place in the country, but—" She looked at her husband doubtfully.

"At least I'd like you to see it," said Alison. But after they'd followed her in their old sedan up the hill (the blacktop not in yet) she was rather sorry; the place looked, she freely acknowledged to herself, simply a mess. The air-conditioning people had taken a lot of tiles off the roof to knock holes for the ducts. There was a forest of brown underbrush and weeds all around the house, and the railing on one balcony was loose; the red tile floor past the great double doors was cracked and filthy. To the eye of love, imagination could see it as it would be, a phoenix of a lovely *estancia*, but possibly the Kearneys just saw an old tumbledown house. She told them about all the plans, the suite for Máiri, the four and a half bathrooms.

"Mercy," said Kate Kearney, "it must be costing a mint. But you'll have a beautiful place—such nice big rooms. And all these nice oak trees. They remind me of home, we had a lot of oaks on the old place."

Presently, after a tramp over the hill, Kearney came back and said, "You could build a right nice corral and riding ring off to the side of that old stable or whatever it is. What I thought," and his blue eyes twinkled, "I wouldn't doubt that pair of yours are young daredevils, and it'd be just as well, when you do get those ponies, to have a place for 'em to practice riding before you turn 'em loose."

"That's a very good idea," said Alison. "Even though there'll be a fence all round—chain-link around the whole four and a half acres." Perhaps on account of being used to the idea of fencing in hundreds of acres, the Kearneys didn't seem impressed with that. "And there are going to be iron gates down where the blacktop begins, with the name of the house. It was an old Spanish grant, and the family who owned it called it *La Casa des Gente Feliz*—the house of happy people."

"Well, so I should think it might be—a fine place for children and animals, when it's all fixed up. You're very lucky, my dear," said Kate Kearney.

"I think it's Fate," said Alison. "Luis says I'm superstitious."

"That'd be your husband," said Kearney cautiously. "Maybe in banking, or oil—"

Alison suddenly realized that the Kearneys were seeing him, a portly figure twenty years older than Alison, who would toss orders at servants in a careless loud voice. "Good heavens, no," she said, amused. At the back of her mind she was thinking about the roofers and deciding that she hadn't been nearly firm enough about not having TV antennas; they must go underground or something, none of them watched TV much anyway. "No, he's a police officer—Robbery-Homicide downtown. Neither of us ever had any money, it was his grandfather turning out to have a lot, but Luis wouldn't know what to do with himself without that thankless job."

"A police officer," they said together, interest and respect in their voices. "Now that's very unusual and interesting," said Kearney.

Alison thought, I really do believe if they say yes, it'll be because they're curious about Luis.

HACKETT HADN'T HAD a chance on Saturday or Sunday to drop in at Kellerman's before the place was open and a crowd started to collect. On Monday morning about eleven he found a parking slot along Vernon Avenue and walked back. One side of the double doors stood open, and a thin black boy was vigorously wielding a broom just inside. Hackett edged past him. "We're not open, sir—"

"That's all right, I'm looking for Mr. Kellerman."

He was there, behind the horseshoe-shaped bar, bent over a thick account book. Metal-framed glasses gave him a queerly studious look. "Well—Sergeant Hackett," he said. He took off the glasses. "Can I do anything for you?"

"Not a thing," said Hackett genially. "I just happened to be passing. I see you've had to take to glasses for close work too. I've just got some. Distance vision as good as ever—for driving, or say, the target practice. Funny how eyes are."

Kellerman shut the account book deliberately and gave him a shuttered look. "That's so."

"I've been hearing some nice things about you," said Hackett, hoisting himself onto one of the bar stools. "From

Mrs. Linker. How you're always nice to the neighborhood kids—and help people out different ways. Rudy Woods, and Ben Blake—how much you always thought of Kathy Fulger.''

Kellerman looked at the scarred bar. His eyes were watchful. He said, "She was Kathy Forbes."

"I suppose you've heard that Jody's got a good job with the bus company. Say, I wonder," said Hackett, "as long as I'm here, if I could have a cup of that coffee, Mr. Kellerman." There was a glass pot keeping bubbly warm on an electric plate behind the bar. In silence Kellerman got out two fat brown mugs, poured coffee, pushed cream and sugar across to Hackett, poured cream in his own coffee. "Thanks. Well, we'll never know now who did shoot Fulger. Big fat mystery, shoved into Pending. And of course, even if we did have some idea, we'd never be able to build a legal case."

"Is that so?" said Kellerman unsmilingly.

Hackett drank coffee and lit a cigarette. "No way," he said comfortably. "We don't like to put cases away unsolved—especially homicides—but sometimes we have to. Can't win 'em all, you know."

"I expect you're right," said Kellerman. The hint of a smile tugged at one corner of his firm mouth.

"And what we heard about Fulger, he's not much loss."

"You might get an argument there from a parson, Sergeant. Worth of individual human souls. I don't know, I never got religion myself."

"Um-hum," said Hackett. "Of course, thinking it over, the way things happened that night, with all that crowd excited and concentrated on Fulger and Kathy, all facing the doors—" he rubbed his nose thoughtfully "—the ideal vantage point to shoot Fulger from would have been right behind that crowd. Say right here at the bar. But he'd have had to be a damn good shot, at that distance with a .22."

"Now you could just be right," said Kellerman in a measured tone. He drank coffee, looked up and met Hackett's eyes across the bar. "It'd be about thirty, forty feet. Of course, if you're going to imagine a man like that—say as it might be about here—the floor behind the bar's raised about a foot, he'd have had a good open view over that crowd."

"Well, that's another point. But I might imagine a fellow here at the bar, while all that was going on—I don't know," said Hackett vaguely, "maybe somebody who'd known Kathy as a kid, felt sorry for her, mad at that mean cuss Fulger."

"I suppose you could imagine that," said Kellerman. "The other barkeep was down in the crowd—and of course I was on the phone calling in the 415."

"Sure," said Hackett.

"We could also maybe imagine," said Kellerman, "that that Police Positive .38 was with my brother on a trip to the mountains that weekend. And I'd fetched out that little peashooter just as insurance. It was right behind the bar."

"Kind of fancy shooting, that distance. But the way I said, a crack shot could have done it. Say an exserviceman."

"We might go on imagining," said Kellerman remotely, "that when the cops dropped on Jody Holt, a fellow like that would have been in a kind of dilemma. Wondering what to do. It could be he decided it was only sense to keep still, because Jody'd only come in for a couple of years. But it could be it bothered him some."

"I could appreciate that," said Hackett. "Little quandary."

"So it was a damn lucky break all round, Sergeant, that you got interested, got Jody to tell you about that gun, and took him off the hook. There's more than the Holts appreciate that."

"Oh, well," said Hackett, "I couldn't help wondering what really happened." He finished his coffee. "Glad it all turned out the way it did. As I say, these cases come along where there's no handle and we have to file 'em away and forget 'em." He slid off the stool. "Thanks for the coffee, Mr. Kellerman."

"You're more than welcome, Sergeant Hackett."

ON WEDNESDAY MORNING the office was humming along a little slower than usual; for once the weekend hadn't produced a new crop of heisters, despite the heat wave. Galeano was in court with Monty Lopez, seeing him indicted; Glasser and Conway—a Conway thinner but just as insouciant as ever—were questioning a suspect in an interrogation room, and Mendoza had just come out of his office with a report in one hand. It was ten-thirty.

"Well, the mountain has moved and produced a mouse," he said to Landers and Grace. "After rechecking the first autopsy results and running some more tests, the doctors now say it appears likely that the Dunlap girl was raped. *Mala suerte*, a final report for one of you to write."

"Oh, Lieutenant," said Lake from the door.

"Yes?" They all looked up.

"I didn't want to bother you at first," said Alice Coulter uncertainly, coming in past Lake. "But the more I thought about it, the more I decided there was something funny about it, and maybe you ought to know. In case it had anything to do with Sue getting killed."

"What's that, Mrs. Coulter?" Grace stood up and offered her his chair.

"Well, when I first saw it, I blamed the phone company, of course, and I called in to complain." She opened her bag and took out a long envelope. "Excuse me, I should have said—this is Sue's phone bill, I've been getting all her things packed up, and of course checking the mail, and this came yesterday. And I couldn't believe—it's nearly eighty dollars, and Sue never used the phone much, and the only long-distance calls she'd made would be to Mother—and when I looked at the statement, here were all these calls to Seattle, and we don't know anybody in Seattle—''

Landers and Grace looked at each other.

''—And at first I thought the company had just made a mistake, but they really don't very often, and I wondered—Seattle of all places—''

And in one voice Landers and Grace said, ''Sidney Putnam!''

''This rings bells in your head?'' asked Mendoza.

''Oh, boy, a dozen chimes at once!'' said Landers. ''Come on, Jase—let's see if we can nail him!''

''But how,'' asked Grace in the elevator, ''did he get in and out?''

''We'll ask him that first.''

At the apartment on Virgil, they rode up to the top floor and pushed the bell of the apartment next to the one where Susan Horgan had lived. After an interval the door half opened. ''Who is it?''

''Us,'' said Landers ungrammatically, and shoved the door all the way open. ''Do you mind telling us, Mr. Putnam, just how you got into Miss Horgan's apartment and out again? We know you were there, because of all the phone calls you made to Seattle on her phone.''

''Oh, God damn it to hell,'' said Putnam. He looked more prosperous than when they'd seen him before; he had on rather sharply tailored sports clothes, and there was more color in his face. ''God damn it. Just when I—Damn it, I thought the family'd just pay the bill, never check. Why should they? I thought—hell, I don't know what I thought.'' He backed away from them. And then he asked petulantly, ''How the hell did you know it was me, for God's sake?''

They were used to dealing with stupid people. ''Because you went out of your way, when we talked to you before, to tell us you'd just come here from Seattle," Grace explained kindly.

"Listen, the phone was all I thought of at first," said Putnam. Suddenly, nervously, he was anxious to explain. "I thought I had a job lined up here when I came—it fell through, I couldn't get another one, and I was running damn low on money. I was pretty sure if I could contact my brother Mort he could send me a couple hundred to tide me over, but I didn't dare run up the phone bill in case— That was all I thought of at first! I knew she was out all day, I just—"

"How in hell did you get in there?" asked Landers.

A kind of inverse pride showed in his expression: something they didn't know. "Well, it was the exterminators," he said. "When they came last month. I was here—I haven't had a job, like I say—and it was then I noticed."

"Noticed what?"

"The crawl space in the closet—for access to the roof and wiring and all that—it goes right through to the next apartment. I heard them talking about it, and after they were gone I looked to see. You just pull yourself up there and crawl about three feet and pull up the other cover and you're in the closet of that bedroom—it backs up to this one."

Landers looked at Grace. So simple when you knew.

"So you got in to use her phone. And then what?"

"It was just an accident!" said Putnam. "I never meant to—do anything—like *that*." He backed up farther and collapsed onto the couch. "I—well, I used the phone. I thought she'd think it was the phone company's mistake. Then I—Mort sent me two hundred but it went, and I was pretty sure I was going to get this job—I did, assistant manager at a movie house—but I had to eat and pay the rent till I got my first paycheck—and I thought, go in and look around for any cash, anything to hock—"

"And you were there that Sunday when she came home," said Grace, and sighed.

"Listen, I meant to pay her back for whatever I took! I'm not a thief," he said sullenly. "But I didn't expect her back so soon, damn it! I'd heard her leave, heard the door slam. I went in, and I was careful—used a handkerchief to open drawers, not that my prints are on file anyplace—didn't make a mess for her to notice—and I hadn't found a damn thing, when all of a sudden she was coming in and locking the damn door—she'd just hooked that chain when she looked round and saw me in the bedroom, and she opened her mouth to yell but nothing came out, she just squeaked a little, and I thought, my God, I got to get out! I didn't think she knew who I was, see, not here long and she never talked to anybody—I just wanted out, and I backhanded her across the head, and down she went and just lay there. I thought she was just knocked out. I took what folding money was in her bag, I went back through the crawl space, and that was—that. And look, my God, when I heard she was dead—police—look, I just gave her a little swipe, to give myself time—it—it couldn't've been that, was it? That *killed* her?"

"Well, I think you know it was," said Landers. Out of curiosity, once they'd given him his rights, they went one by one to look inside the closet at that innocuous-looking square cover in the ceiling.

"We had better," said Grace, "come back and tell Kowalsky about that, Tom. Security these days is important to tenants, and I'll bet that's one he never thought of, any more than we did."

WHEN MENDOZA CAME IN on Friday morning he had hardly sat down when Lake was buzzing him. Traffic was engaged in handling a major gang rumble at a local high school, and reported one body already and probably more to come. Every man in the office went out on that, and it turned out to be quite a day, with one teacher dead and three so-called students, little sense to be made out of any of it, and a mountain of paperwork to be done. By the time they had finished what questioning they could do, gotten the relevant statements, sorted out the ones they might bring some charge on and booked them into jail, they were all feeling exhausted and frustrated. None of these vicious, mindless punk kids would get much of a sentence, the blood and death was for nothing, and it was another day they had wasted on necessary routine that accomplished nothing at all.

WHEN PALLISER GOT HOME he was pounced on by a loving Trina, and was only academically pleased when she dropped obediently on command. "Good day, darling?" Roberta's voice floated from the kitchen.

"No," said Palliser. "One hell of a day. I'm going to quit this damned job, Robin, and we'll move to the country and raise poultry or something. For one thing, the city's no place to raise kids."

"Oh, now—remember all the seniority you've got built up. Take a deep breath, sit down and relax. I'll get you a drink before dinner, and you'll feel better."

WHEN HIGGINS CAME IN the back door, he stood a moment feeling dimly grateful to be home. The place was not quiet or peaceful. Mary was cleaning fresh strawberries at the sink, a mound of them in a bowl beside her already—that meant strawberry shortcake with her hot baking-powder biscuits—and Steve was insistently demanding that she stop just a second to look at this super negative. Laura was pounding lustily on the piano, Brucie was barking loudly at the neighbor's cat in the drive, and the baby was wailing.

"Not now, Steve—for heaven's sake, you're dripping it all over, you'll poison the strawberries—and that's the baby—"

"Hey, George!" Steve had just noticed him. "Take a look at these super shots I got of the class play rehearsal! All flash, and they're really—"

"Oh, George, you do look tired to death," said Mary, wiping her hands. "For heaven's sake, Steve, go tell Laura to stop! George needs some peace and quiet when he comes home."

"Not necessarily," said Higgins. He bent and kissed her. "I wouldn't know it was home, so to speak, if it was peaceful. Never mind, it's good to be here."

LANDERS WENT DOWN to R. and I. at six o'clock to see if Phil had left. She hadn't; they'd had a busy day there too.

"The hell with the money," he told her. "I'm taking you out to dinner. Some place quiet and fairly elegant—not The Castaway on account I want air conditioning. And we'll have several drinks first."

"I won't argue with you," said Phil.

COMFORTABLY FULL of dinner, Hackett was assured that Angel didn't need any help with the dishes. "After the day you've had, go and sit down and relax. And I had a thought, Art—if you let Sheila just look at the glasses when you're not wearing them, get used to feeling them, she might get over being afraid."

"It's an idea." Hackett went into the front room and picked up the *Herald* from the couch. Mark was busy over a coloring book on the floor, and Sheila nattering happily to a stuffed cat. He picked her up and sat down in his big armchair, and she cooed at him. "That's my good girl. Now, look, these silly things are nothing to be afraid of, see?" He brought out the glasses. Off his face, they didn't seem to scare her. She grabbed them firmly and started to chew one of the bows.

Hackett rescued them hastily. "Not one of your mother's better ideas," he told her, "considering what they cost me."

MENDOZA WAS READING an autopsy report at nine o'clock on Saturday morning when Farrell buzzed him. "I've got a call I think you'll want," he said. "A civilian has something to say about a diamond ring, the desk just relayed it up."

"*¿Cómo dice?* Shoot it through. Yes?"

"—This notice about this ring," said a cautious voice. "Diamonds and emeralds. The two-and-a-half carat center stone. This is Isaacs and Jacobs, pawnbrokers, Exposition Boulevard. I'm Isaacs."

"Yes. You've seen that ring at some time? When?"

"I've got it."

"What? Since when? Are you sure—"

"I'm sure. The description, you couldn't mistake. Good stones. I took it in yesterday."

"*¡qQué sé yo?*" said Mendoza to himself incredulously. What the hell was this? "Yesterday?"

"I thought I better call, if it's that hot for a special notice."

"We'll be right down!" said Mendoza, banged the phone down and leaped up. "Art!"

It was a good-sized pawnshop, empty when they got there except for Abe Isaacs on a stool behind the counter. He studied the badges, said, "Can't be too careful," brought from under the counter a small box and opened it. "Is that it?"

"*¡Diez millones de dominios desde el infierno!*" said Mendoza softly, and picked it up. It was, of course, it had to be, Anita Chesney's diamond and emerald ring. It was dirty; dust had collected around the settings of the big diamonds, the emeralds were dull. But it was Anita's ring, part of her, always worn. "So, tell! Where'd you get it? You said yesterday, for God's sake?"

"Yesterday. I had to look twice, see it wasn't junk. They're good stones. This is just like my luck," said Isaacs sadly. "I been away on vacation. My God, my partner'll clobber me, but it was his fault as much. I come back, he takes off. That notice he'd have seen, but does he think to tell me about it? No, of course not. Who expects such a thing to show up here? Listen, am I a fool? Of course, I looked at it, saw what it was, I have a good look at the current hot list. It's not on it. So is it my business how she comes to have it? It was not. And this morning I find that damned notice where Jake stuck it, under the cash box in the register."

"Who brought it in?"

"A fat black dame. Sure, she left an address—the regular form." He produced it promptly.

Before he looked at it, Mendoza asked curiously, "What did you give on it?"

"Don't ask. I could kill myself. Five hundred."

"¡Válgame Dios! You're a damned bloodsucker, you Shylock."

"I know what it's worth," said Isaacs even more sadly. "Now it's police business, you give me a receipt and I kiss the gelt good-bye."

The little scrawled slip bore an address on Thirty-ninth; the name was Martha Terry.

She was fat and black and worried-looking; she looked a good deal more worried when she saw the badge in Mendoza's hand. He opened the other and showed her the ring. "Where did you get this, Mrs. Terry? When?"

"There's somethin' wrong about it," she whispered. "I knowed there was when he give me all that money. More money 'n I ever see in my life all at once. For Tessy's li'l ole junk jewelry ring Tom give her. Was it stole? I never liked that no-count black boy worth a hoot."

"Yes, it was stolen. Who's Tessy? She had it?"

"She's my girl—my daughter." Suddenly she began to cry quietly. "She's in the hospital, she's bad—they say she's gonna die, it's this tuber-somethin', but she don't know—that she's gonna die, I mean. An' you got to humor sick folk, do whatever they want. I was to see her Thursday night, her cousin Rachel was there too, and she says to me—Tessy I mean, grabbed my arm real strong she did, she says, Mama, you got to promise get shut o' that ring—you know, ole thing Tom give me—you throw it away, put it in the garbage, she says. I said I would—just get it out o' the house, she says—but I allus thought it was kind of pretty, might get five bucks for it at Isaacs', an' I sure could use any money. You coulda knocked me over—all that money, five hundred bucks! I knowed there was somethin' wrong then. Police comin'—it's gonna kill Tessy, whatever it—"

"Who's Tom?"

"Tom Atkins— You can't go an' see Tessy, ask her a lot o' questions—it'll kill her!"

"You know where he lives?" asked Hackett.

Dumbly she nodded. "His sister got a whole house up in Hollywood. Ada Atkins, she's a real nice woman, but that Tom— It's Manhattan Place. We useta live pretty near, more money before my man walked out—that's how Tessy took up with him— Please don't go upset Tessy, sir! I dunno what it's all about, but Tessy never done nothin' wrong—Anythin' wrong done it'll be that no-good Atkins boy—Listen, she had it a long time—years she had it—"

"I know that," said Mendoza grimly.

THE BADGE GOT THEM into the tuberculosis ward. That was all. The thin black girl in the bed just looked at the badge and her face was a mask of terror. Mendoza showed her the ring, and the face turned gray-green.

"Do you know where this came from?"

She just shut her eyes blindly. After a few minutes the nurse shooed them out.

THE HOUSE ON Manhattan Place was bastard Spanish, an uncompromising square box painted pink. There was brown discouraged grass in the front yard, an old Ford in the drive. The woman who answered the door was about thirty-five, a scrawny, dark-brown woman in a dowdy beige cotton dress.

"Miss Atkins?" said Mendoza, and showed the badge. A little spasm of feeling flicked across her face, too brief for emotion to be identified. "We've got some questions to ask you. Let us in, please." She stepped back silently and they went in. The living room was inhumanly neat and very hot; there wasn't even an electric fan. "Does your brother live here with you—Tom Atkins?"

"Sometimes."

"Do you recognize this? Ever see it before?" He opened his hand on the ring.

She looked at it in silence while her mouth grew bitter and tight. "I never saw it before." Suddenly she came out with one soft, unexpected, ugly obscenity. "All that time back, and who was to know now? What did it matter? But just because that Goddamn fool got scared—" She was contemptuous on that. "And I could guess, them two silly bitches think that could tie them in— They'd be that sort of fools."

"Tessy Terry, and who's the other one?" asked Mendoza sharply.

"You needn't look at me. You can't tie me in, I never had anythin' to do with it. Tom never told me till after. Besides, it was mostly an accident anyway. I can see, whatever I say or don't say, it'll all come out now. That Goddamned fool. Keep quiet, nobody ever need know."

"But you knew about it," said Mendoza.

She wasn't a fool; she knew they'd try to tie her in; but the rage was for all the stupid fools who had done that, not the police. "I never knew till after! You don't dare try put it on me!"

"Where's Tom?" asked Mendoza.

She turned her back. "They picked him up for burglary yesterday. He's in jail. You go tell him what a damn fool he is."

HE SAT IN THE LITTLE wooden chair in the interrogation room at the jail, and looked at the ring in Mendoza's hand. "There wasn't no call—worry about that, I guess," he said in a dull voice. He wasn't as sharp as his sister: a big hulk of a man about twenty-seven, with an Afro hairdo and huge hands. "I guess Rachel got scared. I never thought anybody'd find out about that."

"We'd like to hear about it now." Hackett offered him a cigarette.

"Huh?" He started. "Oh. I was just thinkin'. Seems a long time ago. Funny, it comin' up again. I'd forgot all about it. So'd Joe. But Joe, he don't remember much anyways, now."

"Joe who?"

"Uh, Joe Ring. We used to hang 'round together about hen."

"So suppose you tell us about the ring," said Mendoza. "About Mrs. Chesney."

"Who's that? It was on account, I read in the paper where hey dug that lady up. I mean, I made out it was about a ody, and that street—I got Ada read it out to me. Where ve put her, so I knew it was that lady. I hadn't thought bout that in a coon's age. Ada said, no never mind, no-ody could ever find out it was us—Joe an' me, I mean. hat time, it gone right outta my head, but then I remem-ered. Wondered if—if there was any way cops could know. 'course, it wasn't no good, try talk to Joe. I told Rachel 'bout it, about that body. She hadn't seen about it. An' I guess she got scared, there was some way cops'd find out.''

"The ring. The lady who had it."

"If you're gonna say we killed her, well, we never. It was all an accident like, the whole thing.''

"So tell us how it happened."

He shuffled his feet, apparently an aid to thought, and asked for another cigarette. "I was broke. So was Joe, and we wanted take our chicks to a show, out dancin' somewheres. Ada, she's my sister, she got a temper on her but I ask, she usual pass me a few bucks. We went up there to ask her.''

"Up on La Loma Road in Pasadena," said Mendoza, and let out a slow breath.

"Yeah. She got a regular job there—still does. Three days a week, cleanin' this lady's house, Mis' Love her name is. Big house all by itself. We was there—Joe an' me—when this lady come to the door. She wants to use the phone, say she got a flat tire. Ada tells her O.K. See, this Mis' Love, she was gone somewhere, but Ada was already mad because she mighta been home an' she wouldn't like us comin', see Ada. But time this lady come in, I was in the dinin' room, get me a li'l drink—Ada was mad as fire about that too, say they think it was her stole their liquor, I only took a li'l one—an' I thought, way earn a couple bucks, I told the lady me an Joe change the tire.''

"Oh, yes," said Mendoza. "I see. And you did."

"It was rainin', you know. Ada asked her in, sit down there. It was a good car.'' And she was going to have it back in running order, in just a few minutes: the obliging house servants of the place she'd picked, at random or because it was nearest, to ask for help: so she hadn't used the phone to call Felicia Russell, announce delay. "Well, we got it changed. She come out an' give us five bucks. She hadda lot of bread in her purse, an' I saw this big ring, looked like di'monds. I never did nothing big-time like that but I thin all of a sudden, maybe her old man's a millionaire, we hold on to her an' ask for a lot o' loot, let her go—but anyways, she had all that bread on her, and Ada wouldn't give me none, she was mad. I just grabbed her purse, the lady's I mean, and she started to yell, we was right by the car, I'd pulled it in the drive—an' I was scared Ada'd hear, so I just grabbed hold o' her then, it was all kind of fast, an' next thing she was passed out, I guess I squeezed her throat a little bit.''

She fell among thieves, thought Mendoza. The random, stupid, unplanning little thieves.

"Well, we didn't want Ada know, see. I had some rope in my truck, we tied her up quick an' Joe put his scarf round her head, keep her shut up. We put her in the Dodge's trunk an' got out, Joe drivin' my truck. There was fifty bucks in her purse, maybe more, I forget. An' it was a nice car. We took the girls out that night, Tessy an' Rachel, had a good time. An'—well, it was just—'' he paused awkwardly ''—I said to Joe later on, we ask like a ransom, let her go, an' he says I'm a damn fool, how we gonna know her old man's name. An' anyway, when we opened the trunk she was dead. I dunno how. We never meant to kill her.''

Suffocation from the tight gag, thought Mendoza, the most likely cause?

"I took that off her." He nodded at the ring on the table between them. "But I look at it, Jeez, they couldn't be real di'monds, they're too big. Just a fake ring to look pretty. I give it to Tessy. She was my girl then, did I say—Rachel was goin' with Joe. She had some earrings on too, we gave Rachel, but she lost those somewheres."

"And why," asked Mendoza, "the house on Sixty-second Place?"

"Huh? We dint know what to do. It was after we took the chicks home, see, it was maybe like two, three inna morning. There she was, dead. We hadda get shut of her. We was at Joe's place, down there—him an' his ma lived on Sixty-

second then. An' he said, good a place as any, this house
empty and gonna be tore down. The floor was all broke in
we just dumped her through, an' put her purse there too
there wasn't no bread left. There was a thing, like fo
checks, but that wasn't no good to us, we threw it awa
somewheres. It was a good car, but we figured it'd be hot
better get rid o' that too. So Joe, he was workin' as porte
down at Union Station then, he just park it in the lot an
leave it." Atkins paused a long time, painfully thinkin
back. "When I give the ring to Tessy, she ast where I got it
an' I tole her. The girls, they didn't b'lieve they been ridin
around with a dead lady in back—well, we dint know sh
was dead, never meant kill her—they was scared then, tim
they believed us—"

And steering wheels usually showed only smudges, no
clean latents. Of course.

"I reckon the girls'd forgot all about it too, but time I tol
Rachel about somebody findin' that lady there, I guess sh
got scared again, an' tole Tessy get rid o' that ring. But
was just a fake one for pretty—"

Mendoza picked it up and turned it in his hand. "*L
veras,*" he said softly. "Just for pretty." The big diamon
caught the light from the little window and shot a rainbo
arc of color against the wall.

Anita Chesney's ring. Anita turning up after all that tim
and then her ring—as if still circling a skeletal finger,
point the way up the cold trail.

He turned it back and forth, and the rainbow arc mov
on the bare wall. Evidence: but eventually the Chesne
would get it back. He wondered whether Ann Chesn
would ever want to wear that ring.

THEY FOUND JOE RING in the psychiatric ward at t
General. After accumulating a short pedigree of burgla
he had succumbed to an advanced case of acute alcoholis

and virulent V.D. He'd be dead before this ever came to trial.

Rachel Taylor hadn't any record; she was just a rather stupid, amoral girl, working as a waitress in a third-class restaurant, and long out of touch with Joe. She might be charged as an accessory, more likely not.

The charge on Tom Atkins would probably be involuntary manslaughter, considering the complete dearth of evidence as to how Anita Chesney had died, the degree of intent, the lack of premeditation. He was already up for burglary. And the death to his account—and the D.A. would also have to consider, how far had Ring been guilty of promoting it?—had happened a long time ago. Almost fifty-two months ago now.

Even if there was any way to reckon it, of course the D.A.'s office couldn't take into account all the side effects—like waves circling out from a thrown rock—of that death. The grief and anxiety and bitterness, and a man dead.

Art Hackett had once coined a phrase for what they were dealing with most of the time: the cupidity and stupidity.

MENDOZA DROVE HOME, late, through the hot dirty streets of Hollywood. He was feeling somnolently satisfied. That eternal imp of curiosity in him, forever unhappy with the unfinished puzzle, the unanswered question, had settled back to sleep.

He hadn't really expected to find out all the answers on Anita. Poor Anita. He would call Costello tonight, tell him what emerged. Costello would be interested.

He turned into the drive of the house on Rayo Grande Avenue. Alison would be interested too.

The twins were shouting and swinging high in the backyard, in the still-bright sunlight. Cedric was barking up a storm, as he switched off the engine in the garage. He could see Alison standing there by the swing laughing, her red hair

bright in the sun and James-or-Luisa bulging out immi-
nently.

He got out of the Ferrari, yawning. Tomorrow, he
thought, was also a day.

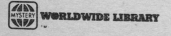

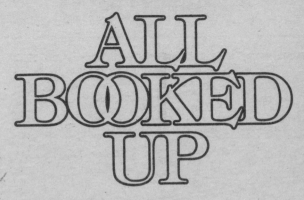
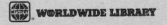

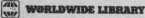

"Suspenseful tale features Gothic atmosphere
and a small-town Southern setting."
—*Booklist*

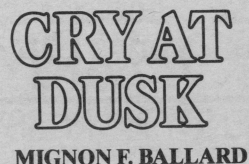

CRY AT DUSK

MIGNON F. BALLARD

A woman comes face-to-face with her darkest nightmare when she returns to her small hometown to investigate the death of her cousin and learns the secret of not
one murder but two.

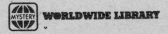

Take 2 books & a surprise gift FREE

SPECIAL LIMITED-TIME OFFER

Mail to: The Mystery Library
901 Fuhrmann Blvd.
P.O. Box 1867
Buffalo, N.Y. 14269-1867

YES! Please send me 2 free books from the Mystery Library and my free surprise gift. Then send me 2 mystery books, first time in paperback, every month. Bill me only $3.50 per book. There is *no* extra charge for shipping and handling! There is no minimum number of books I must purchase. I can always return a shipment and cancel at any time. Even if I never buy another book from The Mystery Library, the 2 free books and the surprise gift are mine to keep forever.

414 BPY BPS9

Name _____ (PLEASE PRINT)

Address _____ Apt. No. _____

City _____ State _____ Zip _____

This offer is limited to one order per household and not valid to present subscribers. Terms and prices subject to change without notice.

MYS-BPA5

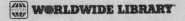